thirty*nine*stars
Austin, Texas

SHROUDED
A Crispin Leads Mystery

A Novel By
MEREDITH LEE

Shrouded

ThirtyNineStars
Austin, TX

ISBN: 978-0-692-88760-8

Library of Congress Cataloging in Publication Data: 2017907109
1.Title. 2. Fiction. 2. Mystery. 3. Suspense

Printed in the United States of America
Written by Dixie Lee Evatt and Sue Meredith Cleveland
Cover Design by Elizabeth MacKey
Paperback Book Design by Elizabeth MacKey
Ebook Design and Conversion by Elizabeth Mackey

ABOUT THE AUTHORS

Meredith Lee owes her half-East Coast, half-southern soul to Texas-based writers Dixie Lee Evatt and Sue Meredith Cleveland. If memory serves, the inspiration for *Shrouded* came one day on the front porch when a fly landed too close to Dixie's gin and tonic. Sue grabbed a 1962 *Life* magazine from a pile destined for recycle, rolled it up, and tried to shoo the fly away. She missed the fly but hit the gin. While cleaning up the mess the ladies noticed the magazine cover featuring the lead story: "Scientists Close in on The Secret of Life." Well, a gin or two later and the rest is history.

DEDICATION

We lovingly dedicate this book to the memory of two women who encouraged us to trust the creative process, our mothers:

Charlotte Shipp and Dorothy Whiteside.

SHROUDED
A Crispin Leads Mystery

A Novel By
MEREDITH LEE

Chapter One

Now three had died. But Crispin didn't know it. She sat propped up on the cold terrazzo floor; her back against the wall in a seated fetal position, her face buried in her knees. It took all of her concentration to control the urge to empty her stomach again; to swallow the acidic foam burning the back of her throat. Her lilac linen dress, wrinkled and soiled beyond redemption, offered little warmth as she shivered alone at the south end of a long Vatican hallway.

Distant sounds of chaos coaxed her eyes open. The other end of the hall was a diorama come to life, populated by firefighters, police, and paramedics; their body bags and gurneys out of place against the ancient tapestries, vaulted ceilings, and intricate geometric patterns in the marble floors. Had she turned this scene on? Could she turn it off again? She reached for an imaginary switch when someone materialized next to her, blocking her line of sight.

Standing beside her was a tall fella with David Bowie eyes, his hands shoved into the pockets of his full-length raincoat. He squatted so that he could make direct eye contact.

"Crispin?"

She gazed sideways into a vaguely familiar face and blinked several times. It was the good-looking guy who'd invited her for cappuccino. It seemed so innocent. Two young strangers meeting up for coffee in Rome. That was before all hell broke loose.

"Roberto?" Crispin paused and then asked, "Who died?"

"Father Mitchel," he replied softly.

The answer upended her carefully catalogued emotional filing system, which in turn triggered a case of giggles. At least that's how it started. But the simple titters were in danger of becoming a full belly laugh, so she covered her mouth with her hands. Definitely not the right response to death—she knew that—but she couldn't make herself stop. Roberto didn't say anything, apparently willing to wait for what might come next.

Crispin didn't know how long the struggle against full-blown hysteria went on, but the shaking in her shoulders loosened something unexpected inside and she began to cry. At least crying, she told herself, showed the proper emotion in view of the circumstances. Embarrassing, yes. But, thank God, appropriate.

Then, just as suddenly as they had started, the tears ended with a deep intake of her breath. She felt as though an internal hard drive had rebooted and she was again in control.

"You must think I'm insane," she said, trying unsuccessfully to smile at Roberto.

"You've had a terrible shock," he replied, standing.

Crispin wiped her cheeks with the sleeve of her bolero jacket, only to realize that her nose was dripping. "You don't happen to have a Kleenex, do you?"

"No, but the lavatory is near the elevator," Roberto said, extending a hand to help Crispin up.

Her legs wobbled as she stood, and a shiver passed up her spine when she tried to smooth the wrinkles from her vomit-stained sundress. "Oh my."

When Roberto began to unbutton his overcoat she noticed that he did not have full use of his left hand. The skin where his pinky should have been was discolored and shriveled. "Here, this will help," he said, draping his coat over her shoulders. It reached nearly to her ankles.

As she turned to face him, Crispin could not suppress her surprise. He wore a clerical collar. "Bejesus."

"Excuse me?"

"I'm sorry, Father. I didn't realize you were a priest."

"I asked you to call me 'Roberto' and you should."

"Tell me again. Where is the bathroom?"

"Let me show you."

In the bathroom, Crispin took her time brushing her teeth with the Tom's of Maine toothpaste she always carried. The taste and aroma of peppermint did not cover the memory of burning flesh. She splashed cool water on her face and tried to douse the images that kept flaming back to life. She used paper towels to wipe the smudges of mascara from under her green eyes. Her thick auburn hair was a hopeless mess. She rummaged through her purse for something to pin it up, but all she could find was a large rubber band. She managed to pull her mane into a mock bun at her neck, but it did little to flatter her heart-shaped face.

The stains on her dress were like the memories of what she'd witnessed, crusty and resistant to attempts to erase them. She dampened paper towels and worked them over the stain. The towels dissolved against the fabric, leaving paper residue down the front of the dress she'd splurged on at Barneys before she left New York. She used Roberto's trench coat to cover the damage, cinched the belt around her waist, and rolled the sleeves up to her wrists. She thought it made her look like a street urchin in a hand-me-down. It'll have to do, she told herself.

She stepped into the hallway and easily spotted Roberto standing with several police officers. He was the only one with blond hair and stood several inches taller than the other men. She hesitated for a moment, but he motioned to her to join them. When she did, he singled out a fifty-something woman and introduced her.

"Detective J. D. Moss, this is Crispin Leads," he said. "Crispin, this officer would like to take your statement when you are ready."

"Ms. Leads?" asked the detective, emphasizing the s in Leads as if it were a third syllable. Her British accent seemed as out of place as Crispin felt.

"I don't know that I have anything to offer."

"Then it shouldn't take too much of your time," Moss replied as she escorted Crispin to a nearby sitting room.

"Do you need anything before we begin? Water?" Moss asked.

"I'm fine," Crispin said, masking her uneasiness with a meaningless social convention. Once she was settled on the couch, the detective pulled up a straight-back chair and opened her notebook. Crispin took a minute to study the well-dressed woman across from her. Instead of the simple suit one might expect of a mid-level police officer, Moss wore expensive tailored pants and had a Hermes scarf draped over one shoulder, held in place at her neck by an emerald-encrusted pin shaped like a peacock. Her body was lean and muscular, but her teeth and fingers were stained with nicotine. "Let's start with a few preliminary questions. Give me your full name."

Crispin hesitated for just a moment before answering. The question made her realize that when Roberto introduced her just now he had used her surname. She was certain she had only ever given him her first name. "Sorry. Would you repeat the question?"

In a rapid-fire series of questions, the detective established that Crispin was an American graduate student from NYU who was in Rome on a summer research grant made possible because of the pope's Year 2000 Jubilee.

"What kind of research?" Moss asked.

"I study death. Well, I should say rituals of death. Burials. Ceremonies and beliefs over time and across cultures."

Instead of a follow-up question, Moss wrote in her notebook. Crispin was all too familiar with the silent response. It was one she had experienced many times with family and friends—an indication that people thought her choice of study was morbid.

"How do you know Father Rossini?" the detective asked.

"Roberto? I don't really. We just happened to run into each other yesterday at Saint Anne's Gate. When I arrived for my appointment with Bishop Pirolla."

"Yesterday?"

"Yes, it's a bit of a coincidence. Nothing really."

"Tell me," the detective urged.

Crispin shrugged and explained that she'd come directly from the airport yesterday afternoon and asked for directions from the first person she saw when her cab let her off near Saint Anne's Gate. "I didn't know he was a priest at the time."

"An easy mistake. He reminds me more of our Beckham than a man of the cloth," the detective said with a suggestive smile.

Crispin's mouth felt suddenly dry. "May I please have that water after all?"

Detective Moss ordered water, then turned back to Crispin.

"Roberto, Father Rossini, was just being kind and offered to help me find the right office," Crispin said. "No big deal. I was afraid I was going to be late, but it turned out that the bishop was not in and I was told to come back this morning."

"By Father Mitchel?"

"No, it was someone else."

"Do you remember who?"

Crispin thought, but was sure the man did not give her a name. "Sorry," she said, shaking her head. "A young man. Twenty or so. Average height. Dark hair."

"Priest?"

"I don't think so. No, I'm sure I would remember that."

Detective Moss flipped through her notepad, made a few more notes.

"Oh, yeah, he had a lisp," Crispin added.

Moss jotted a few more notes and asked Crispin to tell her what had happened this morning.

Crispin queued up her memory so events rolled through her mind like a scene from a movie. "I didn't want to take any chance at being late. I arrived at Bishop Pirolla's office at 9:45 a.m., on the dot. A solid fifteen minutes ahead of my appointment. I was eager to get the meeting behind me since I assumed it would be a routine, you know, welcome-aboard session." She stopped for a moment and took a deep breath as if thinking about what to say next. Then she said, simply, "I was wrong."

There was a tap on the door and a uniformed officer came in with a bottle of water. Crispin took a drink before continuing. "When I walked into Pirolla's outer office, that's when I met Father Mitchel. He was trying to drag a humongous desk away from the wall. He was not much taller than me and round," she said, making a circle with her arms around her middle, almost smiling before her memory turned sad. "Father Rossini told me that Father Mitchel was the one who died."

"Please continue. What happened next?"

"He was getting precious little help from two techs who sat on the windowsill watching. The third guy was on a ladder pulling cable through an opening in the ceiling."

"Tell me about him."

"Tall," Crispin said, concentrating while trying to visualize the scene. "Dressed in baggy jeans. Black T-shirt. Shaggy blond ponytail."

"Do you remember his face?"

Crispin locked eyes with the detective and took another long drink of water before replying. "I only got a quick peek at his face when he glanced down. But what I remember best was his sour expression. I couldn't tell if he resented the lack of help from the other two or if he was just a naturally dour sort of fellow. You know, a pickle face."

"What about the other two?"

"Like you, they were sitting with the sun at their backs," Crispin said. "So I didn't get a good look at their faces, but my impression was they were average in height and I would guess they were fairly young. Sorry, I can't help more."

Crispin couldn't read the detective's expression, so she had no way of knowing how the other woman was reacting. She was sure Moss had intentionally positioned herself to make it difficult for Crispin to see her face. It was an advantage that was not lost on Crispin despite her emotional state. The detective did not acknowledge Crispin's comment. But she paused to make a few notes before continuing her questioning. "What happened next?"

"Father Mitchel was a real talker. He was out of breath, but that didn't stop him from telling me that he wasn't notified ahead of time and that the techs had just shown up unannounced that morning, disrupting the strict order that the bishop expects of his office. He was clearly not a happy camper."

"Did he introduce the men?"

"Oh no. If you ask me they weren't too happy with each other either. I told him about my ten o'clock appointment. He made it clear that I must be wrong. He alone was the keeper of the bishop's appointment book and had no record of my meeting. Besides, he explained, the bishop never arrived before noon."

"What did you do?"

"What could I do?" Crispin said, unconsciously rubbing her right wrist with the palm of her hand. "It was the second time in as many days I'd been stood up." She stopped talking, pulling her hands up into the sleeves of Roberto's coat.

The detective let Crispin take her time, allowing silence to create the kind of void that yearns to be filled.

"So, I left," Crispin finally said. "That's when I ran into Father Rossini for the second time."

"Ah?"

"Literally. Because I was stepping backward into the hall as I closed the door behind me. I ran right into his path and stepped on his foot. I felt like a real ass," Crispin said, crossing her arms across her chest and tucking her hands under her armpits. "He was nice about it. Told me he was there to drop off some papers and invited me for coffee. Since my morning was free, I figured, Why not?"

"How long was he in the office?"

"I'm not sure. I was down the hall looking at some of the art. Does it matter?"

"It might. We'll see."

Crispin unfolded her arms and reached for the water bottle, but instead of taking a drink she started to twist the cap on and off. After a brief moment of reflection, she began to describe how she'd gotten caught up studying the detail of a richly colored, hand-tied Flemish tapestry that covered most of one wall. It depicted Christ's lifeless body draped over the lap of Mary while the Magdalene stood weeping at her side.

"I guess I lost track of time because I've rarely seen a piece of tapestry that extraordinary up close. From its age, I'll bet it had once hung in a Gothic cathedral for hundreds of years. The inscription read, 'It was the women who came to claim Him. It was their tears that washed Him . . .'" Crispin stopped mid sentence when Moss interrupted her.

"What happened next?"

"That's when the lights started to flicker." Crispin took a deep breath and re-crossed her arms, pulling Roberto's coat tighter around her waist. Although she had brushed her teeth, the sharp, bitter taste of bile lingered in the back of her mouth, stinging her throat when she tried to speak. She could detect a faint smell of souring milk beginning to emanate from the stains on her dress.

The detective sat back for a moment and let Crispin collect herself.

"Then screaming. I've never heard a sound like that. A trapped animal being pulled through an underground pit that is collapsing around it. Loud. Painful wails. The wails came out of silence and then receded to finally disappear again into silence." As she talked, Crispin's voice grew faint to a near whisper.

Detective Moss urged her to continue talking. "What did you do?"

"I followed the sound. All the lights went out just as I opened the bishop's office door."

"What did you see?"

"Just a glimpse," Crispin said, the vivid image, a snapshot, frozen in her mind. "The room was dark except for sunlight from the window, like a spotlight washing over the priest, slumped at his desk."

Crispin didn't speak for a while, again playing with the water bottle cap. "His head was charred and pitted," she said with a shiver.

For a long time Crispin studied her feet in silence. Moss pressed her. "Go on."

"Then there was the smell. Metallic. Like burning metal."

"Ah."

"Was it?" Crispin whispered.

"Electrocution is an ugly way to die."

"I've smelled burning metal before," Crispin said in a voice that was barely audible.

Detective Moss did not seem to notice. "Did anyone leave the bishop's office?"

"I tried to run away from the smell, but didn't make it far. It was dark. I couldn't see."

"Did you hear anything?"

"Maybe. I heard a door open. Footsteps. But not in the main hall."

"This is important. Did you or did you not hear footsteps?"

"There was so much confusion I can't be certain, but, maybe, there was something behind me, in the side hall, the one next to the elevator."

The detective closed her notebook and stood to go.

"You will be hearing from me as our inquiry progresses. If you think of anything else, call me." She handed Crispin her business card. "Take your time. Nothing will disturb you here," the detective said as she left, closing the door behind her.

"That's what you think," Crispin murmured, her feelings so raw that as the door closed, the click of the latch hitting the strike plate sounded like a gunshot, metal on metal. What she'd witnessed had awakened memories of a childhood death, the guilt that traveled with it, and the need to numb the pain.

When she finally collected herself and opened the door, the voices in the hallway were subsiding as the police and firefighters concluded their business so she went to find her backpack.

Roberto separated from a group of police officers and Vatican workers and joined her. "How did your interview with the detective go?"

"I don't think I was able to help much. Why?"

"I was concerned. You were clearly so upset by what you saw. What will you do now?"

"I need to go back to my hotel," she said, starting to unbutton his coat.

"No, please, keep it. Tell me where you are staying and I will make arrangements to retrieve it."

Crispin's Lizard Brain began to twitch. Giving a stranger her contact information was risky. But he was, after all, a priest. How dangerous could he be?

Chapter Two

Crispin picked at the cellophane on a package of single-edge razor blades, the thin crimson lines on her wrists being pale testaments to the agony of old wounds at war with solemn promises. She struggled to fend off the savage rebellion of memories, of death and of guilt. *Haven't I prevailed for 1,278 days? I can make it through one more. Then one more after that. Then one more.*

The counterpunch was a thought so vicious that it rattled her teeth, causing her to gnaw through her lip until it bled. *Yes, but none of those days were like today. None of those days smelled like today. None of those sounded like today.* She tightened the hotel's oversized bath towel around her waist and rocked as the trolls of memory dragged her back in time.

Crispin fought back. *You don't have to do this,* she told herself. *You have more than a thousand days of success.* But none of those days smelled like death. None of those days looked like death, the troll voice taunted.

The hard edge of the hotel's porcelain tub offered no more comfort now than the tile floor had then. She saw that blood from her lip had dripped onto the white bath towel. As she pulled a swatch of toilet paper to dab her lip, the rattle of the roller distorted into a squeal much like the peculiar screech she'd followed through the flickering lights a few hours ago. She covered her ears and rocked back and forth, feeling her will weaken with each passing moment until finally she picked up the package of razor blades again.

She broke the seal on the package and peeled back the cellophane. Just one small cut will erase it all, she bargained, just as her cell phone startled her with the opening notes of Beethoven's Fifth. The dedicated ringtone told her it was her dad, The Professor, Daniel Leads, Ph.D. Caught in the act. She dropped the package and hunted in her purse, trying to catch the call before it rolled to voicemail. "Hi. I'm here. It's me."

"Hello, my dear. I had expected you to call before now."

"Sorry about that," she said, tapping her fingers along the edge of the sink as if playing invisible piano keys. "It's been a bit crazy."

"Any problems with the flight? How was your meeting at the Vatican?"

"Haven't met with the bishop."

"Were you late for the appointment yesterday?"

"Why do you always assume that? I was right on time. There was a scheduling mix-up in his office. And, then today there was . . ."

"Really, Crispin," he said, interrupting her. "That's the kind of detail on which you must focus."

"You're not listening to me," she said, her voice growing louder. "It's not my fault. You see . . ."

"Do I need to make a call?"

"No! No. I'm on top of it," she said, trying to control the growing anger in her voice, giving the package of blades a kick that sent it sliding across the damp floor.

Her phone vibrated, signaling that another call was waiting. She recognized the number. She told her dad that she was getting another call and added, "Please, whatever you do, don't interfere," she pleaded.

"Have it your way, but promise you will stay on top of things," her dad said. "Love you."

"Love you more," Crispin said, slamming the lid on the toilet and taking a seat, adjusting the bath towel around her chest before switching to the incoming call.

"Roberto?"

"I hope I'm not disturbing you. How are you feeling?"

"Better now."

"Do you need anything?"

"No. Nothing. Thanks for the call and for helping this morning."

"I called to tell you that I spoke to Bishop Pirolla and he'd like you to return to his office this afternoon. I explained that you were upset and needed time to . . ."

"I'll be there. I'll be there," Crispin interrupted.

"Are you sure? So soon?"

They agreed on a four o'clock appointment.

When the call ended Crispin changed several times before deciding on a pair of charcoal gray knit slacks and red cotton sweater set. Sitting at the end of the bed, she dug around in her jewelry bag for her grandmother's black pearl earrings in an antique sterling setting.

Since she had extra time before she left for her appointment, she called the hotel valet service to pick up her lilac dress. She decided to send Roberto's overcoat along. As she folded his coat for the cleaning bag, she felt papers in the deep side pockets. She tossed them on the bed. After the valet left, she found an envelope for Roberto's papers. She scanned them as she folded each one. The smallest was a photocopy of a newspaper clipping about a silversmith who had died cleaning a hunting rifle. The other was a four-page autopsy report for a fifty-year-old woman who'd died a few days before of anaphylaxis.

Before sealing the envelope she took them back out and laid them side by side. The silversmith and nun had the same last name. She refolded them and stuffed the envelope in her backpack, making sure she had everything she needed for her meeting with Pirolla. Before leaving she double-checked her image one last time in the mirror, smoothing Vaseline over her lips in an attempt to cover faint bloody marks where she'd chewed on the corners. As she turned to leave, she spotted the half open packet of razor blades on the floor. She picked it up and threw it in the trash.

* * *

Roberto searched for a quiet corner in the small courtyard to place a call. He knew he would only have a few minutes alone before it would fill with other priests since the Villa Stritch was a popular residence for foreign clerics visiting Rome, especially Americans.

"We have a problem," he said, without introductory formalities. "Crispin Leads was there when Father Mitchel was executed."

He listened for a minute before responding. "I know," he said, holding his left hand in his pocket and the phone close to his mouth with his right hand, while pacing the sidewalk. "Bishop Pirolla is another problem." A group of loud men was coming his way so he rushed to end the call. "I'll do what I can."

Roberto hung up and removed the cell phone's SIM card. He crushed it beneath his shoe and tossed it in a nearby trash barrel. He carried the cell phone with him to the street and disposed of it in a dumpster behind a trattoria.

Chapter Three

Crispin's hand trembled the moment she touched the door-knob. She turned and ran for the familiar safety of the bathroom. The second the door swung closed she dropped her backpack and grabbed the sink to brace herself. When she looked in the mirror the woman staring at her was a brittle silhouette of the Crispin who had confidently donned her heirloom earrings just an hour earlier. Her chest felt sodden and unnaturally heavy, like laundry waiting for the ringer. It was a shitty idea to come back so soon after what she'd witnessed this morning, she told herself. Why do I let Dad rent space in my head?

She clutched the porcelain so tightly that her wrists ached. "Get a grip, girl," she said, her voice echoing around the empty stalls. Deep breathing. Cold water. Time. Control. A crooked grin slowly crept onto the corner of her mouth as she talked herself through the calming ritual she'd learned in therapy. Her heart rate slowed and her breathing calmed. She was ready to try again.

Back at Pirolla's office door she squared her shoulders and turned the knob. Inside, the space was museum tidy and hospital clean. Quiet. Sterile. Antiseptic. Expectant. Made ready as if something might happen, but showing no sign of what had happened. Instead of police tape, slashes of sunlight fingered across the room. Crispin hadn't known what to expect when she returned, but it wasn't complete whitewashing with such speed and efficiency. The gigantic desk that had confounded Father

Mitchel was again where it should be. The surface was clean and polished. She saw no hint of fire residue or computer cabling. She noticed an exit door in the rear, one she hadn't noticed that morning.

She could hear Pirolla on the phone through the open door to his inner office so she waited at the threshold for him to see her. He glanced up and motioned for her to enter. The office was a stark contrast to the foyer and outer hallways. Its dark paneled walls and heavy drapes gave it a sense of gloom, and the furnishings gave the impression that they hadn't been rearranged or updated in decades. The lone upholstered chair had a worn-out quality, and the office did not appear to have even the most rudimentary form of technology. A Dictaphone sat next to a well-used Rolodex bulging with handwritten notes and business cards. Pirolla ignored her while she took a seat on the straight-back wooden chair across from his desk. It gave her a chance to size him up. He looked like he was at least seventy, a bit older than she'd expected, and clearly didn't spend much time in the gym. She guessed his BMI probably exceeded 30. Wisps of hair poked out the sides of his skullcap and his face was rough, dry and scaly as if he was experiencing an outbreak of eczema. When he finally hung up the phone, she had a chance to greet him.

"Good afternoon, Bishop. I'm Crispin Leads from NYU. I want to thank you for making time for me in your schedule," she said, easing her backpack onto the floor and removing a notebook and pen out of habit. "I hope you will accept my condolences for Father Mitchel. I only met him just this morning, but he was kind to me."

"Father Mitchel is no concern of yours," Pirolla said, ignoring her. "I know all about American graduate students. You are all arrogant and you, no doubt, expect special favors because of your father's connections."

"Excuse me? My research proposal to work with the Macken diaries has nothing to do with my family connections," Crispin said, crossing and uncrossing her legs and adjusting her position in the chair, fearful that her tone betrayed her uncertainty.

Pirolla didn't bother to reply as he rifled through the stack of papers that cluttered his desk until he found what he was searching for and raised it with a triumphant gesture. "The Holy Father's letter was an invitation, not a passport," the bishop snapped, his bushy gray eyebrows pointed straight up as he handed her three neatly typed sheets. "Here are the conditions you will have to meet. They are not negotiable." The maddening smirk revealing the bishop's crooked teeth told Crispin that she was in trouble.

Her papal research grant gave Crispin only one month's access to the ancient diaries she was here to study. Under Pirolla's limitations she would not see the originals. A clerk would photocopy only those portions that directly related to the narrowest confines of her study. Everything else would be blacked out. In addition, Crispin would be given access to one week of diary entries at a time. She would have to return the photocopies before receiving the next set. Nothing could leave the archives save her personal notes.

Most damning of all were the restrictions on publication. Pirolla surely knew that the right to publish is the very lifeblood of an academician. The stipulations severely restricted Crispin's ability to quote directly from the diaries. If she did use a direct quote, the Vatican had the right to review and approve any manuscripts prior to publication.

"You are required to sign this agreement before you begin. That is all," Pirolla said, picking up the receiver and dismissing her with a wave of his hand before beginning to dial.

Crispin gathered her things to leave, struggling to appear in control, even defiant. Something in her wouldn't give him the reaction she felt he expected, even wanted. If he anticipated a scene, she'd disappoint.

"I will review the requirements," she said, while folding the stipulations into her notebook. She reminded herself that she was, after all, a Leads. That meant proper manners are required in public, regardless of the provocation. The exit was difficult, but she pulled it off, remaining controlled, disciplined, even dignified. It wasn't until Crispin was safely downstairs in a small reception area that she sat down to reread the paperwork he'd given her. "God damn it to Hell and back!"

She wadded the sheets into a ball and flung them at the wall. Too late; she noticed two nuns on a nearby bench. Mortified, Crispin raced into the courtyard. Blinded by anger and frustration, only vaguely aware of the people she passed, she wandered aimlessly through a maze of unfamiliar ancient hedges until she found a fountain topped by a statue of some obscure saint. Rimmed with high-backed wooden benches, it created an alcove that offered unexpected but welcome seclusion.

Crispin threw her backpack down and dropped onto a seat. She slumped forward, covering her face with her hands. The deafening sound of blood pulsing in her ears began to quiet and she became aware of a scratching sound.

A plump, black-and-white cat, with markings that made him appear to be wearing a wimple, backed down an overhanging tree. He studied Crispin for a minute, then began rubbing against her leg, demanding attention. When she patted her knee, the cat leapt easily onto her lap almost as if to say, "Aren't I special?" The sheen to his ebony coat was evidence of his privileged life. He coaxed her hands with his head, demanding to be stroked. She was tentative at first, but with each stroke she felt calmer as her senses reconnected with her surroundings. The slightly oily smell of warm asphalt blended with the freshly trimmed lawn on each side of a driveway that was barely visible through the hedges. The hum of a generator kicked on, drowning out the soft motorboat growling from the cat's throat. The deep green of the hedges of her refuge were almost blue in contrast to the gray tones of the marble statue. She bent over and, face to face with the cat, asked, "Are you a mindfulness exercise wrapped up in feline form?" He didn't answer but commanded that she rub him under his chin.

As Crispin obeyed, one of the nuns she had seen earlier caught up with her.

"Crispin, I've been looking for you."

It took Crispin only a second before she recognized her friend from grade school.

"Ellen. Is that really you?" Crispin said, dumping the cat as she jumped up and embraced the nun.

"It's Sister Mary Llewellyn, if you please," she said with a grin. "But my friends here call me Lew."

"You'll always be 'Ellen' to me. Anyway, you have to admit, back in the day your style ran more to punk when we colored your hair purple and tried that faux nose ring to freak out the camp counselors."

"Please don't remind me," Lew said, covering her mouth with her delicate hands.

"I meant to call when I landed but it's been crazy. Let's sit and I'll tell you about it," Crispin said, motioning to the bench where the capricious cat chose just that moment to arch his back and spit at Crispin.

"Is Trinity bothering you?" Sister Lew asked.

Trinity, like a fickle lover, began to rub his cheeks up against the nun's skirts.

"Is this fella your cat?"

"Does a cat really ever belong to anyone?" Lew answered, taking a seat and lifting Trinity into her lap.

Although Sister Lew was covered from her forehead to her ankles, her face had changed little from the shy, dark-haired girl that Crispin had first met on the playground at Saint Teresa's Primary School in Torino. Her features were plain and her nose a bit wide, but her skin was still as perfect as it was when she was a teenager, especially considering that she wore no makeup.

"I don't think you will ever age," Crispin said.

"You say that every time we see each other," Lew responded with a smile. "Now, tell me how are you?"

"Fine as frog's hair."

"Crispin, I don't know another American who talks like that," Lew said, giggling. "For someone who has mastered as many foreign languages as you have, I think your English idioms might qualify as an additional language too."

"I get all my best expressions from Great Aunt Tilde," Crispin said, smiling.

"Aunt Tilde. How long has it been?"

"I think it was four or, no, five years ago," Crispin said, remembering the month that she spent with her brother and Ellen at Tilde's cabin in Connecticut.

"How is she?"

"Crazy. Funny. Full of spit and vinegar for a ninety-year-old."

"And Clinton?"

"You know my twin. Perfect. Right now, he's somewhere on a research trip in the Andes. I wished him luck, surviving six weeks without cell service."

"And, how is Dr. Leads?"

"Still caught up in Cornell University politics," Crispin replied with a shrug. "And what about your mother? I would love to finally meet her while I am in Italy."

"I'll call her. The train ride from here to Torino is easy."

Trinity began batting at a ball of paper in Lew's hand. Lew swatted him away a few times before lifting him onto the ground. "I think Trinity wants us to discuss this," she said, handing Crispin a wad of crumpled paper.

Crispin unrolled Pirolla's stipulations and smoothed them out.

"I apologize for my language earlier but it's been a rough day. You might say it started with a bang and ended with a whimper," Crispin said, reaching to stroke Trinity. "Did you hear about the priest who died this morning?"

"You mean Father Mitchel?"

"Did you know him?"

"Not well. We consulted on several matters. His death will raise questions. How do you know about it?"

Trinity, no longer able to command sufficient attention, skulked away with a twitch of his tail.

"I was there when it happened," Crispin said, unconsciously rubbing her wrists. "The police wanted to talk to me."

Sister Lew scooted closer to her friend and took her hands in silence, gently rubbing her wrists.

"Still counting each day?"

Crispin nodded.

After several moments, Lew told Crispin, "You don't have to tell me unless you want to. When you are up to it, I would also like to know what happened in the bishop's office."

"I'm not sure I could trust myself to use language fit for your ears," Crispin said, her neck and face flushing red.

"Clearly, he made you angry."

Crispin thought about what to share and what to keep to herself. "I suppose the short answer is I thought I would be less restricted in my access to Vatican documents and I'm disappointed."

"How about this? I was on my way to my office. Come with me."

"I'd like that."

The route to Lew's office took them past a large picture window that provided an unfettered view of Saint Peter's, where the nun paused to take in the view. "I pass this place many times a day and often am struck by the notion that we see things not as they are but through the mind we bring. See there, the dome. Viewed by an architect, she is a magnificent inspiration of form."

"Viewed by an historian," Crispin countered. "It is an icon representing the consequences on world affairs of Emperor Constantine's conversion experience."

Sister Lew touched the rosary that hung around her neck. "Viewed by a theologian she could symbolize the personal guidance of God's own hand on earth."

Crispin took a turn. "Since much of the marble in the basilica was harvested from the ancient Roman Coliseum, an archeologist might see it as a metaphor for the way one treasure in time often is destroyed to build another."

"Enough. You win!" Lew said, smiling.

They soon arrived at Lew's office door and made arrangements to meet for lunch the next day in a popular café on the Vatican grounds. Crispin gave Lew an affectionate hug good-bye. It wasn't until she turned to leave that Crispin noticed the sign on the wall next to the office door. The plaque, translated from Latin, read: Office for Documentation of Relics—Holy Shroud of Turin. *Dad, what are you up to now? This cannot be just a coincidence.*

She started to knock on Lew's door, but her hand paused in midair as the day caught up with her. Her mind turned to mush and the tensions she'd suppressed all day washed over her. How could one day hold so much misery? Witness to bloody mayhem. Coming within a whisper of falling back into an addiction. Disappointing Dad, once again. Confrontation over her research. There just wasn't room in this day for one more thing. Not one. All she could think about was a quick meal and a long night's sleep. "Sufficient unto the day are the troubles thereof," she told herself.

Crispin's route out of the building took her past the picture window, where she stopped again to look at Saint Peter's. "You're right about that dome, Ellen," she mumbled to herself, her thoughts turning to the dark images of the dead priest. "For me, a scholar of burial rituals, it is a tomb. A magnificent tomb to be sure, but, ultimately, a tomb."

At the Hotel Ponte Sisto Crispin ordered a simple room service supper of linguine pesto and a salad of Gorgonzola and apples with a glass of pinot grigio. She curled up in bed with her laptop intending to sort through a backlog of emails, but her eyelids grew heavy and she had trouble concentrating. Just before she pulled the covers over her head she sat up and jumped from the bed. She dug through the trash and retrieved the razor blades.

She wrapped the package in a sock and stowed it in the bottom drawer of her dresser before turning out her lights for the night.

* * *

Roberto stopped short. The door to his basement office was open and the fluorescent light was on. He wasn't expecting anyone this time of the night. He stood at the threshold for a minute before tapping softly on the door.

"Good evening," he said in a muted voice for fear of startling the woman sitting at his desk with her back to him.

Sister Llewellyn turned and smiled. "You were right, Father. Your files are a complete mess."

"I didn't intend for you to work this late," he said, knowing she'd slept little since the death of Sister Sarah.

"If you have time, I can show you what I've organized for you."

Roberto joined her, pulling several file cartons from along the wall to form a makeshift stool next to the desk. He listened as she explained each of the stacks of papers she had arranged on the desk. On top of each one she had placed several handwritten pages of summary material.

"This should help you finalize the reports on Jubilee events," she said. "Everything is arranged chronologically and cross referenced by type of event. Once these are entered into the database, I think it should go quickly."

"Thank you. And this can remain between just the two of us?" Roberto said. "The bishop has been in a black mood for weeks."

"I know! A friend of mine from the States met with him today. She felt he treated her unfairly."

"Are you talking about Crispin Leads?"

"Yes. How do you know her?"

"Coincidence. Nothing really. And you?"

"We've been friends since grade school when her father was working on the Holy Shroud." Sister Lew turned toward the desk, her back to Roberto. "Crispin told me she was there when Father Mitchel died."

"What else did she tell you?"

Sister Lew turned around to face Roberto. "Father, don't you see?" She lowered her voice. "Now three have died."

"Your grief may be coloring your judgment."

Sister Lew crossed herself. "Yes, but there is something more. I feel it."

Roberto shook his head as he stood and shoved a carton to its original location along the wall. When he turned around Sister Lew was watching him.

"Did Crispin put those ideas in your head? Do you know what the police told her when they interviewed her?" Roberto asked.

"We haven't had time to talk about what happened."

"She was obviously traumatized by what she saw. It was as if her soul had been torn out."

"Crispin had an early childhood loss that made today especially difficult."

"That explains it. When I first met her, she was so bright. So happy. But, afterwards, when I found her on the floor, I almost didn't recognize her."

"Father, I do not intend to step out of place, but I . . ." Lew didn't finish the sentence and instead looked down and held onto her rosary.

"Please, say what you have to say."

"It's just this. Although she is not a flirtatious woman, Crispin is not always conscious of how attractive she can be."

And this, thought Roberto, is the challenge of working with someone who knows my past. "Your point is well taken, Sister," he responded, working another carton back into place along the wall. When he turned back to face the desk, Sister Lew was attempting to suppress a yawn.

"You've done more than I ever expected and I'm grateful," he said. "But it has been a long day. Please try to get some rest."

After Sister Lew left, Roberto locked his office door and returned to his desk. Removing a key from a chain around his neck, he opened the bottom desk drawer and took out a large accordion file. Scanning the contents, he inserted sheets one by one into a desktop shredder and watched as they turned into confetti.

Chapter Four

The pages of the Macken diary that the Vatican librarian gave Crispin looked like they were covered with grocery store barcodes on steroids. Huge sections were blacked out, and some sentences were so distorted by the rampant censoring that it was impossible to understand the context of the monk's observations. Staring at the excerpts, Crispin heard her inner voice mock her arrogance. "Silly girl, did you really think this was your big break? It's either a discourse on funeral rites or a recipe for Mulligan stew," she muttered as she flipped over the final page in disgust.

"Excuse me, Crispin?"

She was startled because she hadn't heard Roberto walk up.

"May I join you?" he asked.

Crispin nodded as he slid into a seat across from the polished oak table.

"You seem well. How do you feel?"

"Much better, Father," she said with a smile. "Thank you for asking."

"Please, 'Roberto.'"

"Okay, Roberto," Crispin said with a grin. "I got some rest and have settled in at the hotel, but I still shudder when I think about Father Mitchel. Have they figured out what went wrong?"

"It's in the hands of the police, but Vatican officials are giving their full cooperation," he replied. "What about you? Has Detective Moss followed up with you?"

"No, and I don't think she will. I've told her all that I know."

"I understand you may have heard someone leave the bishop's office after the lights went out."

"I told her I couldn't be certain," she said, wondering who had told him that.

Roberto nodded. "It's unfortunate that your introduction to our Holy City was so ugly. I pray that the rest of your stay will be peaceful and productive. Tell me, is your research off to a good start?"

"What can I say?" she replied, hoping her face didn't betray her frustration.

"If it would not interrupt your work, I would like to hear more."

"Are you sure? I can go on and on."

Leaning forward on his elbows, he wrapped his good hand around his bad and gestured her to talk. "I wouldn't ask if I didn't think it was interesting."

"In a broad sense, I am working on a hypothesis that the ritualizing of burial customs is universal for all of mankind over time, across cultures and across society," she said, tenting her fingers as if it were the beginning of a speech she'd given more than once. "Did you know that the Neanderthals, our closest evolutionary relatives, sometimes buried their dead? You might say the need to ritualize death is in our DNA."

"I see. And the research you're doing here adds to that work."

"This is the diary of Father John Macken," she said, indicating the pages on the table. "They document death rituals from 600 A.D. Although Macken was an Irish monk, he spent most of his life in the Middle East. Lucky for me, he was meticulous, recording extensive interviews about ancient funerary practices in far-away lands. His diaries will help me to fill in one section on my global map of ancient burial rituals."

"You are fortunate that your research request came this year."

"I know. The Call for Proposals specifically indicated that the Vatican would entertain requests from scholars as a way to highlight the significance of the Year 2000 because it marks the third millennium of the Christian faith," Crispin replied before realizing she'd told Roberto what every priest already knew.

"You might be surprised at the number and scope of projects that the Holy Father has blessed—scholarship, restoration, education, and outreach—in the name of the new millennium," Roberto said. "Just keeping track of all the avenues and initiatives has proven a challenge."

"Well, things along this particular avenue aren't going exactly as I planned. You might say there are a few dead ends and off ramps on this scholarship road," Crispin admitted, as Roberto picked up the censored diary entries.

"Why, Crispin . . . ," he said, flipping through pages that had more blacked-out passages than readable text.

"My idea of 'access' differs from that of Bishop Pirolla."

"Crispin, do you have the pope's letter inviting you to the Vatican?"

Crispin pulled her precious letter from her backpack and gave it to him.

"I was thrilled when I got the papal grant," she said, a touch of regret in her voice. "Apparently, to quote the bishop, the letter is 'an invitation, not a passport.'"

Crispin handed Pirolla's stipulations to Roberto. He flattened out the wrinkled pages, but only read the first page when he abruptly stood. "Excuse me one moment."

She lost sight of him when he disappeared around the corner of bookshelves at the end of the room. She turned over the sad diary pages and again tried to make sense of them, jotting down the few sentences and random phrases that had not been censored.

Crispin thought back to the first time she'd learned of Macken, a reference in an obscure footnote at the end of an article she'd been reading in an academic journal. When she asked questions of her professor, he made an off-handed comment that only a handful of scholars had seen parts of the diaries and no one, to his knowledge, had ever had access to the full life work of the monk. Within two weeks, she'd prepared her grant application, acquired glowing letters of endorsement from her NYU professors, and submitted it to the Vatican for consideration.

She'd applied for grants before, but somehow this one felt different. It tugged at her, and she found herself checking her email dozens of times a day in anticipation of a response. So when she opened the mailbox at her father's house in Ithaca two weeks after the semester ended at NYU, she was elated to find the envelope addressed to her stuffed in with her father's journals, newsprint grocery ads, and junk mail. On reflection, she realized that a formal written notification, as opposed to email, suited an organization such as the Vatican. She took her time enjoying the feel of the thing before her, the weight of the paper stock and elegant letterhead. Although her address was typewritten, the use of Chancery typeface gave it a mock-calligraphy appearance and feel. The acceptance letter meant that she was to be the first secular scholar given access to the diaries.

Now her victory was dissolving into defeat. Why waste time? Pirolla had won. Crispin started packing her notebook and pens, along with her aspirations.

Roberto returned before she finished. "I hope you don't mind, but I have made arrangements. The clerk has made a private study area available to you," he said. "You can leave your material there each day."

"I'm not sure that will be necessary," she said.

"Will you, at least, consider it?" he asked, with a gesture and a nod indicating the direction of the study area.

Crispin shrugged, picked up her backpack, and followed Roberto to a cubical in the rear of the library. When he turned on the light and unlocked the storage cabinet above the desk, she was stunned to see the Macken volumes neatly lined up on the shelf. It took a moment for Crispin to realize what was sitting on the shelf within arm's reach. "How?"

"I have certain privileges."

"I can't let you do this. This is my fight. Won't you get in trouble?"

"Do not concern yourself."

"No, Roberto, it will never work. It's better that I quit instead of have Pirolla accuse me of something underhanded," she said, closing the bin and returning the key to Roberto.

"The invitation that the Holy Father sent to you was clear. He granted access to the diaries. I offer no more."

"What if Pirolla finds out?"

"Let me worry about the bishop," Roberto said, laying the key back on the desk and turning to leave.

Before he was too far away Crispin called after him to remind him that she had his overcoat, and they arranged to meet at her hotel lobby that evening so that she could return it.

"Supper too?" she added, but he responded with a noncommittal nod and waved good-bye.

Yes? No? Maybe? These Italians aren't so easy to read.

Minutes ticked by as Crispin sat eyeing the key and considering her options, her mind racing through the arguments for and against the opportunity before her. She longed to stand her ground, but she'd played too many card games not to recognize when she'd been dealt a losing hand. The censored diaries were useless. If she refused Roberto's offer, what would she tell her dad? And that snooty Dr. Pierce? Crispin unconsciously mouthed a caricature of Laurie Pierce's admonition, with its condescending tone of feigned concern. "My dear, you mustn't feel bad. Not all of us are cut out for serious research."

The person she most dreaded telling was Clinton. While her twin brother would, without a doubt, support her, like he always did, he really couldn't understand. She saw him the way she pictured the character that Robert Redford played in the 1970s film *The Way We Were*. Like Redford, for Clinton, "everything came too easy." From the first time she saw the movie, Crispin identified with the character played by Barbra Streisand. She'd worked harder and with more passion than her male counterpart, but still never quite caught up with him. Like the Redford character, Clinton was often unaware of how attractive he was. When they were growing up, Clinton was the one with the irresistible charm that other children gravitated to. All he had to do was enter a room and, before long, the others would surround him, laughing and jostling to be the one to sit nearest him.

Clinton was the person she was most connected to. It was more than the fact that they had been together even before they were born. It was their loss, that day on the tarmac in Egypt, that forever bound them.

The question that he'd asked her more than once over the years echoed in her head: "Crispin, you don't really believe we're on this earth to win a competition, do you?" She'd always answered with a lie, pretending that she didn't think that way. Today, however, she couldn't lie to herself. Clinton's excursion in the Andes promised to put his line of research on the map. She couldn't face the prospect of returning to New York a failure. She wouldn't let her twin beat her this time. She stared at the opportunity Roberto had put before her and felt the hard core of her resolve turn to applesauce. Roberto's right, she told herself. A pope trumps a bishop. She unlocked the bin, opened a notebook, and began taking notes from the first volume of the diary. Three long, exhausting, exciting hours later Crispin turned in her photocopies from the first diary. "I'll be back," she told the librarian. She almost skipped out of the library for her lunch date.

Chapter Five

Lew was saving her a place in the plaza café where tourists and Vatican regulars sat elbow close at small metal tables so they could grab a serving of fresh air with their soup. Once the waiter had taken their order, Crispin swallowed hard and confronted Lew with the question that had been gnawing at her since yesterday.

"I saw the sign at your office so I have to ask. Just how is your job related to the Shroud of Turin?"

"I am a documentarian for the Holy Shroud and . . . ," Lew said, stopping in mid sentence. "What's the matter? I get the feeling that I've said something wrong."

"Is Dad pulling strings again?"

"What do you mean?"

They were interrupted when the waiter delivered a generous plate of hot bread with a side of spiced olive oil for dipping. Crispin grabbed a hunk of bread from the loaf and began methodically tearing it into smaller and smaller pieces while Lew watched.

"I have to know. Did he call you?" Crispin asked with bitterness she couldn't hide.

"No, Crispin. It's not like that at all. Our mutual interest in Shroud research has kept us in contact over the years, but he did not call me. I promise."

Crispin dropped the bread and started rubbing her wrists. "One more question. Will you tell me the truth?"

"If I can."

"Did my dad have anything to do with the fact that my research grant was approved?"

Lew took her time responding. "It was a blind review. I don't see how he could have influenced the outcome."

Crispin didn't answer, scraping the emaciated bread into her hand and returning it to the basket.

Lew watched her friend and added, "Your grant proposal was well thought out. Well written. Supported by scholars in your field. It was a first-rate proposal that succeeded on its own merit. Why can't you see that?"

Crispin tore off a hunk of bread and dipped it into the spicy garlic oil and began to eat. She wanted to believe Lew, but she knew her dad too well.

"It's not your fault. It's me. I always have the feeling he's pulling the strings. I'm sorry if I sounded like a bit . . ." Crispin caught herself before completing the sentence. "Enough about me. Tell me how you wound up in the Vatican working on the Shroud."

"I suppose I've known since I was a child that someday I would be here, doing this work. People have been coming to Torino for five hundred years to see where the burial cloth of Jesus is kept. So, I guess, I grew up taking it for granted, the way children do. That changed when they put the Shroud on public display. I was eight when we went to the roof of a movie theater across the street from the Cathedral to watch the pilgrims. Remember?"

"I do remember," Crispin said, interrupting Lew. "I went with you because Dad had been working night and day in the weeks before the opening so his team could gather additional samples from blood stains on the linen. They were rushing to finish before the Shroud grand opening. I wanted to see what all the fuss was about."

"You only went with me that first day. What I didn't tell you was that I went back every day after school, watching as the people lined up for hours to file pass the relic. They came seeking tangible proof of God's presence on Earth," Lew said. "I'm sure that we don't give children enough credit for genuine revelation but, Crispin, as I watched them, day after day, I was moved, in a profound way, by their simple act of faith, and I knew that I was called to this service."

The waiter arrived with their order: fish soup flavored with clams and bitter orange peels for Lew and cold gazpacho and soft tetilla cheese with crusty toast points for Crispin. For a few minutes the two hungry women concentrated on lunch.

"Doesn't it bother you that scientists like Dad keep trying to prove the Shroud is a nothing more than an elaborate medieval hoax concocted more than a thousand years after the crucifixion followed by, shall I say, a rather fuzzy history until the Savoys took possession?"

"You may be surprised to know that I consider science to be a friend of faith," the nun explained. "We have nothing to fear from legitimate scientific inquiry because it cannot disprove what *is*. What is, simply is," she said.

"Scientists can come down on both sides of the dialogue, and clerics—even though they want to believe—can find themselves turned into skeptics by the evidence," Sister Lew said. "With each new technological breakthrough, whether it be radiocarbon dating or new photo imaging techniques from space, scientists have tried to use their toys to settle the question of authenticity."

The waiter interrupted Lew to clear the table and asked if they wanted dessert.

"I will if you will," Crispin said in a conspiratorial tone. They ordered a sweet custard and coffee.

"I'm sure that science cannot prove the Holy Cloth to be a fake or to be genuine. Such questions belong to the realm of faith, not the realm of science," Lew said. Motioning to the buildings and grounds of the Vatican, she said simply, "We build our foundation on faith because proof is impossible."

"But to find truth, you must seek proof," Crispin replied. "The beauty of science is its precision. Its impartiality. I hope that doesn't sound disrespectful."

"Not at all. For all their three-dimensional images, pollen analysis, blood tests, carbon dating, and textile history, they have not, they cannot, affect the meaning in the Shroud. What I learned when I watched those pilgrims serves me today. It doesn't matter whether the Holy Shroud is a hoax or a genuine relic. Either way, it was surely the work of God because it inspires people to examine their faith."

Crispin smiled. "As Saint Thomas Aquinas reminds us, 'To one who has faith, no explanation is necessary. To one without faith, no explanation is possible.'"

"So you haven't forgotten our school days," Lew smiled.

After finishing lunch, Crispin and Lew gave each other a long good-bye embrace, agreeing to meet again the next day.

* * *

With a productive afternoon under her belt Crispin returned to her hotel intent on the prospect of delivering a positive progress report to her father, especially after yesterday's phone call. Today reminded Crispin of all that she loved about doing research. Holding the ancient diaries that had been lovingly carried thousands of miles made Crispin feel a link with their author. Crispin imagined Macken, hundreds of years ago, sitting on the hardscrabble ground of some long-forgotten Middle Eastern village, patiently probing a village elder with questions about his grandparents' burial customs.

She learned that in these remote desert villages it was the mothers and grandmothers who prepared their dead by washing them with what was their most precious commodity: water. The magnitude of this gesture of devotion filled Crispin with admiration. She felt, as she had so many times before when she learned of new burial customs, that she had tapped into the truest vein of human nature, and it was tender and transcendent.

Eager to tell her father, she sat cross-legged on the bed and dialed his number in New York. With the six-hour time difference she was sure she'd be able to catch him at home. The phone rang once before a woman picked it up. The woman giggled as if someone were tickling her toes as she said, "Hello."

"May I speak to Dr. Leads?"

"Who may I say is calling?"

"This is Crispin. Crispin Leads."

Crispin could hear the woman whisper. "Daniel, it's your daughter."

"Hello, Crispin."

For the first time in her life, her dad's voice sounded like that of a stranger.

"Who was that?" Crispin asked.

"You remember Laurie, don't you?"

Had she caught them in coitus? It was too weird to contemplate. Before she could think of an exit strategy Crispin was saved by a knock on the door. "Sorry, Dad, can't talk after all. There's someone at the door. I'll send you a long email."

"And call me tomorrow. I expect a full report."

"Will do. Love you."

"Love you more."

Crispin hopped off the bed and opened the door. It was the hotel valet service with her dry cleaning. After he left, she paced up and down, but she couldn't shake the mental image of her dad in bed with Laurie Pierce.

"What does Dad see in that blonde ass-kisser with a pedestrian curriculum vitae who pranced around campus in short skirts, advertising her wares?" Crispin said to herself, randomly opening and closing drawers without taking anything out or putting anything in. She brushed her teeth, combed her hair, and tried opening email, but nothing worked. So, finally, she did what she often did when confronted with something she didn't want to think about. She went in search of a cemetery.

Chapter Six

This is where it started, this fascination with the rituals of death. As a child she was as much at home in a graveyard as a playground. Crispin couldn't understand why her friends thought they were creepy. For Crispin, graves and graveyards were a tangible, earthbound connection to those who came before, those whose DNA soup made us who we are. That's where Crispin found signs of life and love in what others called dead places. It was also there that she could imagine her mother's soft voice in shadowed memories of long walks and secret talks. Her mother would hold her hand as they strolled the neat rows, reading the faded inscriptions out loud. Even now, Crispin could hear her voice. "What does that say, Little One?"

She knew the game well. Her mother was asking her to do more than simply recite the words on the stones. She wanted her daughter to understand the whole message. She wanted her to think about the question beneath the question. "What does it say?" was her way of asking, "What story does the grave tell you? Look carefully, Little One. Use more than your eyes. Use your mind. What do you see? What does it mean?"

Crispin would go through all the possibilities. Is it part of a cozy family plot, or does it stand alone amid strangers? How much is written on the marker about the person? Name, date of birth, date of death? Or, is there more? Does it quote scripture? Song? Poem? Does it seem as if a loved one wrote the inscription?

Are the words part of a fuller life story? Do they give shape to the life narrative or do they hide it? How about the stone? Its shape? Its size? Is there an emblem, statue, or carving or is it unadorned?

"Listen to everything. Listen deeply with your heart as well as your head. That is where you will find meaning," her mother would remind her.

It was during these question games that Crispin came to appreciate how words alone don't tell a story. You have to see the whole text as well as the context. What is left unsaid as well as what is said. How it is said. Where and when it is said. The words may lie, or evade, but the text never does.

For tonight's escape to a graveyard, the hotel concierge recommended the Campo Cestro, Rome's legendary cemetery for non-Catholics. On her way out of the hotel, Crispin left a note for Roberto and hurried before the fading light would make it difficult to read the marble markers.

At the cemetery gate she met up with a gardener weeding a bed of iris. He told her she only had about twenty-five minutes before he would lock up for the night. As she made her way through the cramped array of aged stones, decapitated carvings, and weeping angels, a pervasive evening gloom soon settled like an unfamiliar weight around her shoulders. Stepping back from one grave, she nearly tripped over tree roots that seemed to reach like a gnarled hand through the soil from the very heart of the grave. At another, the stone carving of a toddler reached out, begging her to lead him away.

She wandered deeper into the cemetery, but tonight most of the graves were close-mouthed and silent, almost mocking. "Talk to me," she said to the bust of the bald man with the craggy face, vacant eyes, and lumpy forehead, tilted backwards against the headstone as if he had been startled. But her concentration was off and she got no reply. Everywhere, there was sadness, wrapped in silence. "Maybe this was a bad idea," she whispered to herself.

Daylight was fading into evening and the birds were roosting in the trees when Crispin realized that she was disoriented. She began to work her way out when she spotted the iconic waist-high marble twin grave markers, one of which commemorated the burial place of the British poet John Keats. By then the light was so bad that she had to lean in close to read the famous inscription: "Here lies One Whose Name was writ in Water." She tilted her head to reflect on the poet's final words when the snap of a twig alarmed the birds in the tree behind her. She ducked as they flew overhead.

When all was silent again she straightened back up, just as something buzzed by her ear. She jerked around to see if anything else was going to fly by but, at first, could see nothing moving except the gardener, who was pushing his mulch-laden wheelbarrow. She started to call to him to ask directions when she spotted a man with a familiar blond ponytail standing near the stone retaining wall. Before she could react, he took off and disappeared into the night.

Chapter Seven

Bishop Pirolla slammed down the receiver and barked at Roberto. "I don't want to deal with that woman again."

"What woman?" Roberto asked.

"That British detective. The one who has been nosing around since Father Mitchel's death."

"Detective Moss?"

"That's the one," Pirolla answered, leaning back in his chair and grabbing a handful of Glitterati mints from the dish on his desk. He began unwrapping one with gusto. "She doesn't understand how things work around here." The bishop polished off three more mints, chewing hard before adding the colorful wrappers to the pile growing on his desk.

"Mitchel's death was an accident. A terrible tragedy. But, she's using it as an excuse to stick her nose into places she doesn't belong. Suggesting someone killed him. Foolishness. Who would do such a thing? He was one of the most efficient assistants I ever had," Pirolla said, picking up the receiver again but pausing before placing the call. "She should close the file and move on. You need to get her in line."

"I'll do what I can."

"You keep telling me that, but I need results. And, I still don't have your reports. When will they be finished? I arranged all manner of clearance for you to expedite your work and, yet, you have nothing to show for it," Pirolla said, dismissing the younger man with a wave of his hand. "See to it."

"Of course," Roberto said, standing to leave.

Three floors down, Roberto unlocked the door to the windowless workroom where he had set up shop. The wall across from his metal desk was still stacked with cardboard boxes full of papers and reports. He locked the office door and settled into the folding chair. He pulled a small radio from the bottom drawer and plugged it into a wall socket, twisting the dial until he was able to receive a clear broadcast of the local sports radio station and tuned it to his favorite rugby team. He surveyed the stack of boxes before removing his shoes, jacket, vest, shirt, and collar, folding each neatly and stacking them on the desk.

The price of my sins, he thought as he examined the deep scars that ran in twisted bands of crimson from his armpit to his deformed hand.

Dressed only in his undershirt and slacks, he took a few minutes to engage in the stretching and flexibility routine he'd learned in physical therapy. Stretching complete, he dropped to the floor and pumped through several dozen one-hand pushups. He followed the floor exercises with a vigorous round of air boxing as if he were in a dual with an unseen enemy. He held his fists in a well-practiced grip, jabbing, bobbing, and weaving until sweat beaded his face and undershirt. The announcer on the radio yelled out the winner of the game and the crowd erupted in cheers as he reached over and turned the radio off.

He went down on his knees, closed his eyes, and cupped his hands in prayer. In time, he let out a sigh, returned to the folding chair, and redressed slowly. He pulled two boxes close to the desk and opened them. Using his good hand he began to unpack the files and arrange them on the desk.

* * *

Crispin raced down the one-way street through the kind of rain that wets everything but doesn't soak through. She glanced back to see if the phantom from the graveyard was following her. He wasn't. Get a grip, she told herself as she sprinted past a group of high-spirited youths parking their motor scooters outside a nightclub. She peeked inside when she passed the open door. The bouncer, a tall guy in skintight pants, motioned for her to join the party.

Crispin brushed him off. Sensing that the weather gods were on the verge of a change in mood, she picked up her pace. She was relieved to see Roberto coming in the opposite direction toward her when she arrived at her hotel. He carried his hat in his right hand as if inviting the rain, which had already dampened his hair into a mass of honey-colored curls, reminding her of profiles of Caesar on ancient coins. She was struck, as she had been in the Vatican, by how he stood out as he walked through the crowd. At that moment, the whole Roman street scene seemed intended for only one purpose: as a backdrop for this man. Even the streetlight cooperated, fighting through the fading evening to suddenly brighten just that spot.

She waved and tried to swing her hair over her shoulder. Since it had come loose from her oversize barrette, the move only succeeded in earning her a mouth full of damp hair as she greeted him under the awning of the hotel. "Looks like you're going to need your raincoat tonight," she told him as she spat her hair out in embarrassment.

"I am not concerned."

"Let me fetch it," she told him as they walked into the lobby.

"I'll wait here," he said, taking a seat.

In her room, Crispin changed into dry clothes and took the time to brush her hair and pin it back into place. Although it was after normal business hours, she called the personal cell phone number that Detective Moss had written on the back of her business card. The detective picked up on the second ring.

"Hello. This is Crispin Leads. Sorry to bother you so late, but you asked me to call if I had any information."

"Yes."

"It may be nothing, but I think I saw the man from Father Mitchel's office tonight."

"Which one?"

"The one with the ponytail."

"Where?"

Crispin filled her in on the encounter at the cemetery.

"It was getting dark and he was running away from me," Crispin said with a note of uncertainty.

"Show me in the morning."

"I plan to work at the Vatican in the morning." Crispin replied, already regretting her impetuous call.

"So, meet me at the cemetery gate at 7:30."

"Okay, if you think it will help," she said, biting her lip to avoid the temptation to complain about the early hour.

In the lobby, Crispin gave Roberto his coat, still in the dry cleaner's bag.

"You've had it cleaned. That wasn't necessary," he told her as he removed his coat from the plastic.

"This was in the pocket," Crispin said, handing him the envelope with the papers she'd removed from his coat.

Roberto accepted the envelope and shoved it into his pocket without comment. "You mentioned dinner together, but with the weather, perhaps another time."

"Please, Roberto. You're about the only good thing that's happened to me since I got to Rome. The least I can do is buy you supper."

Smiling, Roberto agreed. "Of course, I would enjoy your company, but I can't let you pay."

"Dutch?"

"Agreed."

They decided to dine in the hotel restaurant since the evening sky had turned ominous. They weren't the only ones seeking shelter. The dining room was crowded, but the host found them the last available table. It was by the door to the kitchen, which flung open as they sat down. A waiter holding a tray over his head rushed past them.

Roberto ordered wine, and the waiter left them each with a large leather-bound menu.

Studying her menu Crispin said, "I could eat a horse."

"I do not believe *cavallo* is a delicacy on the Roman menu."

"Oh, that's not what I meant. It's just an expression."

Roberto was grinning, almost laughing.

"You're pulling my leg, right?" When he abruptly stopped smiling, she grappled for an explanation. "Just another expression."

"I get it," he said, his smile returning.

She was grateful when the waiter interrupted with a bottle of Sangiovese and bread. He uncorked the wine and poured a small amount into Roberto's glass. Roberto tasted it and motioned for the waiter to fill their glasses.

"I have a confession," Crispin said.

"Ah, I didn't realize you were Catholic."

"I'm not. I went to a parochial school for a few years but I was raised Presbyterian. Besides, it's not that kind of confession."

"What is your confession?" Roberto asked as the kitchen door flung open again and several waiters whisked past them with trays laden with food, leaving in their wake the aroma of tomatoes, roasted peppers, and hot oil.

Crispin fidgeted with her napkin, hoping Roberto didn't notice she was blushing. "I read your papers."

Roberto picked up his glass of wine and studied it for a while before taking a drink. He set it down before he replied. "I see."

Before he could say more, the waiter returned and took their order. Once they were alone again, Crispin returned the conversation to the papers she'd found in his pocket.

"Who are they? The two who died? Ms. Sarah Anne and Kevin Doyle? I couldn't help but notice they were related. Irish?"

"Two unfortunate souls."

Crispin waited for Roberto to say more. He didn't. She let the subject drop, but she couldn't help herself from pointing out the obvious. "You are not exactly one to chat it up, are you?"

Roberto helped himself to bread, dipping it into the olive oil, before responding.

"I would rather listen to you. Were your research efforts today a success?"

"Were they ever! People don't write like that anymore. Beautiful, long passages, full of description and observation. And, details, details, details. I hit the mother lode. How can I ever repay you?"

"That isn't really necessary. But if you insist, I would like to know more about your research."

The waiter interrupted them again, setting out their first course. "My research paper will probably only be read by a few dozen other scholars in a dusty academic journal, but I hope someday I'll find a way to get a broader audience because I believe the theme is universal," Crispin said, taking a big bite of her mozzarella and sweet corn salad.

"I think I understand."

"There is something in all of us, some innately human trait that is drawn to ritual. Don't you think?"

"It is, of course, comforting to rely on the certainty of the sacrament, in times of joy but also, especially, in times of pain."

"Burial rituals come in so many forms. Even the obituaries in the newspaper are a form of ritual," Crispin said. "Sometimes when you read them, your heart aches because you didn't get to know the person and now it is too late. I've even memorized some. Little life poems really, published in death."

"I've never heard anyone say it in just that way. Do you have an example?"

Crispin paused to think. "It's not that I can't think of one. It's that I can think of so many. My dilemma is which to choose."

Roberto smiled. "Please, no hurry."

"Here's one I liked," she said, clearing her throat. "'She loved lost causes, her grandmother's chipped china cups, a bad-tempered parrot that will outlive us all, anything handwritten, something sweet first thing in the morning, and a quilt of uncertain origins (not necessarily in that order).'"

After the waiter cleared their first course and served the pasta dishes, Roberto asked, "I wonder if the person who wrote that obituary ever told her what he felt, how special she was?"

"Probably not. Life gets in the way of feelings."

"You think you have time and then you don't," he said.

"Death can come dangerously quick."

"Unwelcome. Uninvited. Unexpected."

Crispin realized that they had both stopped eating, the words suspended in a still place without air, or breath, or sound.

Chapter Eight

Crispin met Detective Moss at the cemetery just as the gates were being unlocked. She'd started to think her imagination was playing tricks on her when their initial search in the early-morning light didn't produce results. That's when the gardener noticed the handle of a knife. The blade was embedded in the dirt beside Keats' grave marker. It was clear that the knife hadn't been there for long.

Moss pulled on a rubber glove and held it up. "Recognize this?"

"It was late and dark. I'm sorry."

Crispin didn't know much about knives, but this one certainly didn't belong in a kitchen. It reminded her of the camping knife Clinton had in Boy Scouts, but much sharper and, somehow, more sinister.

"I'll take this in for analysis," Moss said, slipping the knife into a plastic evidence bag.

* * *

Just before noon it was a restive Crispin who waited in the Vatican gardens for her second lunch date with Lew. Her restlessness was in part the product of an adrenaline high because she'd accomplished so much with the Macken diaries during the morning. Years of tedium in libraries had taught her that often the really good days in research were scattered thinly across the calendar. Most days it was a tight race to see whether procrastination, laziness, or boredom would overtake her first. Today, however, was like winning a treasure hunt. Holding the ancient pages made her feel as if she could span the centuries and actually touch the author.

She'd bought a folder of Macken quotations with her to share with Lew. Unable to suppress her excitement, Crispin decided to surprise Sister Lew in her office rather than wait for her in the gardens. She found Sister Lew's office door open and assumed it meant that Lew hadn't gone far. Instead of sitting patiently in an armchair, Crispin did what many do while waiting. She fingered the bric-a-brac like a bargain hunter at a tag sale, turning over small items on Lew's desk to read the imprints on the bottom. The pencil holder was vintage English sterling. The coffee cup and saucer were Rosenthal.

In a small brass framed photo, Lew stood between a woman and a distinguished, bearded man with a cane. The woman was a ringer for Sister Lew, just a bit older. It reminded Crispin of a photo taken when she graduated from college, with Dad beaming on one side and Clinton on the other, so she surmised this was Lew's family photo, taken when she finished her tutelage before taking holy orders. The woman must be her mother and the gentleman her beloved Uncle Angelo. As a girl Lew often told stories of her uncle, who filled a void after the untimely death of her father.

The stern voice of Professor Leads invaded Crispin's subconscious: "There you go again, Crispin, fabricating a conclusion based on little more than rank speculation and emotional supposition. Where is the empirical evidence? Where is the proof?" She found herself where she so often did at moments like this, caught between her mother's teachings to draw meaning from the text and the rigid, sometimes hard quantification imposed by her father. Crispin conceded her dad's mental criticism. She didn't have the first clue about the events depicted in the photograph.

Near it on the desk was something less ambiguous: an open file of newspaper clippings. More from idle curiosity and boredom than from genuine interest, she leafed through them. They were about the fire that destroyed most of Turin's San Giovanni Cathedral in 1997. There were pictures of the Cathedral before and after the fire, and dramatic shots of the fire itself. One showed a young fireman dashing from the Cathedral carrying the silver casket that contained the Shroud of Turin.

The heroic rescue of the Shroud made all of the major newspapers around the world. A lone fireman dodged falling timbers to reach the alcove, where the casket was encased in heavy bulletproof glass. After he'd freed the relic, he'd made it to safety just as the burning roof collapsed behind him. The dramatic photo of the bareheaded fireman emerging as if from the devil's own kiln was featured prominently in several of the news clippings. In one, the scene was cropped to show the fireman close up and in sharp focus.

It was Roberto.

His left hand gripped the bottom of the hot metal casket because the handle on that side was broken. Smoke and flames were visible near the cuff of his jacket, but his face betrayed no pain. Mesmerized by the photo, Crispin didn't hear Sister Lew return.

"Now you know our Father Rossini's turning," she said as she unloaded a handful of books onto a side table.

"Caught in the act," Crispin said, fumbling to replace the folders on the desk. "You know how I can let my curiosity get the better of me. It's a nasty habit. Unforgivable—shameful, really."

"The lure of the Holy Shroud can be powerful," Lew answered, without a hint of judgment in her voice.

"You're too forgiving. I'll just wait in the hall while you close up."

"Crispin, you don't need to do that. It will only take a minute and I'll be ready."

Lew replaced the file of news clippings in a cardboard storage box with painstaking care. She slid the box inside a twelve-foot-tall wooden cabinet. A brass bolt ran the height of the cabinet and rested in a deep floor grommet. The latch on the bolting mechanism was secured with a four-inch steel padlock. Lew gave the lock a test shake before stowing the key in a compartment at the base of a reading lamp on her desk. Her office door stuck a little and Lew had to pull it sharply to get it to shut completely before she could lock it.

She suggested they enjoy the fresh air of the Pigna Courtyard before lunch to avoid the crowds at the café.

"Will you tell me about Roberto?" Crispin asked as they strolled.

"That depends on your motive," Sister Lew teased.

"Curiosity."

"Ah, your 'nasty habit,'" Sister Lew said, as she tucked her arm comfortably through Crispin's. She recommended that they circumnavigate the perimeter to avoid the crowds of visitors filling the pathways that crisscrossed the popular gathering place. Roberto's personal story began to unfold as they walked.

"How do you know so much about him?" Crispin asked.

"Many things. We are both from Torino and we both lost parents as children. At least I had my mother and Uncle Angelo. He was an orphan as a toddler."

Lew pulled Crispin closer to her, a reminder that their childhood losses bound them.

For a microsecond Crispin's mind flashed back to the fire on the tarmac, but she quickly slammed the door. "We each have our memories," she said.

"Mama's stories about Papa are so vivid that I feel as if I was there when they happened. Sometimes it is hard to separate my own memories from the stories my mother told me," Lew said.

"It is an ancient belief, but I think a true one, that a person is not really gone until no one is still alive who can remember them," Crispin said.

"Then my papa is alive because I remember him."

"My mother didn't die until I was five and I had my brother, Clinton, to help me keep her memory fresh. For so long it was Clinton, Dad, and me. We were a team. *Les Trois Mousquetaires.*"

"Has that changed?"

"Sort of. But, we were talking about Roberto and you. Tell me more."

Lew told Crispin that her personal connection with Father Rossini was strengthened when she interviewed him as part of her archive work for the Shroud. "I got the impression that he spent more time at university playing sports and playing around than going to class, but still he managed to squeak by."

He was on the path to graduate when something happened. He never disclosed exactly what, but he dropped out before finishing and joined the National Fire Service. He'd been on active duty only a few months when the Cathedral caught fire. After a long hospitalization and rehabilitation, he began the process of entering the priesthood.

"The Holy Shroud has a way of imposing its power when least expected. There is no choice. There is no chance," Sister Lew said.

"I had dinner with him last night," Crispin said.

"You and Father Rossini?"

"We talked about death." The silence that often accompanies the mention of death flicked between them for an instant.

"What do you mean, you talked about death?"

"Well, actually, it was mostly me. I thought, maybe, his work involved grief counseling since I found an obituary and autopsy report in the coat he loaned me. But, I guess priests don't talk about that kind of thing."

They were interrupted briefly by a group of Japanese schoolgirls with name tags and matching baseball caps following in close order behind their docent, listening to her explanation of the "Sphere Within a Sphere," a metallic sculpture in the courtyard similar to those in cities from Dublin to Tehran. It was supposed to suggest the complexity of the world. The schoolgirls were not impressed.

After the bored girls passed, Lew asked Crispin for more information. "Did you say 'autopsy report'?"

"A brother and sister, Sarah Doyle and Kevin Doyle."

"Sister Sarah was a friend of mine. Her death was unexpected. What was in the report? What do you remember?" Lew asked, her voice projecting an almost fearful tone.

"I read it pretty quickly so I don't remember any details. I'm sorry."

Sister Lew sat down on a nearby bench, and for the first time since Crispin had known her, her face turned pale.

"Are you all right?"

"What else did you say he had?"

"Just an obituary from the newspaper. It was for her brother. I made the connection because it listed Sarah as next of kin. Did you know her brother?"

Sister Lew glanced around as if checking to see who was nearby and replied, "Not here. Not now."

Lew was on the verge of asking another question, but swallowed her words as Roberto waved to them from across the courtyard. He joined them with a message for Lew. "Bishop Pirolla is ready to finalize plans for your trip."

"What trip?" Crispin asked.

"My order will work on the Shroud in preparation for the pope's Jubilee. We will reinforce the lining so it can be exhibited," Sister Lew explained. "My assignment will be to videotape the restoration."

"The bishop is expecting us both," Roberto said.

"I'm sorry, Crispin, but we will have lunch another time. We'll continue our discussion then."

"You bet," Crispin replied in an attempt to sound encouraging. It wasn't until that moment that Crispin remembered she'd left her Macken notes in Lew's office. Since Sister Lew had an appointment to keep, she promised to retrieve her file at another time. Crispin gave Sister Lew a good-bye hug that was warm, but cursory. It was the kind of hug you give someone you expect to see again.

Chapter Nine

The phone next to her bed rang just as Crispin opened the door to her hotel room. She wanted to ignore it since she was running late, but changed her mind and grabbed it on the third ring. "Good morning, Crispin Leads."

"J. D. Moss. We have lab results from the knife."

"Oh," Crispin said, sitting down on the bed and dropping her backpack on the floor.

"We traced the prints through Interpol. Your friend with the ponytail has an unfortunate history."

"Okay. Thank you for calling."

"This is not a courtesy call, Ms. Leads. I need you to come down to the station and ID him."

"But, you said you have the fingerprints."

"We need to be sure we have the right person. Someone will pick you up. At your hotel?"

"I'm on my way out the door. Is it okay if I call you from the Vatican to make arrangements?"

"I will expect a call," the detective said, hanging up.

Now the call from Moss had made her late, so she stopped by a coffee shop before dashing to the Vatican, determined to get in a few hours of work. She pushed open the library door with her foot while balancing a cup of espresso and a flakey pastry with one hand and her backpack with the other. The librarian stopped her at the door. "Ms. Leads, you are to go straight to Bishop Pirolla's office."

"No problem."

Crispin turned quickly so the young man couldn't see the mix of guilt and embarrassment traveling in a crimson flush from her collar to her crown. Had Bishop Pirolla somehow gotten wind of her arrangement with Roberto for accessing the Macken diaries? In the elevator Crispin tried to think up a story that would dance just this side of mendacity.

When she entered the now familiar foyer, Pirolla's new assistant gestured Crispin toward the bishop's inner office. The first person she saw when she walked in was Roberto, who stood up stiffly, offering her his seat. Damn, she thought, the gig is up.

Pirolla made no pretense of courtesy. "Ms. Leads, you have violated the terms of your research grant."

Crispin slumped into the chair, absentmindedly tucking her pastry into her backpack. "I don't understand."

"Do not insult me with a denial," Pirolla said. "You searched Sister Llewellyn's office when she was not present."

"But I . . ."

Pirolla rammed on, talking over her, warming to the sound of his own voice. "This is a breach of common courtesy, not to mention a total lack of ethics. I am not surprised, considering your father." Directing his comments to Roberto, he continued, "Dr. Leads is one of those scientists who will do anything to undermine us. You know what I mean. And now he stoops so low as to send his own daughter into the sacred halls of the Holy See to spy."

Crispin was prepared to tolerate his harangue against her, but she drew the line when he impugned her father's integrity. As usual when she was trying to control her emotions, she resorted to a formal and precise way of speaking. The words she chose were defiant.

"That is where you are mistaken. He did not even know I was applying for the grant. I intentionally kept it a secret from him until I was sure I had been approved. He is a man of unimpeachable honesty. He has no reason to resort to trickery. You are guilty not only of fallacious reasoning, but hubris of the most malicious kind if you think you can twist an innocent mistake of mine into an indictment of my father."

Crispin was on the verge of letting her anger get the best of her when something in Roberto's impassive face caused her to swallow hard and rein in her growing fury. "Let me assure you, Bishop Pirolla, that my visits with Sister Lew are no more than casual conversations based on our childhood friendship."

"Do you expect me to believe that story?"

"Certainly. It is, after all, the unequivocal truth. I . . ."

Again Pirolla talked over her, jabbing his finger in the air to punctuate his words. "Ms. Leads, you have not only compromised yourself, but you have implicated a splendid young nun and put a blot on what promises to be a brilliant future."

Crispin's stomach began to pitch as the effect of the strong Italian coffee on an empty stomach collided with the guilty suggestion that her actions might have caused trouble for her friend. Since Pirolla hadn't mentioned Roberto's help with the Macken diaries, Crispin wasn't sure how much he knew, so she picked her way through the estuary between truth and lie. Crispin wondered if couching her denial was just another brand of deceit. "If you will just ask Sister Llewellyn, she will confirm that she . . ."

"That will not be possible. Sister Llewellyn is no longer in Rome."

Roberto's face betrayed surprise at Pirolla's bombshell, but still he didn't say a word.

"You're in violation of your research agreement, and I intend to initiate steps to suspend your privileges," Pirolla said. "You would save us a lot of trouble and yourself a great deal of embarrassment if you withdraw immediately."

Crispin gathered herself with as much dignity as she could muster, but in doing so she spilled coffee on the bishop's carpet. Without so much as acknowledging the mess, she tried to read

Roberto but he remained passively silent. So, she gave up and heard herself repeat what Roberto had suggested in the library. "My commission is from the Holy Father himself, and only he can withdraw the invitation. Until I receive word directly from him, I intend to continue my work." She turned on her heel and left.

If she'd said one more word, Crispin was sure she would have lost it. If her anger didn't seep through, her tears did. This time the anger won when she was safely in the Vatican garden. While Crispin dodged the prying eyes of passersby she replayed the scene with Pirolla. He was probably already on the phone to the authorities. Her score so far with meetings in this office was Bishop: 3, Crispin: 0. Three times she'd been in the bishop's office and three times she'd lost it.

After months of preparation, her disappointment was nothing compared to the dread of facing her dad. If Pirolla succeeded in giving her the boot, the thin folder of handwritten notes that she'd left in Lew's office represented the only tangible thing she had to show from this wreck of a Roman holiday. Determined not to leave empty handed, she fished for her cell phone. First things first, she thought as she called Detective Moss.

Chapter Ten

Crispin sorted through the file that Moss gave her, pausing occasionally to read some of the material in detail and scanning other parts. After a while, she closed the file and put it back on the table.

"I'm not sure what to think."

"Is he the man?"

"I think so."

"You aren't sure?"

"The man in the recent photos looks right, but I'm not sure about the one in the older pictures."

"I need you to be sure," Moss told her. "Is he the man you saw in the bishop's office?"

Crispin stood up and went to the window in an attempt to catch a breeze. The day was sultry and the police building did not have air conditioning. The tiny conference room further restricted air circulation. "Yes, it's the same man. What I don't understand is why he followed me to the graveyard."

"Why do you think?"

"I thought he might be a stalker or psycho."

"What do you think now?"

Crispin could tell by the detective's tone that she was annoyed, but didn't understand why she couldn't be more direct. "Are you trying to tell me that there's more to Father Mitchel's death? That it wasn't an accident?"

Moss didn't respond but joined her at the window, leaning on the windowsill, facing Crispin so that the light obscured her face the way it had during their first interview. "You did the right thing calling us after you saw him in the graveyard."

"You didn't answer me when I asked why you thought he followed me there," Crispin said, conscious that the other woman was once again playing with her.

"You missed the more important question," Moss said in an impatient tone punctuated by her digging in her pocket for her cigarette case.

"How did he find me?"

Moss tapped a cigarette against the palm of her hand. "Smart girl. Who besides me knew where you were staying and how to reach you?"

Crispin thought about it and realized that there were only four people in Rome who knew where she was staying.

"I think you already know the answer, don't you?" Crispin said. "There's the man with the lisp in the bishop's office the first day, Father Mitchel, and Father Rossini."

"Is that all?"

"Well, my friend, Sister Llewellyn."

"Who is she?"

Crispin explained her friendship with the nun.

"You didn't answer me when I asked why you thought this guy followed me to the graveyard," Crispin said. "Is it because I could identify him?"

"That's one possibility."

"What other reason could there be?"

"What indeed? What do you make of that episode with the knife?"

"I don't understand your question."

"Think about. A man with his kind of history uses such a clumsy weapon, leaving fingerprints for us to find. What do you think he is trying to tell you?"

Suddenly, Crispin felt tired of games and tired of defending herself. The fight with Pirolla, the likelihood of her research grant being revoked, and, now, a game of cat-and-mouse with the police brought her to the end of patience. "Who knows? I'm probably not going to be in Rome much longer anyway. Is there anything else you need from me?" she asked as she gathered her things to leave.

"That's all for now. But I should caution you that our friend is a dangerous man. If you stay in Rome, you should change hotels. And, Ms. Leads, be sure to stay in touch with me," Moss said. "The sergeant will show you out."

Crispin left without saying good-bye.

Moss stopped working when the sergeant returned. "Get Father Roberto Rossini on the line."

* * *

Crispin went straight to Lew's office. As she rounded the corner she saw Roberto. Something in his manner made her hang back. Besides, she was not sure where she stood with him. On the one hand, he had helped her with the Macken diaries. On the other, he had done nothing to defend her in front of Pirolla. Now he was snooping.

She stayed out of sight and watched as he felt above the doorframe for a key. He checked to make sure the hallway was clear and then used the key to let himself in. Fortunately for Crispin, the pesky door was playing its tricks again. Instead of remaining solidly closed, it popped open. Crispin tiptoed up to the opening so she could peer through the slit to see what Roberto was up to. He was trying, without success, to open the wall cabinet. After a few tries at the cabinet, Roberto gave the lock a vigorous shake and turned to leave. Crispin had just ducked back out of sight when he stepped into the hallway and locked the door, returning the key to its hiding place. When he was gone, Crispin retrieved the key and let herself into Lew's office.

Her notes were not on the arm of the side chair where she thought she had left them. Thinking that Sister Lew may have inadvertently scooped up her Macken folder with the papers in the cabinet, Crispin took the key from its hiding place in the desk lamp and opened the wooden cabinet.

Sister Lew was nothing if not organized. Each box was carefully labeled with a black marker and neat script. One contained a dozen or so catalogued videotapes. Most held paper files. She didn't relish a long search, but she told herself that a girl's gotta try. And, anyway, what more can Pirolla do to hurt me?

She moved several boxes to the floor and sat down next to them, cross-legged behind Sister Lew's desk. It wasn't long before she found herself reading the files. The bulk of the material dated from 1983 when the House of Savoy gave the Shroud to the Holy See. The Savoy family had assured the safekeeping of the cloth and its occasional exhibition since its first documented appearance in the fourteenth century. There was a complete set of files dedicated just to fires that had endangered the Shroud. As she scanned through it, Crispin learned there had been several fires in the storied life of the Shroud—some accidental, some intentional.

One of the more compelling files was devoted exclusively to the guests at the gala on the night of the most recent Turin fire, the one where Roberto saved the Shroud. Among those attending had been the chairman of Fiat, politicians, noted clerics, and some of Italy's wealthiest industrialists. It read like a Who's Who of influential Italians. The reproduced black-and-white photographs from the newspapers showed the dignitaries arriving in Rolls-Royces. The event was more like a glitzy Hollywood premiere, complete with paparazzi, than a church function next door to a holy Christian relic.

Sister Lew had constructed a thumbnail biography for each dinner guest, neatly typed and alphabetized. There were symbols and numbers next to each name. Crispin had spent enough time in libraries and archives to recognize a catalogue cross-reference system when she saw one. These notations, however, were unfamiliar. She assumed there was a code key somewhere that would explain the notations.

Crispin had lost track of time when she heard the office door slowly opening. Roberto slipped in and closed the door quietly behind him, locking it securely. She jumped up and began to dust herself off, trying to think of a plausible explanation for her presence. Roberto turned around, startled to see Crispin. The pair stared at each other without speaking before Roberto broke the silence.

"What are you doing here?"

"I might ask the same question. Now I suppose you're going to go straight to the bishop and rat me out for breaking and entering."

"I'm not who you think I am."

"Well, who the hell are you then?"

"Please, Crispin, there's an explanation. My intention has always been to help."

"You weren't much help this morning, were you?"

"I know you have a lot of questions about my behavior, but I don't have time to answer them right now. If you care about Sister Mary Llewellyn, I ask that you believe me."

"What do you mean?"

"Bishop Pirolla moved the date for the repair work on the Shroud and sent her away last night, but she never made it to her convent."

"Where is she?"

"We don't know. She was apparently traveling without an escort and didn't arrive when expected. At this moment, no one knows her whereabouts."

"Did anyone call her mother?"

"Yes."

"Then call the police."

"We have. Bishop Pirolla believes she intentionally disobeyed his order to return to her convent. He plans to search her office and confiscate her files."

"What? Roberto, that doesn't make any sense."

"Sense or not, we don't have long before agents come to lock up her office, perhaps as early as this evening. I rarely agree with Pirolla, but this time I think he's correct."

"That she disobeyed him?"

"No, of course not. The answer to her disappearance might be somewhere in her files. She contacted me, very excited. She discovered something about the Shroud, but left before she could tell me what she found. If we find out what she knew, maybe it will help us locate her. Crispin, will you help me?"

"Of course. But, I remind you that I might be a spy. Doesn't that bother you?"

Roberto shrugged his shoulders. "Expediency. You're here. You care. And there is no love lost between you and the bishop. For now, that is enough for me to trust you."

"But, can I trust you?"

"That is not for me to say."

Crispin took a deep breath and responded in the only way she felt made sense. "So what are we looking for?"

"That, I don't know. Perhaps, we'll know it when we see it. We have so little time."

Chapter Eleven

Whatever it was that Lew had planned to tell Roberto, she'd left no clues behind. Crispin and Roberto found nothing in her files that hinted at her secret revelation.

"I can make no sense of these marks," Roberto said, indicating the sister's notations as he attached a final paperclip to the guest list for the gala, adding it to the stack they'd tagged for photocopying.

"My brain is fried," Crispin replied, as she stood to stretch, her hips and legs numb from sitting crossed-legged on the floor. "Shall I make the copies?"

"No, I'll take care of that."

"Okay, but I still need to poke around for my Macken notes. They're all I have now that the bishop has cut me off."

"I'm sorry, of course. Let me help."

Crispin opened the drawers in Lew's desk. The first two had office supplies and personal effects, but she pulled two manila envelopes out of the bottom drawer and stacked them on the desktop. "Maybe there is something here."

The first contained a hodgepodge of postcards and family photos. The second had a duplicate of the autopsy report of Sarah Anne Doyle and the news clipping about the death of Kevin Doyle.

"Can you tell me about these?" she asked.

Roberto took the material from her and laid each item out on the desk. "She asked me about these yesterday. She said you told her about them, so I gave her copies."

"What else did you tell her?"

"I'm afraid there was little that she did not already know or suspect."

"Tell me."

"I'll begin with Sister Mary Sarah," he said, picking up the autopsy report. "Her death was unexpected, especially coming so soon after that of her brother. Although she had no history of allergies, she died of a severe idiopathic allergic reaction, which the coroner could not define. Her death was ruled an accident of unknown origin. Sister Llewellyn could not accept the circumstances under which she passed."

"How did her brother die?"

"He was a talented master of silverwork. That is why he was commissioned to repair the handle on the Shroud crypt. He died while cleaning his rifle. He was a careful man who had been a lifelong hunter. Sister Sarah swore that he would not have made such a pedestrian mistake. She talked to Sister Llewellyn about it endlessly."

"So you think there was a connection between her death and his?"

"Sister Llewellyn was convinced there was also a connection back to Father Mitchel. For the life of me I fail to see a tie-in. I tried to allay her concerns but the bishop kept pushing to close the cases. Meanwhile, the police were digging around, asking questions about all three who died."

"Detective Moss?"

"Yes. Why do you ask?"

"It's a long story," Crispin said, wondering how much she should share with him from her conversation with the police. "Let's not waste any more time trying to find my notes. That is a lost cause."

Crispin pulled a crate full of videotapes off the shelf. "Perhaps there will be something on these that will help us. I have a VCR in my hotel room. Should I take them with me?"

Roberto shook his head. "It will help if I watch them with you. If we only knew what we were after."

"Is there somewhere else that is private?"

His shoulders slumped in silent resignation. "I will meet you on the street so we are not seen together on Vatican grounds." He loaded the videotapes into a canvas tote bag he found hanging on the back of the door, put on his coat, and, without a backward glance, slipped into the hall.

Crispin counted to one hundred and followed, locking the door behind her and returning the key to its unimaginative hiding place above the doorsill. The coast was clear so she quickened her pace and soon caught up with Roberto waiting for her outside Saint Anne's Gate.

After a brisk walk they arrived at her hotel. When they got off the elevator they nearly bumped into a couple entwined in a passionate kiss. The young man cupped the woman's rear end and the woman's hands were busy in a way that caused him to moan. The girl gave Crispin a look of sisterhood that signaled she assumed Crispin was also about to engage in an afternoon tryst.

"If she only knew," Crispin mumbled.

"Excuse me?" Roberto responded, but Crispin shook him off. "I was talking to myself. Another nasty habit."

There were only two seating options in the small hotel room: either the bed or an armchair. Roberto motioned her to the chair and slipped off his raincoat. He also removed his jacket, folding both and stacking them on the bed. He then eased down on the floor, propping his back against the bed for support. Crispin removed her shoes before sitting in the chair with her legs tucked under her. "I know we don't have a lot of time, but before we begin you owe me an explanation," she said.

"About what happened today in the bishop's office."

"What am I supposed to think?"

"That too is a long story. And, we don't have enough time for all of it right now. For now, understand that the bishop summoned me to his office and told me he was going to revoke your grant. I assumed he'd found out about the diaries. Before I could explain that it was all my idea, he launched into an explanation that a reliable source told him you were guilty of espionage and spying on Sister Llewellyn. He ordered me to remain silent. There is more to tell but I pray you believe me when I say that I had no choice."

"Okay, for now. But only for now." Crispin put the canvas bag on her lap and opened the top. "What secrets are you going to tell us?" she said, talking into the bag.

Roberto smiled at her silliness, and for a microsecond she caught a glimpse of the young man behind the collar. But, the image flashed and was gone, leaving only a suggestion of it, like the haze that remains after a sunset. Keep your mind on the task at hand, she chastised herself with a mental finger wag.

Over the next two hours their work fell into a rhythm. After each viewing, Roberto would unload a tape while Crispin selected the next. After the fifth tape of celebrations, ceremonies, and long-winded interviews, Roberto sighed with frustration. "Another dead end."

"Let's take a break," she said. "Would you like something to drink? They have room service here."

She thought he was going to refuse, but something, perhaps just good manners, prevailed. While they waited for service, Crispin opened the window, leaning her hands on the sill and breathing in the smells and sounds of a city that drifted up from the busy street below.

Behind her, Roberto followed her every move and then, as if shaking off some demon, he willed a casual, conversational tone. "This morning you said you kept your application for a papal grant a secret from your father. Why secret?"

Crispin sat back on the bed near him, stretching her arms and back, and rubbed her feet. After a pause to gather her thoughts she began her story.

"Two reasons, I think. First, I would have been embarrassed if I weren't selected."

"Why embarrassed?"

"My dad is like Midas, a touch of magic for anything he wants. He's as envied as he is admired, although he's blind to the way others react to him."

"Even you?"

"Especially me. Maybe he can't see it because envy and admiration are emotions and, therefore, illogical."

"But that wasn't all. You said there were two reasons."

"It's complicated."

"I don't mind."

"Since Mother died, it's been just the three of us. My dad, my brother, and me." Crispin crossed her arms over her chest in a self-embrace.

"Now that has changed. How?"

"My dad has a girlfriend."

"Ah."

There was a knock on the door and room service delivered a tray. Crispin put it on the floor next to Roberto and sat across from him.

"I feel like we're on a picnic," she told him as she offered him a glass of San Pellegrino and a plate of cheese.

"You were telling me why you kept your grant application a secret."

"It all sounds childish when I explain it, but I wanted to spring the news on the guys for maximum effect. You see, Wednesdays are supposed to be a family night. Just the three of us, so when I got the letter I thought that would be a perfect time to tell them. It's tradition for me to make Yankee Noodle Casserole."

"I'm not familiar with this dish."

"I'm not surprised. It relies on an American secret ingredient, Campbell's chicken noodle soup, made better because you top it with tons of New York cheddar cheese. I mastered the complexities of this culinary masterpiece when I was ten years old. I was putting the casserole in the oven when Dad's secretary called to tell me that Dr. Pierce would be joining us."

"So your father invited a work friend to family night?" Roberto asked.

"That's right. Exactly! And she arrived early, if you can believe it, before I'd even had time to clean up or comb my hair or anything. I felt like a scullery maid in my grease-stained apron compared to her yellow silk suit and Prada knockoffs. Well, her contribution was a dish of *coq au vin* that smelled as if came from Emeril's kitchen," Crispin said, unable to mask the bitterness in her voice.

Later when Clinton brought in the large serving dishes from the table, Crispin said she could feel her jealousy grow. The men had almost licked clean the fancy French chicken with wine sauce cooked by Dr. Pierce, but Crispin's noodle casserole was practically untouched. It didn't help when Clinton said, "But we have your chicken every week."

"Clinton never meant to hurt me, but bottom line, things are changing and I don't like it," she asked, helping herself to cheese and toast from the room service tray. "No advice?"

"Do you want advice?"

"Not really. Sometimes it's enough to just have someone listen."

They nibbled on the food for a few minutes when Crispin broke the silence.

"Okay, Father Rossini. If you were going to give advice, what might that advice be?"

Roberto stood up and went to where Crispin had previously stood by the window. With his back to her he took his time before answering. When he turned around she was struck by the change in his demeanor. As they'd worked together in Lew's office and then watched the tapes, he acted like a friend or teammate. But standing there with his hands in his pockets leaning against the windowsill, he was remote, serious, and somehow inaccessible.

"I don't have advice exactly. But I'd like to tell you a story. It's about shopkeeper in the neighborhood where I grew up. My buddies and I passed his shop on the way to school. He was friendly, but the stuff in his store was awful. You know how boys are. We wanted the latest sneakers and T-shirts. His merchandise was out of date, and sometimes, we would cut up and make rude comments. His wife died young so he raised his children alone. They moved away after college and he lived alone for forty-seven years. Everything stayed just the way it was when his wife was alive. He didn't change anything. He tried to hold on to something that was not there anymore. A life trapped in amber. A life only half lived."

Crispin took a few minutes to absorb the lesson before conceding to herself that Father Rossini had a point. Okay. I get it. Move on, she told herself.

"I just wish Dad had better taste in women," she said.

"You are blessed to have a family that loves you, but you know that already. Not all are so fortunate."

"You sound like you're speaking from personal experience," Crispin said, before she caught herself, remembering what Lew had told her about Roberto's childhood. "Hey, enough family drama. Let's get back to work," Crispin said, standing up, dusting crumbs from her slacks, and finishing off a bottle of fizzy water.

"Of course," Roberto said, returning to the canvas bag and picking out another video and sliding it into the VCR.

"Oh, great. Another exciting short subject," Crispin said, turning the cardboard sleeve so she could read the title. Unlike the others, the sleeve for this one was unmarked. It must have been in the bottom of the canvas bag all along since Crispin was sure the ones they'd taken from the cabinet were all labeled. For a moment, she thought, this is it!

Again disappointment.

The tape was of a solemn religious ceremony led by Pirolla. The priests were installing the Shroud casket in an alcove of a small chapel. An onion dome of blue inlay, a miniature of the kind in Red Square, graced the alcove. As the procession droned on, Crispin tried to suppress a yawn.

"I am sorry," Roberto said. "You are tired and I have asked too much of you. I will find a way to finish this." He started packing up.

"Why don't you leave the rest of the videotapes, and I'll watch them. If I find anything interesting, I promise that I'll let you know right away."

"If we just knew what Sister Llewellyn wanted to tell me before she disappeared."

After Roberto left, Crispin ordered supper. While waiting for her food she loaded another tape into the VCR without first reading the label on the spine. This one was different. It was an interview with Roberto.

He was in a hospital room. Crispin could hear Sister Lew asking questions off-camera.

Hearing Lew's voice filled Crispin with a renewed concern for her friend. Lew, where are you? Are you safe? Did you discover something that put you in harm's way? Did you leave of your own free will, or has someone taken you?

Crispin shook the thoughts from her head and forced herself to again concentrate on the tape. Although they spoke Italian, the pace and intonation of Lew and Roberto's recorded conversation was slow, clear, and measured, which made it possible for Crispin to follow what they said. The tape appeared to be one of a series because it began in the middle of a conversation.

"The fire chief said he told you that the heat was too intense and ordered you to stay outside. You disobeyed and risked your life. Tell me about that," Lew asked in a soft voice.

In a muted yet certain response, Roberto explained that he was drawn into the fire by a force that he could neither explain nor resist. "It was as much that force, pulling me forward, as it was any conscious decision. I knew my destiny was inside that church. I simply . . . knew."

Roberto stopped talking for a long time and, to her credit, Sister Lew didn't rush him. When he started his story again, he turned toward the camera. After a thoughtful pause, he began to speak again. "When I joined the Fire Service I thought I was running away, escaping, my mistakes. I thought I could make up for them through public service. I actually thought about military or police work, but I didn't think I could do anything that required me to use a weapon. Fighting fires was a better fit. Then that night at the Cathedral I knew I'd had it all wrong. I hadn't been running away. All this time I'd been running toward something and it was in there, in the Cathedral. I know how I must sound to you. Some of the guys I used to hang out with would take pills and they'd talk out of their heads. I must sound that way, but I swear to you what happened was not that way."

Again, Roberto paused and seemed hesitant to say more. Sister Lew responded, "What did you feel?"

"It was as if a fresh wind moved ahead of me, hollowing out a course through the smoke and heat. With every step, my old path, like my old life, crumbled and fell away behind me. All I had to do was lean into the new way opening up before me."

"How did you know where to find the Holy Shroud?"

"I just knew."

The relic and its silver casket were inside a glass, bulletproof case.

"I had an axe, but the glass would not yield. I raised it again and again and again with all the force I had in my body, and each time my heart screamed, 'Help me, oh Lord, send me out. Oh Lord, find me another life. Oh Lord.'"

"What happened?"

"The screams became a prayer and the prayer was answered."

"The glass shattered?"

"Yes. I took the coffin and started out of the building. I felt as if I were in a cocoon of certainty. I felt no fear. I felt no heat, no pain. The fire yielded before me."

A loud knock on the door broke the spell that had mesmerized Crispin as she watched Roberto. Her hand shook as she pushed the Stop button on the machine. Should she open the door this late at night? What if the Vatican had sent someone to search her room? Crispin squinted through the peephole. A young woman stood in the hallway. She was holding a tray covered with a linen napkin. Dolt, thought Crispin, it's just room service.

She opened the door to accept the tray. As she ate, she couldn't help but wonder what her mother would make of Roberto's account of the mystical pull of forces that are part intuition and part inspiration, forces that lead you in directions you never anticipated. She was sure that her dad, who trusted only what he could prove or hold in his hand, but never what he could only feel, would not understand.

I don't know what Mother would say, but she would surely recommend sleep after a day like today, Crispin thought, setting her tray in the hall and stretching out on her bed without undressing. Before long she was dreaming.

In the dream she was a child sitting on the floor sharing secrets with her mother whose face was obscured by sun spilling in through floor-to-ceiling windows. A loud rap at one of the windows interrupted them. A girl outside the window made a rude face and stuck her tongue out. Crispin tried to pull down the shade, but it flew out of her hand, rolling up to the top of the window with a loud *clap, clap, clap* sound that made her think she was being shot at with a BB gun, so she ducked and buried her face in a pillow. Soon there were girls at every window, mocking Crispin and laughing at her. She searched for a door, but the room only had windows. There was no escape. Her tormenters began to open the windows and climb into the room. "You can't come in unless I invite you," she yelled. But they kept coming, crowding in uncomfortably close, poking at her and making fun of her, turning her name into a schoolyard joke. She woke, sweating and crying, tangled in her bed sheets.

That familiar nightmare hadn't haunted her for years. The first time she'd had the dream was right after her cabin mates at summer camp in the Adirondacks found her diary and taunted her for days. When they finally returned the precious notebook it was soiled and mutilated with their pornographic drawings and ribald comments. That summer was also the first time Crispin had used razor blades to soothe fear and cut away pain.

Crispin got out of bed, ejected the Roberto tape from the VCR, and returned it to the cardboard sleeve without watching the rest of his interview. She was certain that Roberto wouldn't want her to see a conversation that private any more than she had wanted her cabin mates to invade the private thoughts in her diary. When something is that personal you don't open the door unless you are invited in.

Chapter Twelve

The green numbers on the digital clock flipped from 5:01 to 5:02 a.m. Crispin could hear sanitation trucks rumble by outside. She hugged the pillow over her face, but could not shake the dread that had haunted her all night. The pills she'd taken for her headache weren't working. The curtains wouldn't close all the way, and the bright light from the streetlight illuminated the room. She needed dark. She needed calm. Caffeine might help. She ordered a double espresso from room service. After it arrived, she ran a steaming hot bath with gardenia salts.

After closing the door to the bathroom, she turned off the lights and eased herself into the water, pressing a hot cloth to her forehead. Questions marched through her head, like a drum line, some in close formation, weaving patterns through the mysteries of the past few days. Others circled outside the parade, as if to their own tune.

Why did Pirolla send Sister Lew away so suddenly? Why did she go without an escort? What is the meaning of the strange notations in Lew's files? What happened to the Macken notes?

Roberto's inconsistency was maddening. One day he was helping and the next he was standing by while the bishop demolished her hopes and insulted her integrity. Then, without a solid explanation, he asked her to help him in a surreptitious search of Lew's files and worked side by side with her as if they were a team. What was he up to? What was he hiding? Roberto's description of what had happened in the fire both moved and, for some reason, left her troubled. She couldn't explain her reaction because she knew it was not rational. Lew clearly trusted him, but could she allow herself to trust him?

Maybe she should call Detective Moss. What would the police detective make of Lew's suspicions regarding the deaths of Sister Sarah and her brother or, more importantly, her disappearance? Nothing so far in Lew's disappearance was directly connected to Father Mitchel. But Crispin didn't believe in coincidence. Father Mitchel had died in Pirolla's office. Pirolla sent Sister Lew away. Pirolla was in that Shroud ceremony. Pirolla was going to confiscate Lew's records. So much, somehow, connected back to Pirolla.

The most nagging question was what to make of the grave-yard incident. Detective Moss implied that someone was playing games with her. Trying to scare her. Why? The more she thought about the conversation with the policewoman, the more con-fused she became.

"I'm in way over my head here," Crispin said out loud. Her voice echoed with a hollow sound in the dark bathroom. She pressed her temples for relief from an incessant barrage of ques-tions that had no answers.

Crispin dried herself and drew on her soft, white terry cloth robe and rolled the hot coffee cup against her forehead. The heat helped to push her headache into the background, but sleep still would not come. The clatter of rambunctious deliverymen on the street made her nerves flinch. She thought about turning on the television when she remembered that she still had videos that she needed to rewind. How many times had she heard her dad say, "Never leave your mess for others to clean up."

She inserted a tape into the VCR. It was the tape about the installation ceremony for the Shroud. As the tape rewound in slow motion, Pirolla and the other bishops and nuns walked backwards from the crypt in a solemn procession. By watching the film in reverse slow motion Crispin found herself noticing tiny details in the vestments and background. It was like the editing trick she'd learned in high school. Read what you've written from the bottom up if you want to catch typos.

Then she spotted it. Why hadn't she noticed before? Crispin stopped the tape in freeze frame. The angle of the shot made it hard to tell. She rewound and stopped the tape several times, until she found a frame with the view of the casket that she wanted. It was only visible for an instant.

"How can that be?" Crispin whispered to herself as if saying it too loudly would make it sound less plausible.

Then came the flood of interrogation from her subconscious. She could almost hear her mother's voice, talking her through the question game.

Okay, I'll play.

What assumptions are you making? It wasn't exactly application of Cartesian skepticism, but it helped to set out all assumptions and challenge them methodically. One by one, assumptions ticked off until one hit pay dirt. What if the fire wasn't an accident after all? What if someone set the fire on purpose? Why? The answer, though implausible, led to an interesting conclusion: A fire would create a perfect diversion for someone intent on stealing the Shroud. The phone rang with a loud shriek, jerking Crispin out of her internal cross-examination. She grabbed it before it rang again.

"Crispin?"

"Roberto, you won't believe what I discovered on one of the tapes. I think . . ."

Roberto interrupted. "We have to get the videotapes back to the Vatican. Immediately. Pirolla is calling for a full criminal investigation . . ."

"What?" Crispin's stomach muscles clenched.

"This morning when I went back to Sister Lew's office to return the files that I'd made copies of, it was a mess. Files were emptied onto the floor and everything was turned upside down. I overheard Pirolla talking with the Swiss Guard. They found your

Macken notes behind an overturned chair. He's accusing you of vandalizing her office."

Crispin pulled on her jeans as she tried to tamp down her growing panic. "That's crazy. We put everything back in place."

"I know."

Crispin pulled her shirt over her head. "Can't you tell him you were with me and . . . ?"

"He's after me too."

"For what?" She had a sinking feeling that she knew the answer.

"Your Macken notes. The librarian told him about our little ruse."

"Shit. I knew we shouldn't . . ."

"Just bring the videotapes to me. The only thing we did that can be interpreted as even mildly criminal was removing the tapes from the Vatican grounds. We need to return them as soon as possible."

They arranged to meet at a small prayer chapel. Roberto gave her directions. "We'll figure out what to do. Just come quickly but, please, be careful," he said, the tone less than certain.

Crispin stuffed the tapes back in the canvas bag as she crammed her feet into her Keds. "Shit, and double shit," she mumbled as she exited the hotel lobby.

Trying not to attract undue attention she walked, instead of ran, toward the Vatican. All she could hear was the loud swooshing of blood coursing through her still tender brain, her heart pumping as if she were in the final stretch of a race.

After a few blocks she stopped to get her bearings. Rough arms from behind tightened around her chest, grabbing at the canvas bag and pulling her toward a nearby car. A gravelly voice shouted, "Give it to me."

Crispin threw her arms up and twisted out of the hold the way her twin brother had taught her. She shouted as the mugger clawed at her shoulders. He was momentarily thrown off guard as her scream swelled to an ear-shattering sensory assault.

Crispin heard Clinton's instruction, as surely as if he were with her: "Use your legs." Turning, she kicked with all the force she could between the man's legs. He crumpled to the ground, and she took off as fast as she could.

After several false turns Crispin finally found the chapel. Inside, Roberto knelt in prayer. Under normal circumstances Crispin would have, out of respect, waited in the rear. Not today. "Hope you are putting in a good word with the Big Guy," she said as she flopped into a pew behind him, bending over to try and catch her breath.

Roberto spun around and took a seat next to her. "Are you all right?"

"Actually, I'm okay," Crispin responded, her breathing beginning to calm. "A guy tried to grab me, but I gave him a kick that would have laid out a pro wrestler," she added, hoping her voice projected an appropriate degree of bravado.

"A street thug?"

"I don't think we need to worry about him right now."

"I want to hear more. We can talk along the way," he said with a fierce urgency, leading the way out of the chapel. "You said you found something."

"Do you remember the videotape of the ceremony installing the Shroud in a new crypt? The one with the pretty blue onion dome? Anyway, when I rewound the video I could see the casket up close."

She couldn't help herself. She paused for dramatic effect, as if her revelation needed to be well seasoned to be appreciated.

"And?"

"Both silver handles were perfect. Neither was broken."

"How is that possible?"

"The casket you saved in the fire, the one with the broken handle, must have been switched with a counterfeit after you rescued it. The video is proof."

The expression on his face told Crispin that her outrageous theory had struck a chord.

"I see," he said. "After the fire the Shroud was left at the cardinal's residence for two days. It was a rare window of vulnerability."

"What should we do now? Call the police?" asked Crispin.

"Wait. First, we have to make sure that Sister Mary Llewellyn is safe."

"But they will be able to help. I could call Detective Moss."

"Not yet. You need to give me some time."

"What do you mean?"

Roberto pulled her into the shadows of a building.

"I'm going to Torino to find her."

"That's a good idea. We could . . ."

"Not we. Me. You must not even consider going with me. It is too dangerous."

"*Et tu*, chauvinist?" Crispin's voice reflected her annoyance. "And staying in Rome isn't dangerous? Give me a break! The guy who just accosted me in the street is our friend with the ponytail from Father Mitchel's office. It's the second time he's come after me."

"What do you mean second time?"

"We can't discuss it here," she replied, noticing the attention they were drawing from passersby. "Let's keep going."

As they walked, Crispin gave him the condensed version of the encounter in the English Graveyard. She intentionally omitted the part when she and Detective Moss returned and found the knife near Keats' grave. She told herself that a little creative deception never hurt anyone since Roberto would be impossible to convince if she told him everything.

Out loud, she made her case to Roberto. "I am the one who uncovered the switch. I'm going with you. Or, I'm calling Moss and filling her in on everything. Lew was my friend. End of discussion."

"We need to first take care of the videos. With one important exception, they must be returned," Roberto told her.

"How? Swiss Guards are posted at Lew's office. How can we get in?"

"There is another place she would have kept them and it is the one place I can't go. But you can."

"Where is that?"

"Her sleeping quarters."

So now he can't do without me, Crispin thought.

Roberto told Crispin how to get to the nun's residence. He said he would return to his resident at Villa Stritch to pack a travel valise and then meet her in the lobby of her hotel.

* * *

Roberto passed the growing queue of tourists lining the early-morning street to see the Sistine Chapel. He had a rendezvous with a street vendor in a few minutes and didn't want to be late. The man at the open-air kiosk greeted him with a toothy smile and a familiar nod. His cart was laden with plastic saints, rosary beads, postcards, and other overpriced memories for tourists to take back home as proof that they had stood at the wall of the Holy See.

"Do you have something for me, Father?" asked the young man with a noticeable lisp.

Roberto handed him the video in exchange for an envelope and slipped into the crowd.

* * *

On the way to the dormitory Crispin tried to plan out how she would talk her way in. Nuns may not own much in the way of worldly possessions, but they don't appreciate anyone rummaging through their belongings at will. In answer to an unspoken wish, Crispin was waylaid by Trinity when the cantankerous cat jumped out of a bush. This time he didn't swat her; he tapped on the cuff of her jeans with his paw, his bravado dampened by hunger. "Come here. I'll take care of you," she cooed to the feckless feline.

Crispin carried Trinity into the nuns' residence, where she was greeted by an elderly nun pulling receptionist duty at a desk tucked into a small alcove by the front door. "Look who I found," Crispin told her, holding up Trinity.

"We'd been wondering where he went," the nun said.

Crispin introduced herself. "I think he's hungry," she said, just as the phone rang.

"Do you mind, dear? I would do it but, as you can see, I'm tied to my post. There's food in Sister Lew's room. Number 16," she said, smiling and waving Crispin toward the hall. "He likes the kind that comes in tins," she added, turning her attention to the call.

"I'll just bet you do," Crispin whispered in Trinity's ear as she held up his paw in a kitty wave to the older woman who returned it, giggling as she waved back.

In Lew's room, Crispin opened a fresh tin for Trinity, but as she served it to him, the ingrate scratched her hand. "You little bugger."

Crispin was making room for the videos on a closet shelf when she noticed Lew's video camera. Now that's an odd thing to leave behind if she's in Turin to film the repairs. "What do you think?" she asked the cat.

A habit hanging neatly in the closet gave Crispin an idea. If she was going to be any help in Turin she might need a disguise. She slipped into Lew's tunic and scapular. It was a little too short, but otherwise a good fit. Crispin took the video camera for good measure and stuffed it into the now empty canvas bag.

Before Crispin left, she poked through Sister Lew's desk drawer, where she found her passport. On an impulse she pocketed it.

"You might as well be hung for a sheep as for a lamb," her grandmother had always said.

Crispin exited through a side door and made a concentrated effort to walk with slow, measured paces, her eyes downcast as Lew's habit flapped around her ankles. Navigating the streets of

Rome, she was acutely aware of how men and women of all ages averted their eyes, some giving her a nod of respect or stepping to the side to allow her to pass.

Concealing herself inside Lew's costume, which covered her from head to ankle, gave her a sense of power because she could disappear into another, different Crispin, one who had no baggage, no history, no fears. Since puberty, Crispin had been self-conscious of her figure, wearing turtlenecks to cover her ample cleavage. She even bought sweats a size larger than necessary since they tended to shrink when washed, and she hated the way they would cling to her hips and breasts. Her first boyfriend in high school teased her about hiding what he referred to as "the merchandise," but her brother just thought she was shy. She knew, however, that her reasons ran deeper. She didn't want her classmates, men or women, and certainly not her professors' impressions of her, to be about her physical appearance. She wanted them to be impressed by her work, not her body.

For all of her efforts in school, she thought, nothing was as complete a cover as the outfit she wore today. At her hotel she sat in the lobby and again had the chance to appreciate the anonymity of her disguise as she waited unrecognized. She sat there for thirty minutes before giving up, admitting to herself that she really hadn't expected him. He had given in a little too quickly when she insisted on going with him to Turin.

Men are so transparent, she thought, as she took the elevator up to her room. She packed a small bag and phoned the front desk to make sure they would hold her room for a few days while she made a quick out-of-town trip. She exited by a rear door and hailed a cab for the Roma Trastevere Station.

Roberto was easy to spot, so she purchased a ticket and found a seat a few feet in front of him, her back to him. Once the train was well out of the station she got up and moved down the aisle to where he was seated.

"Excuse me, Father, may I join you?"

Chapter Thirteen

"This is never going to work. You do realize that, don't you?" Roberto asked.

He had converted their tickets to a first-class, private compartment so they could talk without drawing unwelcome attention while she explained her plans.

"I fooled you, didn't I? Anyway, it's probably safer this way."

Roberto sat up straight. "What do you mean?"

"I didn't tell you the whole story about our friend with the ponytail."

Crispin filled Roberto in on what she had learned from Detective Moss about the man's criminal record. The file on him started in the mid-1980s when he was with the Central Intelligence Agency. He spent the first few years in the United States at the agency's main office in Virginia. He didn't appear to be a field agent, more of an analyst. After he left Langley the record was vague about his overseas assignments. He spent time in Europe, including Italy and France. In 1994 he left the agency.

"I think he was fired because of something that happened in Spain. The final sections of the file indicate he became a gun-for-hire."

"Mercenary?"

"Pretty much. He has worked under any number of aliases, but the name he had at the CIA was Thomas Cross," Crispin said.

"Sounds like the kind of name you would give a player in a board game."

Roberto appeared puzzled so Crispin explained. "You know, Doubting Thomas and Holy Cross?"

"I see," he replied without conviction.

"I believed that he would lose interest in me once I made a police identification, but something made him come after me again today," Crispin said. "Frankly, I feel safer leaving Rome right now, and I don't think he'll trace me to a convent." She swept her hand, indicating her disguise.

For a while they rode in silence.

Silence was a place where Crispin's long-time adversary, her personal chorus of conflict, sometimes came calling, loud, bitchy, and insistent. The Shroud puzzle chimed in first, asking for answers, followed quickly by a dialogue about her emotional ambivalence toward Roberto, which had been awakened during the partial interview she'd seen on the video. Just when she thought she'd heard enough, a yapping sub-chorus from left field, her anger over her dad's relationship with Laurie Pierce, joined the cacophony in her head. Enough, she told herself, wrenching control again. All that matters now is Lew.

Time slowed to a crawl, the way it did when she practiced meditation during therapy sessions. As with those exercises in mindfulness, she closed her eyes and tuned in to her senses. She could feel the course cloth of her costume rubbing her arm and the unfamiliar weight of the heavy crucifix at her neck. The sounds of the train's engine and wheels churning on the track imposed itself on the silence, then emerged from silence and returned again into the silence from which it came, creating an almost, but not quite, seamless noise. She could feel each breath move over and through her nostrils, a sensation just shy of a tickle. She could feel the loose strands of hair against her skin where they had escaped from under the coif. Even the gentle sounds of each breath as she exhaled were vivid against the moisture that accumulated on her tongue and nostrils. A sense of lightheadedness reminded her that she needed to eat or she would soon have another headache, and she tried to push the unwelcome thought away like a log floating down a river.

The spell was broken when Roberto spoke in a soft but resolute tone as if he'd come to a difficult conclusion.

"Your theory of an *extractum ex originali* is radical, but it is not out of the question. Sister Llewellyn may have come to a similar conclusion. If someone did substitute a fake Shroud for the real one, I pray it is a misguided collector of relics rather than one who would desecrate the Cloth."

Crispin stood and picked up the canvas bag. "I appreciate your agreement," she said, with a tone of slight annoyance, "but right now, I am feeling a headache coming on and need to eat. Is there a dining car on this train?"

"Of course. I'll show you."

After they had settled at the corner table in the club car and ordered, Roberto continued. "Tell me, even if you are able to get direct access to the Shroud, how will we know if it is counterfeit?"

"That's the best part," Crispin explained. "We just need to see if there is a strand of Francine's hair in the lining."

Then she told him a story. It was one that she had learned from her dad when she was growing up. One of her dad's best friends in college was Gilbert Rose. When they were seniors they both fell for a feisty redhead named Francine Russell. In the end, Francine chose Gilbert. Crispin's dad was best man at their wedding.

"Two years later while working as a graduate fellow on a project involving the Shroud," Crispin said, "Dad received a desperate call from Gilbert. Francine had ALS, or Lou Gehrig's disease, and she was convinced that the Shroud could cure her."

Francine got the idea from reading the story of Josephine Woollam, a ten-year-old Gloucester girl with osteomyelitis. In 1955, after authorities let the little girl touch the Shroud, her condition miraculously improved. Francine convinced herself that if she could touch the Shroud, she too would be cured.

"Although he believed the whole enterprise was irrational, his affection for them caused him to agree to a bizarre scheme."

Since Francine was physically unable to travel, she would send him a lock of her hair. Her waist-length, copper hair, which was the color of a Japanese maple leaf in the autumn, was her fetish.

"While she never dyed it, the shade was so unusual that people assumed it came from a bottle," Crispin explained. "Dad's task was to find a way to bring the lock of hair into contact with the Shroud. After several attempts, he succeeded," she said, with pride. "It turned out to be easier than he thought."

He was assisting a scientist using cellophane tape to lift pollen and dust samples from the Shroud. As the other researcher worked, her dad's job was to carefully replace the folds of the Shroud. This gave him the access he needed. When no one could see him, he wove a few strands of Francine's hair into the silk lining on the top left corner of the Shroud.

"Because it was attached to the lining rather than the Shroud itself, he rationalized that his action did not violate the relic," Crispin said. "Once the lining was folded over the Shroud to create a border, Francine's hair was in contact with the Shroud, but out of sight. He planned to remove it, but he never got the chance."

"If the hair strands are still there, it is the authentic Shroud," Crispin said, with a hint of drama. "If not, we have a ringer."

Roberto sat without talking for some time after Crispin finished her story.

"What happened to Francine?"

"She died," Crispin said, and then added after a pause, "I think she committed suicide rather than face the slow, painful agony of the disease."

"Your father sounds like a complex man. He was willing to risk being discredited to perform a favor in which he did not believe, all in the name of an irrational emotion."

"He never told anyone else about his actions. I think he was embarrassed. He only told me the story to demonstrate the futility of actions inspired by emotion."

"You are like your father, willing to take a great risk to help a friend in trouble."

"I've never thought about it that way."

The thought of Lew brought an abrupt end to the conversation, and the pair escaped into their private memories as the train rolled toward Turin.

Eventually Roberto broke the silence. "If you're determined to go through with this, I will do what I can to help."

"Thank you for believing in me," Crispin said, her voice just above a whisper.

"However, there is more to distinguish between the ordained and laity than a simple change of clothes."

"Then teach me."

They returned to their compartment, where after two hours of lessons in such basics as the rosary, simple liturgies, and accepted customs of address and comportment, Crispin begged for a break.

"If I try to take in any more, I will just confuse myself."

"Then let's talk strategy," Roberto agreed.

Their first order of business would be to find out what they could about Sister Lew. The logical place to start was Lew's family home in a historical district near the center of Turin.

"Did you grow up near there?" Crispin asked.

"No. My family lived near the industrial plants close to the Po River. Our friend came from a line of traditionalists who held on to the family villa," he told her. "Many of the streets in her part of town now have designations for historical preservation."

"I prefer older parts of town, but I like them with a little dirt," she told him. "At least in Turin they haven't power-washed everything like they did in Paris and London to get ready for the millennium celebration. I've always felt there's a sort of honesty in the layers of soot that have accumulated for more than five hundred years. The dirt is like the lines on a strong woman's face; it shows she's lived a rich and interesting life."

There's a dishonesty too, Roberto thought, since that dirt masks what's built up underneath, hidden away and forgotten in the mist of time.

Chapter Fourteen

The taxi easily located 112 Strada del Gandolfo. Sun-drop and grotto-colored tiles were imbedded in the wall beside the wooden front door that, like so many in Italy, was painted a fanciful color. The Sato door was washed in turquoise. Mediterranean shutters, the color of an overcast ocean, were the only other adornment on walls finished with salmon pâté-colored plaster.

The villa faced a street so narrow that pedestrians had to flatten up against a wall to allow a car to pass. Other than the occasional window box, little about the buildings had been updated in centuries. Crispin half imagined she would see gray-haired matriarchs in heavy stockings and long black dresses carrying baskets of fresh pasta. Of course, there were none.

Lew's mother met them at the door. She was a contemporary Italian woman dressed in comfortable slacks and a stylish cotton twill shirt. Although the physical resemblance to her daughter was even more striking than in the picture on Lew's desk, she had none of Sister Lew's serenity. She was like a wind-up toy, all movement and chatter. After Roberto explained to Madam Sato they were friends of Sister Lew's from the Vatican, she invited them to her kitchen, where preparations for an enormous meal were underway. They sat at the harvest table in the center of the room while Lew's mother kept returning to food preparations.

"Tell me, Father, what have you heard about my *bambina*?"

"I was hoping you could tell us. We know only that she did not arrive as expected."

"I have had no news since last night when Mother Mary Kathryn called. She did not tell me she was coming. So unusual. Always she let's me know. Now no word to me or to anyone."

Without asking whether or not they were hungry, Madam Sato set out platters of hard rolls, homemade jam, butter, roasted peppers, and cheese.

Crispin told her it had been a long time since she'd tasted food as good as what was being served, all the while secretly wondering if her ravenous appetite would appear out of place for the kind of discipline expected of a nun.

Once she was satisfied that she'd filled her duties as a hostess, Madam Sato turned her full attention to Roberto.

"Forgive me, Father, but I cannot sit still. I must stay busy," Madam Sato said as tears began to roll down her cheeks.

Roberto offered to pray with her, escorting her to the garden. Crispin could see the pair out the large window and was again struck by the duality of Roberto's personality. When she was with him she could too easily forget that he was a priest. At dinner he was funny, almost carefree, and interested in her research. But the man sitting next to Madam Sato was someone else. He was the wise Father Rossini who had told Crispin the story about the shopkeeper with the half-lived life. He was a minister. A priest. A comforter. Madam Sato was clinging to him and he was clearly a source of solace.

Crispin felt like she was invading their privacy, so she began to stroll around the spacious kitchen. Although it was upgraded with modern appliances, it had the original brick oven recessed into the wall opposite a window with a view of an expansive interior courtyard, filled with fruit trees. Crispin could envision Sister Lew and her family eating meals at the table, and it made her feel closer to Lew. When Roberto and Madam Sato returned, the older woman appeared calmer.

"You must dine with us," she told them, as she began kneading dough in a large wooden bowl. "My brother-in-law, Angelo, he's coming from Spain. I expect him any minute. He has important friends with the government."

In her rapid, nervous chatter, Madam Sato told them that Uncle Angelo was the only brother of her deceased husband. He was a successful industrialist who'd moved to Seville before Sister Lew was born.

"After we lost Giovanni, Angelo became like a papa to my little girl."

"What can I do to help?" Crispin offered.

"All I can ask now are your prayers."

Madam Sato's straightforward, humble request made Crispin feel self-conscious and deceitful. Before she could think of an appropriate response, she was jolted by a loud knock at the door.

"Ah, Angelo," Madam Sato said, dashing out of the kitchen to the door.

When Madam Sato returned with her guest, Angelo greeted Roberto and Crispin with a warm embrace as if they were long lost friends. Crispin recognized him as the man in the photo on Sister Lew's desk. He was a little taller than Roberto and sported an elegant Vandyke beard. His Armani suit and Arienti shirt were, like his Continental manners, impeccable. Although he was nearly old enough to be her father, his manner had a suave, ageless appeal that Crispin found both surprising and a little embarrassing, so she made a conscious effort to hide her attraction.

She couldn't say as much about Angelo's obsequious manservant. Introduced only as Estabin, the man was almost as tall as Angelo but beefier. He had a short neck and badly pocked skin.

Madam Sato insisted that the arrivals sit and eat. Estabin declined the offer to join them with a cloying deference to his boss. He assisted Angelo with his coat, and after Angelo was seated took command of his walking stick. It was an elegant work of art topped with an elaborate ivory handle, carved to resemble a roaring lion. Estabin excused himself to unload the limousine.

"I have just come from the police. Although they normally do not become involved in a case of a missing adult until seventy-two hours have passed, they are making an exception for our Little Sparrow," Angelo told them.

"I knew you would be able to talk to them in a way that they would listen," Madam Sato said, almost fawning over her influential relative.

"I am not happy to report that the investigators still have no leads," he said. "But they are looking."

"My child will soon be found, I am sure," Madam Sato responded, as Angelo rocked her in a hug that tented the tiny woman in his embrace.

"There is likely a misunderstanding or miscommunication. She has probably had a stopover somewhere and will laugh at us for making such a fuss," Angelo said.

Madam Sato wiped her tears with her handkerchief and implored the group, "Please, sit, eat."

Estabin returned but didn't join them at the table. Instead, he positioned himself nearby so he could attend to Angelo's every need.

"You know, Father, I considered the priesthood," Angelo said as he helped himself to a generous serving of tomatoes stuffed with tuna and capers. "But, for me, I knew that I could never honor the vow of poverty," he added, with a deep chuckle that suggested while he intended this comment to be humorous there was truth in the jibe. "How much did you know of our Sparrow's investigations?" Angelo asked Roberto.

"I'm not sure I understand."

"The fire. She told me she was certain that the criticism of the Church regarding the gala was unfounded and she found evidence that would clear all suspicions. Surely, she shared this with you, of all people."

Before Roberto could answer, Angelo directed his attention to Madam Sato.

"My dear, you are a wonder. This fish is perfect. The herbs are the best in all of Italy. You have outdone yourself. Did I not tell you, Estabin, that my sister-in-law was a magnificent hostess?"

Madam Sato blushed and brought a platter of roasted vegetables and peppers to the table along with another platter of cheese and freshly baked bread, smiling for the first time that evening.

"Save room for the rum cake and sweet cream," Madam Sato said.

Angelo gave her hand a squeeze and patted his stomach. "I always do." Turning to Roberto he continued, "Go on, Father, I interrupted you."

"We had discussions on the matter. After the fire, media and politicians suggested the Church was negligent by allowing the gala to be staged in such close proximity to the relic and to the Cathedral." Turning to Crispin Roberto added, "She thought the criticism was wrong and she spent hours going over the official record. It demonstrated that reasonable precautions were taken since food was prepared off premises and, therefore, her assessment exonerated the Church."

"Yes, yes. Go on," Angelo said.

"You appear to be more informed than I."

"Yet, you have the training from the National Fire Service, do you not?"

"Forgive me, but I do not know what you would like me to say."

"If it was not an accident then there must be another cause, yes?"

"What are you saying?"

"Intentionally set, of course. Arson," Angelo said, smiling. "It wouldn't be the first time, now would it?" he said, waving his glass to Estabin indicating he wanted more sangria.

Sensing Roberto's caution at divulging too much information, Crispin attempted to follow suit. "Is that what Lew told you?" she asked.

"Ah, I wondered when you would get it," Angelo responded. "Arson presents interesting possibilities, does it not, Roberto? Will you please explain to the good sister the motives that drive one to set a fire? You know this, yes? From your training, of course."

Visibly uncomfortable, Roberto addressed Crispin. "Except in the rare case of genuine pyromania, there are three motives for arson: revenge, profit, or to cover up another crime."

As if the word "crime" were a theatrical cue, the doorbell rang and Estabin hurried to answer it. He returned almost immediately followed by three police officers, only one of whom spoke.

Crispin had to fight to keep from screaming at the police, No! Don't say it. Then it will be too late. Once the dreadful words are spoken they can never be taken back. Lew will be gone.

The policemen were quick and to the point. They had found her. Someone would have to go with them to identify the body.

"The body," Crispin thought. What a perverted way to refer to Lew.

Chapter Fifteen

The morgue attendant pulled the sheet away from Lew's face. He'd tried to clean the blood off, but she was so badly injured that it was difficult, at first, to recognize her. Her skull was crushed, hair matted, and body deformed under the covers.

"Dear God, how could it have come to this?" Angelo asked. "How could my Little Sparrow be in such a lonely place?"

"Faith does not protect us from life," Roberto responded.

"Or death," Angelo added, as he choked back a sob.

Angelo made the necessary identification and then asked to speak to the police investigators.

"Before I leave, I would like a moment alone," Roberto said.

"Of course," the morgue attendant replied, recovering Lew and excusing himself.

Roberto pulled the crisp white sheet back and stared at the mutilated face of his lost friend. He reached into his left pocket for a silver crucifix but fumbled and dropped it to the floor, where the sound of metal striking the tile resonated in the oppressive silence of the room. He reached to retrieve the cross but his hands were shaking, and as he stood the chain caught on the corner of the metal table. It was as if the cross were resisting him, pulling him away from his task, challenging him. Finally he placed it at Lew's neck and said prayers. He covered her again and with a final whisper said, "How can I ever ask forgiveness for such sins as I have committed? I never intended for you to come to harm. You must know that."

Roberto caught up with Angelo, talking to a police officer in his office.

"Tell him what you told me," Angelo ordered the man behind the desk.

The police captain, no stranger to high profile cases and the political tightrope a man in his position was forced to walk, stood and greeted Roberto. "Pardon me, Father, we have few chairs. I will retrieve another."

"Damn incompetence," Angelo said, as the captain left. "They didn't even conduct a search. Mushroom pickers found her. Mushroom pickers!"

The captain returned with a chair, and Roberto thanked him. "I am Father Roberto Rossini," he said, shaking the other man's hand. "I knew the sister in Rome." The policeman registered surprise that he tried, too late, to cover up.

"Captain Magro," he said, returning Roberto's handshake and then taking his place behind the desk.

"These idiots don't even know how she died," Angelo told Roberto. "Her body was at the bottom of a ravine. She evidently fell from one of the hiking trails above."

"An accident?"

"I seriously doubt it. She grew up on those trails. My Sparrow could navigate them blindfolded," Angelo replied.

"Surely not suicide," Roberto said in a horse whisper.

"Not a possibility! She was a happy, healthy woman in her prime, and such an act would be a violation of everything she believed," Angelo said.

"That only leaves . . . ," Magro offered.

"Homicide?" Angelo scoffed.

"We will know more after the autopsy," the policeman explained. "You must allow us time to gather the evidence."

"If you imbeciles had been doing your job, you would have found her when we first reported her missing and she would be alive today," Angelo yelled, scraping back his chair to leave. "Let's get out of here."

Estabin materialized from the hallway and helped his employer with his overcoat.

After they were gone, Captain Magro dialed the Vatican.

* * *

It was late in the night when Angelo and Roberto returned to the Sato villa. Madam Sato was waiting for them at her kitchen table, clinging to Crispin's hands.

"Tell me. Was it her? Was it my child?"

Angelo answered with a silent nod and moved to her side, enfolding Madam Sato into his arms. Her sobs rose to that ethereal place inhabited only by women who have lost a child. It is reserved and held sacred by the Blessed Mother for women whose children have died in birth, women who have miscarried, or women who have buried a toddler or lost a grown child to war or accident, suicide or disease. All know the pain. To see a child who was grown from your womb, from your body, your bone, live and then die is a kind of agony that only a mother can know and only a mother can speak of to another. In that moment Crispin saw Madam Sato go to that Pietà and knew she would forever inhabit that company of lost loves.

Crispin didn't move until Roberto spoke. "Angelo, I must escort Sister Crispin to her convent. She is expected."

Madam Sato turned to Roberto, grabbing his hands and begging. "Don't leave me, Father, please don't leave me."

"I promise, Madam, I will come back," Roberto replied.

Angelo offered to have Estabin drive them, but Crispin found her voice. "That is kind, Angelo, but I need some time to collect my thoughts, and a walk will help."

"The convent is not far from here," Roberto added. "I will return as soon as I can."

Crispin gathered her belongings and said good-bye to Madam Sato, although the distraught woman was oblivious. They left her in the consolation of Angelo's arms.

A block from the Sato home, Roberto turned to Crispin. "We are not going to the convent. You need to leave Turin. Right away."

"See here, Roberto, we've been through this before. It's not your decision. Tell me what you know and I'll decide whether I'm in or out."

"Sister Llewellyn. Her death may not have been an accident. I think it is somehow connected to whatever she found out about the Shroud. And, if I'm right, the local police are on the phone to the bishop right now to let him know I'm in Turin. It is too dangerous for you to continue."

The narrow street spilled into a small plaza with a fountain in the middle. Although the water in the fountain was only a trickle, the broad stones and colored tiles surrounding it offered a bench where Crispin and Roberto could sit.

Roberto told her that Lew had been found at the bottom of a ravine in an area she had hiked all her life. "I know the area well. The trails are well marked and maintained. Even at night, I don't see how she would fall or lose her way. That is why police do not believe it was an accident."

Crispin didn't answer immediately, but when she did she was resolute. "Let me tell you what happened after you left with the police. Madam Sato was near collapse so she asked me to make her a cup of tea. When I brought it to her in the drawing room she was holding a box of photographs. She showed me several of me with Lew in New York and Connecticut. She wasn't angry but told me that she'd recognized me when we arrived and she knew I was wearing Lew's clothes. She wasn't sure if you knew who I was, so she kept quiet. She demanded an explanation."

"What did you tell her?" Roberto asked.

"Everything."

"How did she take it?"

"I couldn't tell exactly, but she told me something important. She said that the last time she talked to Lew, her daughter was worried, even frightened. She kept telling her mother that if something happened to her that she would always watch over her. It was so unlike Lew, who was an eternal optimist."

"I see."

"Madam Sato made me promise to finish the investigation, regardless of what happens. She made me promise. So don't think you can frighten me or change my mind. Ever since the police came to the front door I've been through every possibility in my mind. I know what we're up against and I'm not backing down."

"I'm sorry if you think I was trying to control you, but I'm concerned for your safety."

"You should be sorry," Crispin said. "What are you going to do if I leave? What is your Plan B?"

Roberto didn't answer.

"Right. I say we go ahead with our plan. I owe it to Lew, and now I owe it to her mother. Besides, I will be safe in the convent tonight. Tomorrow we'll have our answer. You can take the information and do what you want with it. Believe me, I'm ready to go back to New York. Agreed?"

"Agreed," Roberto responded, with an uncertain resolve.

From the plaza to the convent was a short distance. In spite of their unusual midnight arrival, Mother Mary Kathryn accepted, without question, when Roberto explained that Crispin was sent to fill in for Sister Lew as videographer. Crispin suspected that Roberto's position in the Vatican and his heroic role in rescuing the Shroud imbued him with unquestionable credibility.

"How appropriate, my dear, that you carry the name of the patron saint of weavers," she said as she welcomed them with few questions.

It was the first time that Crispin had realized that her name-sake, Saint Crispian, was connected to weavers. She knew only that Crispian and his brother had worked as cobblers at night to support their evangelical efforts, but it was their martyrdom, as much as their ministry to the makers of useful things, that won the pair their place in Catholic devotion.

"May Saint Crispian bless our work," Mother Mary Kathryn told Roberto as he said his farewell.

Chapter Sixteen

Crispin was grateful that their late arrival gave her a logical reason to excuse herself and escape to the safety of her sleeping quarters. She had a big day ahead and didn't want to risk tripping herself up. The veneer of religious instruction she would have to rely on tomorrow was thin and she knew it.

It took no time to settle into the narrow bed. Once safe under the covers, the pain of loss was so intense that it left Crispin feeling strangely numb; the way a hand or foot feels when pressed so firmly for a long period until all sensation bleeds away. She was laying on her back staring up at a ceiling she couldn't see in the darkness, surrounded by a silence violated only by the faint sound of her breath. She felt her mind drifting back over the events of the past few days. Back to Roberto's suspicions about Lew's death. If Lew was killed, then she was the second death this week. Father Mitchel was the first. Or was he? What about Sarah and her brother? Was Cross connected to them in some way? As she paired the names of those involved—Lew and Sarah; Sarah and Cross; Cross and Mitchel; Cross and Lew—Crispin realized a rhythm was emerging. But it had nothing to do with solving the mystery of the Shroud. It had everything to do with the cadence of her heart. Frustrated and needing to be prepared for tomorrow's events, she turned over, curled up with the pillow, and tried to sleep.

She was awake long before sunrise. Her first waking thoughts were so muddled that she'd decided to get up and dress long before the daylight told her it was time. The tears she'd shed during the night left her eyes swollen and burning and her cheeks caked with salt. The scent of verbena bath soap and vanilla candles permeated the fabric of her clothes, a tangible residue that reminded her of Lew, a smell Crispin could inhale the way she did as a little girl when she would bury her face in the sleeves of her lost mother's dresses, inhaling the memory that still lived in the cloth. She tried to turn away, but grief beckoned her from the folds of the fabric. It called her to lean into it, to absorb it.

I can't. Not now, she told herself. This was neither the time nor the place to be vulnerable. Today, Crispin had to store the pain behind pylons, safely out of the way for now. There would be time later for a full expression of grief.

Crispin paced the cold stone floor. With every step across the cell she was aware that she had become the undercover agent Pirolla accused her of being. She felt relief when Mother Mary Kathryn knocked on the door. "Now it begins," Crispin whispered to herself.

She fell into line with a column of nuns. Heads bowed, they filed into a windowless workroom with halogen floodlights suspended over a rectangular table nearly as long as the room. As those in the solemn procession took seats in armless metal chairs down each side of the table, Crispin chose one by the top left corner, where she unpacked the camera and then joined in silent meditation. After a few minutes, Mother Mary Kathryn led them in a brief prayer that their restoration work would succeed.

The silence was interrupted when the door opened to admit four hearty monks carrying the silver Shroud casket. They placed it with great reverence on the table in front of the seated nuns. From where she was positioned, Crispin had a clear view of the casket. The handle was broken. How is that possible? How could it be broken on the night of the fire, intact when placed in its new crypt in the video, and now broken again?

Crispin struggled to process this revelation while hiding her confusion by fiddling with the dials on Sister Lew's video camera as the monks carefully opened the casket and spread the fourteen-foot-long cloth down the length of the table. She had guessed right so she didn't have to reposition her perspective. The Francine corner was next to her on the table.

Face to face with one of the most mysterious and revered relics in Christianity, Crispin realized that pictures she'd seen over the years didn't do it justice. The patched, cream-colored linen cloth, long enough to easily enfold a tall man, bore signs of its age, including severe scorching from near destruction in 1534. Was this imprint the body of the true Christ, or, as some believed, no more than an elaborate medieval hoax concocted at least a thousand or more years after the crucifixion?

Even though Crispin had come here to determine whether or not this particular piece of fabric was a counterfeit, she was intimidated by its direct connection to more than two thousand years of Christian faith. Crispin could almost hear Lew's soft voice whispering to her: "Those who come into contact with the Holy Shroud are called. There is no choice, no chance."

For the moment, however, Crispin's concerns were less about cosmic callings than with the practical considerations of ceremony. The nuns had again bowed their heads in prayer. What was she supposed to be doing? Her cowl obscured her view of the nun to her right. She needed to imitate her companion's actions. Crispin didn't want to risk attracting attention by staring at the nuns across the table from her, so she cast her eyes down and tried a sideways glance as she coughed lightly.

Crispin then reached over and turned on the camera, making sure it recorded a close-up of the casket handle before adjusting the line of sight to encompass the whole room. She tried to mimic the solemnity of the others, all the while fighting the electrical charges of adrenaline on her nerves. One nun across the table was unable to restrain herself and placed her finger on the edge of the Shroud. Mother Mary Kathryn saw her. "Patience, Sister Lucia."

Sister Lucia's cheeks turned cherry red with embarrassment, and Crispin diverted her gaze. Once the monks left, it was time for the nuns to go to work on the raveled edges of the Holland Cloth, or lining, with precise, delicate stitches as if each thread were sacred. It was now or never. Crispin's stomach churned as she thought of what she was about to do.

Crispin stood up, readied the video camera, and then fingered the top of the border. The frayed edge pulled away. Crispin had only a moment. It had to count. Her heart rate accelerated, reaching the rhythm she achieved after a jog in the park. Guilt, fear, excitement all hammered in her chest. Lew's admonishment the last time she saw her alive again sounded in her brain, "There is no chance, no choice."

When no one was looking her way, Crispin lifted the border as far as she could. It was all over in an instant. In plain view were the distinctive copper strands of hair that her dad had woven there for Francine. Unmistakable. A beat, a deep breath, and then Crispin covered her discovery. What she'd seen only confused her more. First the handle, and now the hair. Her theory was wrong. Crispin hid behind the video camera, hoping the shock wasn't written on her face.

In a near trance, she moved around the chamber filming when loud male voices shattered the peace of the chamber as the door flew open. Crispin almost dropped the camera. She steadied herself and aimed the camera in the direction of the commotion. At first, her lens was filled with black. As she focused, Bishop Pirolla's red face materialized in the viewfinder.

"Impostor!" he screamed, pointing at Crispin. Stunned, the nuns stopped working and watched, but said nothing as Bishop Pirolla grabbed Crispin by the arm. His companions confiscated the camera. Pirolla roughly escorted her into an adjoining room. Mother Mary Kathryn followed them, clasping her hands to her mouth. "Bishop Pirolla, what does this mean? Father Rossini brought Sister Crispin to us. We were told you sent her as Sister Llewellyn's replacement."

"This woman is a spy. She is a liar, a cheater, and a thief. She was sent here to desecrate the Shroud. Father Rossini was too foolish to see it and now he is implicated as well."

"But, you said you were her friend," Mother Mary Kathryn said to Crispin.

"I'm . . ."

"Silence!" Pirolla commanded as he took Crispin roughly by the arm and pulled her out into the hall.

Mother Mary Kathryn excused herself and returned to the Shroud work, leaving Crispin alone with her enemy.

Chapter Seventeen

Crispin's fight and bravado were battered into submission inside a tornado of unanswered questions and confusion as Pirolla escorted her to a narrow, windowless room. He motioned her to a chair and ordered her to sit.

"You have a great deal to answer for, Ms. Leads. I'll be back," he said as he turned to leave. "And, please, show some respect and remove that ridiculous disguise."

He locked the door to the hall as he left.

Crispin, more from embarrassment than obedience, removed Lew's veil and coif and twisted them into a ball with her hands.

"I'm a fool," she told herself. "A first-class fool. Why did I think I could pull off a con like this? Now I've humiliated myself. What will I tell Dad? I've failed Lew. I've failed Madam Sato."

Crispin felt like crying, but her tears had dried up and emptied out on the convent pillow the night before. All her sadness was now covered over by guilt, shame, and fear. Minutes ticked by. The longer she sat, the more anxious she grew. She got up and began to pace, talking to herself.

What will he do to me? What *can* he do to me? she wondered. Is it against the law to impersonate a nun? They will charge me with vandalism, but they can't prove anything because I didn't do anything wrong. My only crime is stupidity.

By then she'd reached the length of the room so she turned and continued to cross-examine herself. What about the funny business with the Macken diaries? And, you did take Lew's clothes and passport. That's, at least, misdemeanor theft. You probably should get a lawyer. Shit, oh shit, oh shit.

She tried the door to the hall, confirming that it was, indeed, locked. As she turned around she saw another door in the far corner of the western wall. She hadn't noticed it before because she'd been sitting with her back to it. When she tried, it resisted her frantic pulls. The doorknob seemed to be more stuck than locked. "Come on. Come on. I've got to get out of here. I've got to," she muttered. She gave the door one final, adrenaline-powered jerk and it yielded.

The door led to a room that was the mirror image of the one she'd just left. Same size. Same layout. Same hallway door. She peeked through the unlocked hallway door and saw Pirolla standing a few yards away, talking to two other priests.

Shit, she thought, carefully closing the door and tiptoeing to the western wall door. On the other side was another identical room. That led, railcar fashion, to the next room. She did her best to block each door as she passed through, propping a chair against one and moving a desk in front of another. Her luck held and she moved through three more rooms until she came to a side door that was locked and would not yield, even though she pulled with all she had in her.

"Damn it to Hell."

Before she could plan her next move, someone inserted a key and unlocked the door from the opposite side. She braced herself for another confrontation. Instead, Roberto popped his head through the open door. Before she could muster words, he put his finger to his lips indicating she should be quiet and motioned her to follow him. After she was safely through, he relocked the door.

"This way."

"Oh, Roberto. I was wrong about everything and the bishop . . ."

He again gestured her to be silent and waved her to follow.

Crispin followed Roberto out to a breezeway that opened to a narrow, metal platform, which offered access to a cast iron spiral staircase. It was so narrow Crispin felt she would have to squeeze her shoulders together just to make the turns. The Slinky toy stairs dropped below them several stories, and for a moment she experienced vertigo at the thought of navigating them.

"You've got to be kidding," she said.

"It's the only way out."

Crispin gathered up the skirt of her habit so she didn't trip, folded it over one arm, and used the other to cling to the stair railing as she followed Roberto, one precarious step after another until they finally reached *terra firma*. There an ancient iron gate was propped open against a stone archway that led to a tunnel that gave off the odor of a neglected toilet or city sewer. Roberto fished a flashlight from his pocket and led the way inside.

"Oh, great. Just what my stomach needed this morning," Crispin said, pinching her nose as she caught the first whiff of stench from the damp interior.

Once they had gone a safe distance, Roberto stopped and handed her a bag. "I retrieved these from Madam Sato's. It would be better if you changed clothes," he told her without further explanation.

Roberto turned his back and she found a niche that gave her a modicum of privacy. While she changed into jeans, a button-down cotton shirt, and Keds, she told him that she knew the answer that they came to Turin to find.

"The Shroud. Francine's hair is there. And the handle is broken, again."

"What do you mean?"

"There was no switch. Don't you see? It's all over?"

"You're wrong. It won't be over until we know why Sister Llewellyn died," he replied.

Crispin stuffed the nun's attire into the bag and followed Roberto through the rat-infested passageways. The tunnel was wide enough in places that they could walk two abreast. In other places, she felt claustrophobic. At times the tunnel would open into large chambers with multiple exits, but Roberto never hesitated, each time choosing their course with certainty. They had been underground for no more than fifteen minutes when Crispin became disoriented.

"Do you have any idea where we are?" she asked.

"These tunnels are from the war," he answered. "We learned about them in the Fire Service."

After another half an hour underground, Crispin saw a light ahead and had to fight the urge to race toward it. The light was coming through a gate, much like the one where they had entered the labyrinth. At first she feared they had been going around in circles, but when they pushed through the gate they stepped out into a small plaza on a street just a few blocks from the Sato villa.

Chapter Eighteen

Angelo greeted them at the familiar turquoise door, but said nothing about Crispin's street clothes. After inviting them in, he told Roberto that Madam Sato was asking for him.

"Come, my dear, we'll take refreshment," Angelo said to Crispin.

She followed the older man into the once-cheerful kitchen, where he poured her a glass of sweet lemonade. She felt the immediate sugar rush on her empty stomach.

"I suppose you are curious about how I'm dressed," she said.

Angelo didn't speak for a moment. He stared at her for a long time over his hands, which were folded in front of him on the table. Finally, he smiled. "I have known your secret all along. The day Sparrow left the Vatican she told me about her beautiful friend, Crispin, who came from the States."

Crispin sniffed. "Why didn't you say something?"

"How could I? You and Father Rossini have a plan. No?"

"Had a plan. It's blown all to . . ."

"Hell?"

Crispin could feel the dull pain behind her eyes warning of an oncoming migraine. Her system was reaching overload and she needed food. She wasn't hungry, but if she didn't eat and take something, she risked being incapacitated.

Angelo saw what was happening. "Estabin, come immediately."

The manservant materialized from another room.

"Our friend needs something to eat and, perhaps, something for a headache?"

"I have medicine in my bag upstairs. Hot tea would help too."

Angelo got up and turned off the kitchen lights. "I too suffer. Estabin knows what to do."

Crispin took her medicine and tea along with a small plate of cheese and fruit. Using the canvas bag as a pillow, she laid her head on the tabletop and closed her eyes.

She woke with a start to the sound of loud voices. It was Roberto and Angelo arguing. She got up and followed the sound to a small sitting room. Roberto was standing near a fire grate. He stopped talking when Crispin came in.

"There you are, my dear," Angelo said. "I hope you are refreshed."

"I am sorry. How long did I sleep?"

"Only a short while. Please join us. This affects you too," Angelo replied.

"What are you talking about?" she asked, as she curled up in a seat near the fireplace.

"Next steps," Angelo said. "To follow your interesting theories."

Roberto started to say something, but Crispin interrupted him. "You mean about the suspicious fire?"

"Yes," Angelo answered. "And, the concerns about Sister Sarah's brother and how he died."

"Did Sister Llewellyn know something about his death?" Roberto asked.

"She shared many concerns, but did not have clear evidence the last time we talked," Angelo replied.

"And then there's the switch," Crispin said.

"That's it!" Angelo added.

"I was so sure that someone had switched out a copy of the Shroud after the fire, until I saw Francine's hair," Crispin said with a sigh, too late to realize from Roberto's expression that perhaps this point hadn't yet come up in his conversation with

Angelo. "That reminds me, does anyone know how Pirolla knew where to find me?"

"I can answer," Roberto said. "Do you remember Sister Mary Elizabeth?"

"No, I don't think so," she said.

"She's the mother superior's secretary," Roberto said. "I had coffee with her this morning to see if a call had come from the police or the Vatican about me. The sweet old woman mentioned that Bishop Pirolla had just arrived. Mother Mary Kathryn called him late last night with the news about Sister Llewellyn. She thanked him for sending you in her place."

"So he knew we were both in Torino?" Crispin said.

"That's right. So I came to find you," Roberto said.

"All our shenanigans and it led to nothing," she said.

Angelo coughed and said, "I fear there is more to it."

"What do you mean?" Roberto asked.

"Captain Magro, from last night, called to warn me about you, Father Rossini. The bishop told him about some troubles at the Vatican and to be on the lookout for you. He called the bishop after we left last night to let him know you were in Torino."

Crispin covered her eyes and began to rock back and forth in her seat. "This is so crazy. What difference does it make? The only thing that matters is that Sister Lew is dead. Sister Lew is dead and the Church is worried about a few files out of place in her office. Give me a break."

"They assume the two events are connected," Roberto said.

"So none of this would have happened if I had just minded my own business?" Crispin said.

"You must not blame yourself," Angelo said.

"All I wanted to do was help," Crispin whispered.

"You still can. It is my hope that you and Father Rossini will honor my Little Sparrow's memory and continue her inquiry. It is important to know the truth."

"How?" Roberto asked.

"Are you familiar with the Sudarium?"

"At the Cathedral of Oviedo? In Toledo?" Crispin asked.

"Yes," Angelo answered.

"I know a little of the Sudarium," Crispin said. "It's certainly more obscure than the Shroud, but some still revere it as the cloth that covered Jesus' face after his death."

"I was able to help my Sparrow arrange interviews with the monks of Oviedo," Angelo said. "Perhaps they will have the answer."

"Is that what Sister Lew thought?" Crispin asked.

"She asked for my help, but I knew little of her reasoning. There was no time," Angelo said, his voice fading to a whisper.

Although he had remained silent for a long time when he spoke, Crispin could tell that Roberto was having trouble controlling his tone. "As I told you last night, Angelo, I can make the trip to Oviedo alone. While I appreciate your offer of transportation, we should not involve Crispin further."

"What do you mean involve? I intend to stay involved until we know what happened to Lew and I clear my name. Besides, we owe it to her memory to figure out the secret of the Shroud. I believe that somehow all of the deaths, including Father Mitchel, are connected. I just don't know how," Crispin said in a tone that left no room for argument.

"I am certain, my Sparrow would expect you to help," Angelo said, again pressing his offer to arrange transportation on his private jet. Although Angelo would need to remain in Turin to help Madam Sato with funeral arrangements, his plane could take them to Spain immediately and return later for him.

"Please accept my offer. By continuing my Little Sparrow's work, you honor what she stood for."

And died for? Crispin thought to herself.

"What better options do either of us have?" Crispin asked Roberto.

"Then it is settled," Angelo said, leaving to make arrangements.

Although Roberto had acquiesced to the plan in near silence, after Angelo left he confronted Crispin. "Are you sure you want to do this?"

"We need a safe place to sort things out," she replied. "Maybe Uncle Angelo is Lew's way of guiding us. Telling us where to go next."

For a minute, Crispin thought he was going to argue with her but, instead, he nodded and left to say good-bye to Madam Sato.

Before leaving, Crispin retrieved her small travel bag that she'd left there the night before. She smoothed and folded Lew's things with care and packed them in the well-traveled canvas bag. She had planned to leave the bag with Madam Sato, but at the last minute changed her mind. Crispin couldn't explain the compulsion, but she felt by keeping a piece of Lew with her she could touch what Lew had touched and, in doing so, still touch her friend. She needed a totem.

Sitting alone in the kitchen waiting, Crispin had an urge to also connect with her dad. Maybe it was the way Madam Sato suffered by not knowing the fate of her daughter? Maybe it was the little girl in Crispin, wanting the familiarity and safety that only a parent can provide? Maybe it was a desire to shake off the residue of her deception and reconnect with her authentic self? It was hard for her to pin down the exact reason that it was so important to her to talk to him. It just was. That's why she was so disappointed, and a bit melancholy, when the machine picked up. A mechanical voice recording is a poor substitute for a parent when you are hurting.

Crispin left a brief voicemail telling him that she was traveling to Spain and could be reached at Señor Angelo Sato's home in Seville.

"Love you," she said as she signed off.

"Love you more," she whispered to herself as she hung up.

Chapter Nineteen

The Falcon 900 lifted off the runway as Crispin studied the jet's lush appointments. Everything—linen napkins, crystal glassware, headrests on the leather seats, lavatory towels—was embossed with the Sato family crest, an angel, her feet planted firmly on the earth, clad in armor, pointing her golden sword heavenward above her outstretched wings. She asked Estabin to interpret the meaning for her. "Loosely translated it means 'God's Instrument on Earth,'" he explained. "The Sato family lineage can be traced to the original Knights Templar."

Once the jet achieved cruising altitude, Estabin excused himself and went to the galley. Roberto, sitting across from Crispin, focused on the contents of a pocket notebook. She watched as he occasionally stopped reading to add or amend notations.

"What were you and Angelo fighting about?"

Roberto closed the notebook and folded it into the empty seat beside him before answering her. "Sister Llewellyn. Deadly danger. You," he said.

"Please, I gathered that much. If we're going to work together, you have to be open with me."

"Agreed," Roberto replied, crossing his legs and shifting slightly in the seat so that he could tuck his left hand into his coat pocket. "Angelo received a call from the coroner not long before you joined us. He had preliminary results. There is no doubt. Sister Llewellyn was murdered."

"Oh."

Estabin interrupted them with a weather report and a tray of bottled water and warm nuts.

"Would you like something else to drink?" he asked. "We have a full bar."

Crispin turned down the offer.

"I'm fine," Roberto said, waiting until they were alone again before continuing. "The final autopsy report should be available tomorrow."

"Wouldn't it be hard to tell that someone actually pushed her into the ravine? Do they have a witness?" Crispin asked.

"The evidence indicates she was dead before her body was thrown over the cliff."

Crispin didn't respond to the revelation, but waited for Roberto to continue.

"She had been tied up. Her wrists were covered with abrasions and bruises from trying to twist out of the coarse ropes," Roberto said.

"I see. But, there's more, isn't there?"

"Do you really want me to tell you everything?"

"No, but yes. I have to know," she answered, as she reached for a drink of water, her hands quivering.

"She was tortured."

The pool of sunshine that had filled the cabin minutes before disappeared as the plane passed through clouds streaked with violet and gold, as if the gruesome shadows in Crispin's mind were controlling the weather.

"Tortured. What do you mean tortured?" she asked.

"The details aren't important."

"I need to know," Crispin said, rubbing her wrists.

Roberto leaned forward and covered her hands with his right hand. His warm, gentle touch helped quell the anxiety she was feeling. When her hands stopped shaking, he leaned back in his seat and continued his explanation. "It is enough to know that it involved repeated near suffocation. I think they were trying to get her to tell them something. We don't know why they did it. We don't know who did it, but something has changed."

"What do you mean?"

"If we assume that the deaths of Father Mitchel, Sister Sarah, and her brother are all connected to Sister Llewellyn's, someone went to a great deal of trouble to make sure the first three looked like an accident. This time no such effort was made."

"What if we are wrong and there is no connection between her death and the Shroud?" Crispin asked. "Should we be thinking about a different motive?"

"As you say in America, we may be chasing geese in the wind."

Crispin almost corrected his use of idiom when the plane jerked and banked suddenly to the right. Within seconds Estabin opened the door from the galley and rushed in. "I apologize, but we are going to experience turbulence. The pilot asks that you remain seated and use your seatbelts," he told them, as he picked up the bottles and stowed loose objects. "I am sorry for the inconvenience, but he will adjust our course and should find a smoother ride shortly."

Estabin buckled himself into an empty seat in the rear of the cabin. After a brief rough ride, the intercom system crackled and the pilot announced that he had achieved a smooth altitude above the storm. Estabin unbuckled his seatbelt and arranged the cabin for the comfort of the passengers before excusing himself and returning to the galley.

"I have been trying to summarize the situation," Roberto said, picking up his notebook. "I've started a list of questions."

Roberto read the list off to her: Why did the bishop change the schedule for the restoration? Is he involved in some way? What was Lew going to tell me about the Shroud? Why did she travel unescorted? Is the clue to be found in the coding scheme connected to the gala? Are the deaths of Father Mitchel, Sister Sarah, and her brother connected? How? Why? What is Thomas Cross up to and who does he work for? Who ransacked Sister Llewellyn's office and why? What did she think she would learn from the Sudarium? What is the answer to the mix-up on the videotape where the Shroud casket clearly had a repaired handle? Who set the fire in Turin?

"That is just a partial list," he told Crispin, tossing the book back on the seat.

They decided to be methodical and review the evidence. The more they talked, however, the more they became frustrated by the endless questions without answers.

"Maybe we will be able to think after a good night's sleep when our brains are clear," Crispin said with a yawn.

Roberto opened his notebook and began to write.

Crispin's thoughts drifted into memories of Lew as a child in Turin and later as a young woman visiting her in New York. She could think of nothing in Lew's actions or attire suggesting she came from a family of wealth or privilege. Crispin wondered if Lew had gone out of her way to give the opposite impression. She remembered waiting with her brother and Lew at the baggage claim at Boston's Logan Airport the first time Lew had come for a summer visit to Aunt Tilde's. They watched the luggage shoot dump the jumbo black canvas bags of the international passengers, one after another, onto the carrousel. "If you see it, let me know and I'll grab it," Clinton told their friend, and Crispin pointed out the sign that warned passengers to make sure they had the right bag before leaving the terminal because so many look alike. We shouldn't have worried, Crispin remembered with a smile. When Lew's bag appeared at the top of the shoot, it was a small, beige leather-and-canvas suitcase that had probably been in service since the 1950s. Lew had packed for a two-week stay in a bag that some Americans would consider a tight squeeze for a weekend excursion. The thought of Lew's well-worn suitcase sitting on the overhead rack in her uncle's luxurious airplane made Crispin ache for her lost friend's company.

"How can you know someone and yet not really know them at all?" Crispin mumbled.

"What did you say?" Roberto said, leaning toward Crispin.

Trying to avoid his gaze she said, "Nothing."

"Your face says something else."

"I can't bear to think that Lew died alone," Crispin whispered after a few minutes of quiet had passed. "We deserve to have loved ones with us."

As is often the case with new grief, past losses intruded to demand a voice.

"My mother also died a violent death," she added.

Roberto didn't say anything, but rather shifted in his seat, rested his chin on his hand, and nodded for her to continue. The movements were so slight and the nod so subtle as to be almost imperceptible. Yet, in that change of posture and that nod of the head, he wasn't Roberto, her traveling companion anymore. He was Father Rossini again, the compassionate counselor, ready to offer guidance and comfort.

"How do you do that?" Crispin asked.

"I don't follow."

"Make yourself open to confession? Are priests taught these moves or do they come naturally?"

"Perhaps it is you who is open?" he said. "Tell me about her, your mother."

Crispin could see her mother, imagine the feel of her soft, olive skin and almost, just almost, convince herself that she could smell her scent; a mixture of magnolia blossoms and fresh mowed spring grass. "My mother's name was Melete. She was from Greece."

Memories moved through Crispin's mind like images passing by the windows of a moving train—well-lit, three-dimensional vignettes illuminating a familiar neighborhood. Slowly, an early memory moved into the spotlight, bursting into frosted color.

Crispin was a little girl at a kitchen table helping her mother fold pale blue linen napkins that smelled starchy and warm from having just been ironed. Then before she could hold onto that moment, the scene dimmed and sank back into the blackness that always drove her fondest memories out of view, the way a schoolyard bully pushes to the front of the line.

Now she was lost in the woods, where towering pine trees shed their needles to form a deep, molding blanket on the floor. She was running scared, crying. She heard her mother's voice calling her name. She started running toward it, to the safe place where nothing could hurt her. Just as the sun broke through the trees and she saw her mother's open arms, the image changed to a train station and she was with her brother. Melete was giving them each bright, helium-filled balloons, red for her and yellow for Clinton. Someone on the platform bumped Crispin's arm, causing her to let go of her balloon and she watched, helpless, as it drifted away into the rafters of the station. In her memory, the little girl sobbed and gasped for breath.

When she shook off the memories and realized she was sitting next to Roberto, she too was fighting back tears. Now she spoke in a whisper as she permitted her most feared memory to surface. "Clinton and I were five when Mother died. We were living in Egypt." Her gut tightened. She was at the airport concentrating on her coloring book, waiting for her mother's plane to land. Melete was returning to Egypt after an emergency trip to New England.

"The metallic gold crayon I was using kept flaking off. Waxy flecks stuck where I didn't want them. I'd brush them off the paper, but they would smear. I was intent on getting an even color but couldn't because the crayon was a cheap one."

Crispin felt her throat tighten, making it difficult to swallow as she envisioned what came next, struggling for the right words that could fully translate the emotional truth of a five-year-old who witnesses a parent's death.

Roberto waited silently, without interrupting her story.

"It's all there in my mind. The light from the fire. The noise from the explosion. The heat melting the crayon. The smell." Crispin's hands were trembling, and she saw that the vigorous rubbing had turned her wrists a bright red, exposing faint, thin white scar lines along each inner wrist. "It's all one thing. One sensation. A smell. A taste. A sound. A color. I've never really been able to separate them. Death is a distinct sense. Unique really to that moment.

"The fire was so intense that Mother's body was burned to ashes. There was nothing left of her dark eyes or her black hair. Nothing of her laugh. Nothing of her smile." She tugged her sleeves over her hands and tucked them under her armpits as she rocked and hugged herself. "At her memorial service, we only had a framed picture of her."

She was keenly aware that Roberto had let her talk without interruption, observation, or comment. After a long sigh, she asked, "Why do we run toward the flame? Do you know?"

"Sometimes we are compelled to lean into the pain, to absorb it, neutralize it like alkaline to acid. Perhaps it is what draws us to the flame. To cauterize the pain," Roberto answered.

"Is that the way it was with you?" Crispin asked in a whisper.

"What do you mean?"

"You don't have to answer. I shouldn't have asked."

Estabin opened the galley door. He was carrying a tray laden with tapenade, black olives, cheeses, cured meat, crackers, and empanadas. After spreading a linen cloth on a table, he placed the charcuterie between them and described the wine choices. They both chose a bold red, and after he served them he excused himself.

When they were alone again, Roberto picked up the broken thread of their conversation. "You asked me a question and I didn't answer."

"I saw the newspaper clippings in Lew's office."

"I see," he said, taking a sip of wine. "I have the feeling there is more you want to say."

"There was a tape. An interview."

"Ah."

"I didn't watch all of it."

"You saw enough to know that, like you, my life was changed by fire."

They sipped wine silently for a few minutes

"It's little wonder you are interested in burial rituals," he said.

"A way to say good-bye?"

"Something you were denied."

"You are not the first to suggest that I use my research as a path to healing."

Helping herself to cheese and crostini, Crispin thought for a minute.

"There may be something to it. But some of my less sympathetic friends assume there is more to it. They accuse me of trying to prove myself by carving out a niche where I can distinguish my career from that of the rest of the Leads clan."

"What do you think?

"If I am honest with myself I have to admit they have a point," she answered, raising her glass.

She told him that when she was a little girl a tutor asked her to fetch a story from the "Harvard Classics" book set in the library. "Next to the volumes devoted to Bacon, Homer, Darwin, and Virgil, I noticed one labeled 'Minor Works.' Even as a child, I thought that while it must be an honor to have your writing selected for a collection of classics, how disappointing it must be to be relegated to a volume with such an ignoble title.

"I assume that's where I'll wind up someday, while Dad and Clinton will have a volume of their own. 'Minor Works,' indeed," she said with a bit of bitterness just as Estabin returned with another bottle of wine.

"But, a 'classic' nonetheless. Surely those minor authors followed your Thoreau," Roberto said. "To go with confidence in the direction of your dreams. Live the life you imagine. As we all should." Roberto reached for the bottle and topped off both their glasses.

"Let's raise our glass to all those who author minor works," Roberto said with a smile and a toast.

"To minor works that are also classics," she replied, smiling for the first time since they'd boarded the plane.

After the plane landed, Estabin escorted them to a waiting limousine. An hour later they approached a gated driveway lined with poplar trees that stood like anorexic sentries on each side of the road. When Estabin keyed in the security code, the metal gate rattled briefly on its hinges before swinging wide. Crispin stuck her head out the window into the sultry Spanish air. The day had been so hot that the long gravel driveway radiated heat. Through the haze she could see Angelo's three-story parador cloaked in a mirage of fading sunlight. Many of Spain's ancestral castles had been converted to high-class hotels. To own one outright was unusual.

Even though they'd arrived in the evening when the household was resting, a meal awaited them by a large fountain at a stone table inlaid with mint and lemon-colored tiles. Roberto and Crispin dined *al fresco* on mescaline salad and a highly seasoned variation of paella served in the regional style with spaghetti instead of saffron rice. They ate in silence. The beauty of their surroundings was lost on them as the tension of the day caught up with them. They were relieved when Estabin appeared from the shadows and offered to show them to their suites.

It took Crispin no time to dress for bed. She could feel her tired body yield willingly to the comfort of her surroundings, sinking into the dense cushions and down duvet surrounded by piles of pillows with embroidered damask covers. A flight of cherubs adorned the fresco on the ten-foot ceiling. The uprights on the walnut bed were deeply carved in rice bowers that ended in finials so high that she couldn't have reached them even if she'd stood on the tips of her toes. The bed offered its occupant a direct view out the beveled glass doors that swung open onto an ornate iron balcony that bordered the courtyard below.

Hours into a deep sleep Crispin dreamed she was a toddler wandering, lost in a Vatican room of bright frescos and marble statutes. One Nativity grouping had a baby Jesus. She mistook it for a doll and ran to the manger to cradle the baby in her arms and sing lullabies. That's when the pope arrived. He was dressed as if for High Mass, his miter giving him the appearance of a magician. He turned from his entourage and pointed an accusing finger at little Crispin. "Bad girl. Put it back where you found it!"

The pontiff was followed by a long procession of clerics and altar boys swinging incense. As each one passed, they repeated the same admonishment, ordering Crispin to return the baby to its crèche. "Put it back. Put it back. Put it back."

Chapter Twenty

The morning sun arrived in slow stages. First, rays of light filled the halls and rooms, softening the grayness of predawn with gold and warming the chill left by the night air. Crispin and Roberto were dressed before dawn, intent on a private farewell ritual for Lew in the affirmation that comes with the first hours of day. The staff didn't bother them as they scouted the kitchen for coffee and sponge cake, which they took with them into the awakening. The bird's morning arias met them in the garden as the sun yawned upwards, illuminating the variations of tone in banks of blood-red sunflowers on sturdy purple stalks while honeybees dipped their feet in the pollen. A scraggly orange tabby crept like a thief among the sunflowers, stopping still and gazing longingly at the birds high above her head.

Crispin imagined her friend as a youngster, playing along these same pathways. Could you name all the birds? Did you play under that tree? she asked, in a silent conversation with Lew's memory.

Since they were not able to attend Lew's funeral, Crispin and Roberto had agreed to hold a simple remembrance that would encompass Lew's appreciation of the natural world. They spread out their morning coffee at a quiet spot beside a small stream, and for a time each drank, lost in their private thoughts.

"Are you ready?" Roberto asked.

Crispin nodded and gathered a handful of flowers, making her way to the bank of the stream where an eddy of smooth rocks blocked the flow and caused the water to bubble and churn. Roberto offered a prayer that ended with a psalm. "I am poured out like water."

When he'd finished, Crispin dropped the flowers into the flowing water and watched silently as they drifted away, some catching on the rocks and others twirling in a steady movement. She started to return to the house when she realized that Roberto was still by the banks of the stream. He was standing with his back to her, his head bent forward. She gently called his name but he didn't answer. He was standing with his right hand half covering his face. Unwilling to disturb his meditation, she waited. After a respectful silence she said, "Roberto, we need to go."

"She was like a sister to me," he said in a quiet, distant reply. "My adoptive parents were good people, but I was a stranger to them. Sister Llewellyn knew who I was. I don't think I'll find that again. Not on this earth." They stood for a while longer before Roberto turned back to Crispin. "We have to leave the garden sometime if we are to take on the world," he told her with an unconvincing smile.

When they returned to the courtyard they were surprised to find Angelo waiting for them. Relaxed but weary, he reclined in a wooden chaise. His feet were bare and his white linen slacks were rolled up. A short-sleeved blue silk shirt complemented his white hair. Holding up a tall glass of orange juice, he saluted them.

"Come. Take some shade."

Roberto remained standing, leaning against the table with his arms folded, but Crispin settled into a camp chair next to Angelo. They were full of questions about Lew's funeral plans and about Bishop Pirolla.

"He arrived not long after you left my sister-in-law's house. I fear he is hoisted by his own petard," Angelo said. "He just assumed that I am as angry with you as he is, so I did not have to say anything and he was deceived by his own misperceptions."

"We see what we want to see," Roberto said.

"Right you are, Father. Right you are."

Estabin interrupted and handed Angelo a note and then excused himself. After he left, Crispin asked about Madam Sato.

"A close friend has come to stay with her. The women will help her. It was better that I had Estabin fetch me home early. There was no need for the women to have to worry about taking care of me. Besides, I was starting to draw attention."

"I don't understand," Crispin said, giving him a puzzled look.

"Some newspapers are digging into the story about the brutal murder of a young nun, making it a sensation. The police leaked her connection to me. Most unfortunate. I am taking steps, but it was best if I did not remain in Turino."

"If that is the case," Roberto said, "I need to leave for Madrid as soon as possible. The Sudarium. Have you made the calls we discussed?"

"Not so fast, my boy," Angelo replied.

Roberto explained that he'd phoned the station and the trip to the capitol city via Córdoba would take just under three hours on the high-speed train. "Once I am in Madrid it is an easy drive to meet with the monks to discuss the Sudarium."

"I understand," Angelo said. "I have made all arrangements, but there is no point for you to leave until tomorrow so, I fear, you are stuck with me one more day. Please let me show you my Seville."

Angelo told them that he had planned a walking tour of the city followed by a night out on the town. When they protested, he feigned insult and insisted that they accept his hospitality.

He reached under his chair and, with a gesture that carried the suggestion of flirtation with it, handed Crispin a package. It was wrapped in ivory tissue paper and secured with a purple satin ribbon.

"What's this?" Crispin asked.

"Something for you to wear tonight."

Crispin pulled out a white sleeveless silk dress. It had a layered skirt embroidered in patterns that had a distinctly Moorish influence, each layer more progressively sheer than the one before it until the final flounce was transparent.

"The women at a nearby village are famous for their embroidery. I hope it will always remind you of España."

"You are kind to have thought of me," she told him. When she stood up to hug him in appreciation, he embraced her and kissed her cheek. She blushed and sat back down, slightly flustered. "I do not want to appear ungrateful, but what I really need is a computer. I left mine in Rome."

"I'm sure that you will want to dress for the day. Be sure to bring a scarf since we will visit several churches," he said. "While you attend to that, I will make sure our agenda includes a stop for electronics."

"I don't think I have a scarf with me."

"Estabin will make sure you get what you need," Angelo said, with a wave of his hand.

After she'd accomplished her shopping mission, Crispin met Angelo and Roberto at the El Buzo bar on Calle Antonia Diaz for the planned tour of the historic port city, where the blending of two continents was written in the architecture, food, and history.

"Even today the slightly menacing underground activities causes officials to caution female tourists not to travel alone in the city," Angelo told them with a hint of pride.

Some of the choices on the itinerary were a bit ghoulish for Crispin's taste, especially paintings in the local charity hospital, like *Finis Gloriae Mundi* (*The End of the World's Glory*), which depicted a casket with the decaying body of a high priest covered with cockroaches. At the Iglesia de la Magdalena, where they stopped to watch restoration work, Angelo made a point to pause at the medieval fresco at the north transept of the baroque church. He told Crispin that it depicted a medieval auto-da-fé, and then asked Roberto to explain the ceremony.

"Literally translated, it means 'act of faith,'" Roberto said. It was a common ceremony during the Inquisition, which was intended as a way to unify Spain under one monolithic ideology. Although the trials of heretics had the trappings of a judicial process, in reality many of the accused were tortured to obtain confessions.

"Before they died, they confessed their faith. That's the key," said Angelo.

She assumed it was just the oppressive Dark Ages atmosphere of the buildings and the morbid art, but Crispin was more than a little relieved when Angelo signaled the end of the tour. I am interested in death rituals, but these paintings are more about bugs and bones than celebration, she thought.

The footsore trio returned to Angelo's home to find a mid-afternoon meal laid out for them. As they settled into a first course of lima beans with cured ham, crusty bread, and a side dish of spicy olives, Angelo took up the thread of the conversation that was left dangling at the church.

"My dear, with your scientific training, I'd like to hear your perspective on the paintings and tapestries we saw today."

Okay, Big Mouth. Remember who you're talking to. How are you going to thread this needle? Crispin thought as she helped herself to more wine and chose her words carefully. "Creativity and imagination, unlike faith, is constantly replenished by our need to question the universe, to give it form and purpose," she told him. She kept the rest of her thinking to herself. That's why it is so dangerous to marry the power of the church to that of government. Only corruption can result.

Roberto seemed about ready to ask a question when the discussion was interrupted as the kitchen staff, led by Estabin, cleared the first course and replaced it with an elaborate salt-crusted fish, baked whole and served with a garlic mayonnaise and a side salad. Just when they felt they could hold no more, Estabin served luscious custard and plates heaped with cinnamon and almond-flavored cookies.

Because the afternoon had grown hot, Angelo suggested they follow the local custom of a siesta. On their way to rest, Crispin found herself alone with Roberto for the first time since their morning benediction. Roberto was restless, but Crispin reminded him that it would be rude to refuse Angelo's offer after he had helped them escape Turin. "I think he's a bit lonely and melancholy. He likes our company as a diversion since we were Lew's friends."

"I'm sympathetic, but we will help him more if we stop wasting time and continue our search for answers," Roberto said.

"Okay. While he rests, we can work. Do you have the list we made on the plane? I'll meet you in the courtyard," she told him.

Crispin found a shaded area near the stone table where they had dined the night they arrived. She had her cell phone and set up her new computer while waiting for Roberto. When he arrived he brought a pitcher of ice water and two glasses and sat across from her. He read the list out loud as she typed it into a spreadsheet so that they could annotate it as they worked. When she was ready, they chose a question they thought they could make progress on: Were the deaths of Father Mitchel, Sister Sarah, and her brother connected?

"Let's call Detective Moss," she told Roberto.

Although he appeared skeptical, he agreed.

Moss picked up on the first ring. "Hello, Crispin," Moss said, recognizing the phone number.

"I'm checking in like I promised," Crispin answered. "I was just wondering if you've found out any more about how Father Mitchel died."

"It is still an open case."

"I understand, but I've been thinking a lot about Thomas Cross and worrying about what happened in the cemetery. Tell me straight up, Detective. I need to know. Do you think Cross killed him?"

"Where are you?"

"Don't you think I have a right to know? Did you ever locate Cross?"

"No, but that's not what I asked," the detective replied. "Tell me where you are."

"Are you saying that you don't know where to find Cross?"

"I'll need you to come back to the station. We've been notified of a death in Turin and I have some questions for you."

"I'll have to call you back," Crispin said, hanging up.

Crispin had put the phone on speaker, so that Roberto had been able to follow the entire conversation. They sat quietly for a while.

"What do you think?" Crispin finally asked.

"The bishop told her what happened in Turino. That you've gone missing," he said. "For that matter, they likely think I'm missing too since I haven't been seen or reported in to the bishop since I left Madam Sato's house."

"Oh, Roberto. I've made a mess of everything."

"You are not responsible. We just need to figure out what happened."

Crispin took a deep breath. "I think I can help with one of the problems, but it may sound wacky."

"I am listening," he said.

"You know how we couldn't figure out how the original Shroud got back in Turin? What if the fire was part of a plan to switch the Shroud, just as we suspected from the beginning? Except, it wasn't to steal the Shroud. It was to put it back."

Roberto took a long drink of water before responding. "How did you come up with an idea like that?"

Crispin was embarrassed to tell him about her prophetic dream about the pope's entourage entreating her to "Put it back," but she needed him to understand. He listened carefully to her explanation, stopping her once or twice to ask clarifying questions.

"It's not the first time I've had a dream like that when I was stumped on a problem and it gave me an idea that led to a solution," she said.

"So your dreams are a way of tapping into your subconscious and displaying your thought patterns in an imaginative way." He poured her a glass of water before continuing. "Do you know the work of Kilton Stewart?"

"Yes, the anthropologist."

"I've read where he said dreams are unopened letters from God."

"It's a bit presumptuous for a Yankee Protestant to think God takes time to write personal dream scripts for me," Crispin said with a smile. "Does it matter?"

"No, I don't think it does. We've assumed from the beginning that the fire was arson. If your idea is right it could explain a lot. It would tell us that this fire was to cover the theft of the Shroud."

"Except the crime, if you can call it that, was to return the Shroud, which was actually stolen at some other time," Crispin added.

"Which means the actual crime was sometime in the past."

"But when? And by whom?"

"Maybe that's the connection Sister Llewellyn tried to make with the Sudarium," Roberto added. "Regardless, at least you've offered an interesting theory. Truthfully, I'm at a loss to come up with a better one. The only question is . . ."

"Who took it? What happened to the Shroud while they had it? What purpose did it serve?"

They were stumped. Every answer led to another question. They decided the best course would be to try to find out when and under what circumstances the Shroud was first taken. That information might help explain the enigma.

Once again Crispin needed to call her dad's office. This time she reached his secretary. Carole said Dr. Leads was out of the office and hadn't told her where he was going.

"You know your dad. He's not the type to explain his absences."

Crispin was grateful that she didn't have to explain what she needed to know to her dad. He would just ask questions and poke holes in her emerging theory. Carole was less inquisitive and more accommodating. When Crispin told her what she needed, Carole promised to pull information from the files about the scientists who participated in various Shroud research projects with Dr. Leads over the years. Since Crispin's dad was still in contact with many of them, Carole's help would save time. Carole promised that as soon as she had the information, she would email it.

Once they had converted the rest of their notes to the spreadsheet and brainstormed additional ideas, they agreed to take a break. After Roberto left, Crispin tried phoning her dad but could reach no one. Disappointed, she returned to her room. She put her new dress on the chair by the window and drew the curtains to block out the intense sunlight and heat. She stripped down to her bra and panties and indulged in a soothing sponge bath before stretching out on the cool sheets.

* * *

Roberto's soft knock woke Crispin from her nap.

"Are you ready?" he asked through the door.

Crispin stretched, feeling invigorated. "I just woke up. Give me twenty minutes and I'll meet you downstairs."

She was conscious of Angelo's appreciative appraisal when she arrived. She had to admit that she was feeling especially feminine. She'd braided her hair into a coronet so that her shoulders were bare. The silk dress felt cool on her skin, although she was a little self-conscious because she knew that the shape of her legs and hips were outlined through the sheer skirt. She couldn't help but wonder what Aunt Tilde would say. "Surely you're not going out in public without pantyhose or a slip?" She mentally reassured herself: Aunt Tilde is in Connecticut and I'm in Spain, so her out-of-date fashion advice doesn't count.

Angelo took them to a back alley club in the heart of the oldest section of Seville. At the center of the steamy room was the polished wooden floor where a man and a woman, dressed for Flamenco, began to dance to sultry guitar music.

"Now you can experience what makes Spain erotic—our dance," he said.

The female dancer oozed around her partner, luring him with her hips and her castanets.

"Rossini, I hope this does not offend you," Angelo said.

Roberto said nothing. His impassive face revealed no hint of what he was thinking or feeling.

Crispin leaned close to Angelo's ear, making him laugh by saying that the dance reminded her of Salome as she begged for the head of John the Baptist. She hadn't intended to move so close, but it was the only way she could make herself understood over the music. The exchange was more intimate and suggestive than she'd intended.

Roberto focused his full attention on the dancers just as the guitar rhythm picked up. The metal taps on the dancer's shoes kept rhythm with the tempo. They controlled their bodies in slow, fluid movements, circling each other in excruciatingly lustful anticipation.

"God, she's about to have sex with him right in front of us," Crispin told Angelo, then blushed when she saw how her comment affected Roberto.

"I need air," he said as he stood. With a quick bow he made an excuse and left, telling them he was going to return to the villa.

Angelo acted delighted to be alone with Crispin, filling her glass with the Crianza.

"Our *vino tinto* is heavy to the mouth, yes?" he whispered. "You like the cherry and the raspberry?"

Maybe it was because Crispin was annoyed that Roberto had left so quickly, but she found herself accepting the attentions of the sophisticated Angelo. What started as innocent flirtation with a mature gentleman became increasingly intimate: a lingering brush of the cheek, a hand resting on a shoulder, a shared glass of wine. Crispin reminded herself that Roberto might be off limits, but not Angelo.

The ancient ritual of a man and a woman each testing the strength of their attraction in the first moments of seduction suddenly came to an end when a delicate chain around Angelo's neck caught Crispin's eye. Suspended on the chain was a gold Sato family crest. She recalled seeing one just like it in a drawer in Lew's bedroom. The memory was like an ice-cold washrag on a hot cheek. It brought her back to reality.

Crispin pulled away, asking Angelo to please take her home. He objected, but she insisted.

"Then we'll go by foot for a while. You will like the Triana District at night. It is alive with music and color."

"Okay. I need the exercise and, frankly, will welcome the night air after the heat of this place," she told Angelo, all the while admitting to herself that the heat she was feeling was not all from the wine.

The evening air was colder than Crispin expected, and it sent a chill through her. Angelo took off his jacket and wrapped it around her shoulders. "My dear, please let me call the car."

"Later. For now, I need the fresh air."

They had gone a few blocks when Crispin thanked him for the tour of Seville.

"It's my first time in your city."

"I feel our local art was not to your taste."

"It's not that. It was the recurring theme of religious fanaticism and persecution. History repeats itself, doesn't it? Ayatollah Khomeini. Khmer Rouge. Spanish Inquisition. Zealots justify any corruption, any act of terrorism, to achieve their end. Even the Nazis had 'Gott mit uns,' 'God With Us,' emblazoned on their buckles."

"Surely you do not equate these movements," Angelo said in a sharp response. It was too dark to see his face, but his tone told Crispin that she had crossed a line again.

"I apologize. I meant no disrespect. It is late and I've had too much to drink. Please forgive me for speaking out of turn."

"Of course, my dear," he replied in the mellow tones she had come to expect from Uncle Angelo.

A man jumped in front of them and snapped a picture. Angelo wrapped his arm around Crispin's waist protectively, raised his cane, and swatted at the man.

"Get out of here! Paparazzi. Get out of here, you devil!"

The man took several more pictures before turning and running away.

Angelo's limousine, which had apparently been following them, materialized from a side street. Estabin jumped out and rushed them into the safety of the back seat.

By the time they arrived at the villa, Angelo had regained his composure. He insisted on escorting Crispin to her suite. When they arrived, he kissed her on the forehead and bid her goodnight.

"Rest in peace."

Chapter Twenty-One

Crispin woke with a start, disoriented. Was she in her hotel in Rome? Bedroom in New York? The convent in Turin? She clinched her fists and lay still, getting her bearings and watching as the moonlight cast shadows along the back wall, forming intricate geometric patterns and shapes. The shadow, shaped like an outline of South America, began to shift. It was no longer plastered on the wall. It was moving. Moving toward her.

She screamed and tossed her bed sheet where she calculated the shadow's head might be. Crispin jumped out on the opposite side of the bed and sprinted for the door, flying out into the dark hall, where she ran into Roberto.

"I heard you scream. What is it?" he asked, grabbing her arms.

"Someone's in there," she said, pointing to her bedroom.

When they reentered her room and turned on the light, it was empty. Crispin's bed sheet was in a pile on the floor, and the window to the balcony was wide open. Roberto stepped outside and peered down into the dark courtyard.

"I don't see anything," he said.

Crispin gathered up the sheet from the floor and wrapped herself in it.

"I don't blame you if you don't believe me," she said. "Hellfire, I'm not even sure I believe it myself. It may have been a nightmare."

She sat down on the edge of the bed and ran her fingers through her hair. "I shouldn't let it get to me."

"Would you like me to sit here until you go back to sleep?" Roberto asked.

"Do you mind?"

"Not at all," he replied, settling into one of the room's throne-like chairs that resembled a holdover from the thirteenth century.

Crispin crawled under the covers and asked him, "How do you do it?"

"Do what?"

"Stay so calm," she answered. "After that scene in the cabaret tonight, I'd think you would be angry with me."

"You need to rest. We have an early start in the morning."

Crispin punched her pillow a few times and turned her back on Roberto, pulling the covers up close to her neck.

Hours later Crispin woke to the sight of Roberto, who was still in the chair where he'd kept vigil through the night. He looked cramped and uncomfortable, his damaged left hand cradled in his good one. Even though his eyes were swollen from the exhaustion of the past few days, he was breathing softly. She lay there watching him sleep.

My very own knight-errant protecting a damsel in distress, she thought.

Roberto's eyes slid open and briefly held her gaze. The intimate moment was gone, however, as he pulled himself up for a long stretch.

"Are you okay?" he asked.

"Slept like a baby. Acted like one too, I guess."

"Don't say that. I'll meet you downstairs and we'll leave for Madrid."

"Yes, sir," she replied with a mock salute.

Breakfast of fruit, cereal, and yogurt was self-service, laid out on a sideboard in the kitchen. Just as Crispin poured a cup of strong coffee, Estabin came in and informed them that Angelo could not join them because he was incapacitated with a headache.

"I can sympathize," she said. "Wine has a way of sneaking up on you, especially in this heat."

"Yes, miss," was all he said, giving her a modest bow at the waist before taking his leave.

* * *

Roberto needed street clothes for the trip to Madrid. While he shopped, Crispin agreed to buy their train tickets. They planned to meet on the platform at Estación de Santa Justa before the train left. After she purchased the tickets, Crispin passed time in shops near the station. In one that specialized in the tourist trade, she was attracted to a rack of embroidered tablecloths that made her think of the dress Angelo had given her. The needle-work on the table linens appeared to be machine crafted instead of hand-stitched and was not nearly so fine as on the sundress she'd left behind. When she'd packed that morning, she'd folded the dress neatly and left it on the bed. The Crispin Leads who'd gone to a club the previous night dressed in revealing clothes and let down her guard long enough to flirt with Angelo would not be traveling with her to Madrid.

She was jolted from her thoughts when she caught a glimpse of a familiar figure. "No way," she murmured. Thomas Cross had dodged, a little too slowly, behind a corner across the street. Crispin tried to convince herself that she was seeing things again, as she exited onto the street where she walked, as calmly as she could, before ducking into a pharmacy. Inside, she positioned herself at a floor spinner of postcards so that she could see the street reflected in the mirror behind the counter. Sure enough, after a few minutes, her stalker emerged from an alley. There was no mistaking him. It was Cross, and he was following her. Crispin did not see Roberto approach from the other side of the street.

"How did you find, me?" he asked, causing her to jump with such a start that she bumped against the wire rack of postcards and several fell on the floor. He grabbed the rack to steady it. "Careful, there," he said with a slight grin.

She whispered a quick explanation to him and surreptitiously pointed to the slim Roman mugger. A short, fleshy man in a wrinkled suit whose garish gold necklace reflected against his black shirt had joined Cross. Just then, the fat man pointed out Roberto to his companion.

"Let's go. Now!" Roberto said, opening the door to the pharmacy and pointing the way toward the train station.

As they turned the corner they found themselves surrounded by a crowd of schoolchildren coming from the opposite direction. The teacher acknowledged Roberto, who was still wearing his clerical collar. He smiled and nodded but did not slow down. After the children passed, he grabbed Crispin's arm and they raced toward the train station. They crossed the street, doubled back, and found an alley where they could hide out of sight across from the train's platform.

While they waited, Roberto whispered to Crispin. "The big man, the one with the necklace," he said. "I saw him at the clothing store. He's working with Cross."

Just before the train started to pull away, they made a dash from their hiding place and boarded.

* * *

In Madrid Roberto and Crispin had hoped to disappear into the crowds of morning commuters after exiting the train at Estación de Atocha. He was the first to spot the newspaper with front-page photos of the two them under a three-column headline: "Nun Killers on the Run." The photo of Roberto wasn't too bad, but the one of Crispin, lifted from her passport, resembled a vacant-eyed criminal instead of a university scholar.

He had changed into street clothes on the train trip, and Crispin had pulled her hair into a tight bun. Their feeling of anonymity, however, was short-lived once they saw the newspaper.

Roberto bought a copy of the tabloid and hustled Crispin to a bench in a quiet part of the terminal.

"What does it say?" Crispin asked.

"We're wanted by the authorities for questioning in connection with the murder of Sister Llewellyn."

The news accounts were full of gruesome details about Lew's tortured death.

"Why did they put all of that in the newspaper?" Crispin said, tears moistening her eyes.

"That makes it sensational. That's why it is on page one," Roberto said, holding the paper up so it hid their faces. "I'm sorry, Crispin, but we can't afford to draw attention. The article says we are traveling together. It would be best if we separate and get back together later to figure out what to do next."

They agreed to meet at an out-of-the-way hotel that was a few blocks from the train station. Roberto took their small suitcases with him and said he would make arrangement for rooms.

Crispin felt vulnerable and exposed the minute Roberto disappeared into the crowd. She slid into the sea of businesspeople, heading away from him in the opposite direction and onto the street. The arched-glass and steel-framed station opened onto the handsome corridor that connected the Prado museums and the Retiro, the great central park of Madrid.

If Madrid were anything like New York City, Crispin figured that the crush of rush hour commuters would last about twenty more minutes. She decided it would be best to simply follow the tide of humanity, staying close on the heels of the determined pedestrians around her. It was another of Aunt Tilde's life lessons from their shopping sprees in Manhattan: You can hide in the crowd. The more people are jammed together, the less they take notice of each other. That's why her aunt preferred services at churches with large congregations. She liked the privacy.

Snapping out of her memories, Crispin shifted her internal warning system to broadband. Her aunt had also taught her the trick of walking on city streets as if she had eyes in the back of her head by keeping one eye on the images reflected in the storefront windows. When she saw the reflection of a police car, she slipped into a cigar stall and bought a pair of sunglasses. She was only back on the street for a few seconds when she saw Cross.

Fighting back panic, Crispin spotted a line of tourists waiting for admittance through glass tube elevators mounted on the outside of a nearby building. She didn't hesitate. She pushed past the people in line and vaulted up the stairs. The top opened into a lobby where banners trumpeted Picasso's masterpiece, *Guernica*.

Crispin grabbed a brochure for the Museo Nacional Centro de Arte Reina Sofía from a nearby rack and stepped into the middle of a docent-led tour that ended in front of a canvas of distorted and emaciated figures cringed in angular anguish under an onslaught of fire and destruction. At another time, or under different circumstances, Crispin would have been moved to long reflection by the unbridled passion of the painting. Instead, she indulged in a momentary kinship with the ghost-like figures who were, like her, caught up in violence they could neither stop nor understand.

She wasn't there to enjoy the art. The museum was just a way to lose her tail. As she exited, she pitched the brochure in a recycle bin and turned up a narrow side street. She couldn't see Cross anywhere. For a moment she dared to hope that her dodge had worked. When she glanced up and down the street to get her bearings, he stepped out of a doorway and grabbed her from behind. She could feel the point of a knife digging into her shoulder blades.

He wouldn't be fooled a second time by amateur karate. He kept her in a close grip and forced her into an abandoned building.

"I'm going to enjoy this," he said, as they treaded their way over the refuse in the building toward the stairs. He straddled a large crate as he used one hand to grab Crispin's wrist and push her to the stairs.

"Let go of me!" Crispin screamed, trying to kick.

He hauled Crispin up three flights of stairs to a narrow hallway that offered him privacy. Instead of slashing her throat, however, he roughly dragged her into a corner, where he kept her pinned down with a heavy, booted foot. He then dumped the contents of her purse and Sister Lew's canvas bag onto the floor and ransacked her belongings.

Cross turned to Crispin, pushing his hands into her pockets, touching far more than the contents. When he felt around under her shirt, bile flooded into Crispin's throat. When he'd finished his search, he grabbed a hunk of her hair, holding it close to his nose. "I like the way you smell. A woman smell." He thrust his tongue into her ear and his saliva seeped down her neck, causing her to gag. Sensing what was coming, Cross slightly loosened his grip. She bolted to a rickety balcony, where she leaned over the railing and threw up. He laughed and grabbed her neck again.

"Not without a fight, you shit," she yelled, or thought she did.

Crispin gripped the railing with both hands while Cross pulled her like a rag doll from side to side, trying to loosen her hold. Below her, a police car cruised up the narrow street and slowed. When the attacker saw it, he let go of her and disappeared down the stairs, taking two at a time. Crispin was left gagging over the balcony, unable to control the renewed turmoil of her stomach.

The police officer got out of his car and called up to her, offering help. In the best Spanish she could muster, she told him it had been no more than a lover's spat. Pointing to her stomach, she told him that she'd had too much to drink last night. The officer laughed, indicating that he understood, and drove away.

* * *

Roberto was waiting outside of the Hotel el Prado.

"Our friend from Seville is here," she told him.

"Quickly," he said, escorting her through the front door.

The hotel had almost no lobby, and the elevator was more like a dumbwaiter than a proper lift. It did the job, however, taking them safely up four flights to a Spartan room with twin beds and clean sheets. Crispin went immediately to the small bathroom and ran a sink full of hot water, scrubbing her face several times. When she returned to the bedroom she was holding a small cloth, drying her face, rubbing her cheek repeatedly.

Crispin gave Roberto a quick report on her confrontation.

"Are you okay?"

"Yes and no. Physically, I am okay. Bruised, but otherwise okay."

"But?"

"I need time to think," she told him. "I'd like to take a bath and clean up. May I have the room to myself?"

"Of course," he said, gathering his coat and hat. Without a word, he left, closing the door behind him.

She locked the door, secured the deadbolt, and wedged a chair under the doorknob. She undressed slowly until she stood naked in front of the dresser mirror. She was right about the bruises. There were large yellow patches on her hips and knees. They would soon turn purple. There was a small cut and another bruise forming behind her ear, but it would be easy to hide. What would be harder to hide would be the memory of Cross' breath, which smelled like an open tin of sardines, and the penetration of his tongue in her ear.

All at once, she needed to feel clean and ran for the shower. Crispin used two of the tiny hotel shampoo bottles to wash her hair and body. She stood under the hot steam until her shoulders, back, and buttocks turned pink. When she finished, she dug through her toiletries for an unopened package of razor blades.

She pulled an extra chair up to the sink and draped it with a towel. She sat, naked, staring into the mirror, the razor blades fanned out before her. The person who looked back at her wasn't the grad student who had left New York on an exciting adventure just a few days earlier. It was a frightened little girl who wanted her mother to tell her what to do. She wanted her dad to tell her she was special. She wanted to feel safe and loved.

"But, I'm not her anymore either, am I?" she finally told herself, her voice near a whisper. "Now, I am Crispin the Spy. I am Crispin the Seducer. I am Crispin the Fugitive. I am Crispin the Street Fighter. I am Crispin the Sleuth."

With each pronouncement of a persona, her voice grew louder and more theatrical, and soon she was giggling to the point of near hysteria, until her laughs turned to bitter tears and she began to cry uncontrollably. The tears washed into hidden places to loosen what was left of her pain, not just of Lew's death but also of deaths that came before. She thought it had all spilled out on the pillow in the convent, but there was still a residue of sadness that came flooding out, triggered by the realization that she had to follow this story to its end. Lew had died in the pursuit of some strange and complex mystery. Crispin would never know why unless she stayed on the path she was on. No matter how dangerous, it had to be followed, no matter where it led her.

Years of fear and shame were written into each slender white scar on her wrists. She reached for one of the razor blades on the counter. Gripping it tightly she began to cut her hair.

I am Crispin the Avenger, she told herself.

* * *

By the time Roberto knocked on the door, Crispin was dressed. She wore slim-fit black slacks and a royal blue jersey top that fit loosely across her shoulders. She was working at her computer at the small desk in the corner of the room. She checked the peephole before opening the door to let him in.

He stared at her hair, now cut in an ear-length bob, for a few seconds before crossing the threshold. Inside, he unloaded several plastic shopping bags.

"I think we had similar ideas," he said, reaching into one bag for a package of hair dye. "I thought you might want to consider a change in color, but I like your solution better."

He'd also brought supper: wine, soft white cheese made of sheep's milk, crusty bread, and bite-size yemas—sugary cakes that resemble egg yolks. The simple food was as welcome as a feast. While they ate, they talked about Crispin's latest escape from the Rome mugger.

"This was no ordinary assault. He was after something specific," she said.

"What?"

They tore apart everything they had with them. Crispin even felt along all the seams of Sister Lew's habit. They examined her passport and emptied her canvas bag. They found nothing.

"The only thing of value is the videotape," Crispin said in frustration.

"Trust me. It is safe," Roberto assured her.

"Besides, that can't be what he's after. He searched me, feeling in my clothes," she said with a slight shiver. "I could never hide a videotape in my pockets. Whatever he was after, it can't be very big."

Roberto didn't respond. Instead he passed Crispin a piece of bread slathered with cheese.

"The Internet connection here is so sluggish that I've made almost no progress," she said, pointing at her open computer on the desk. "I'm not cut out for all this international intrigue. All I'm good at is plain, old-fashioned research, the kind that is methodical, careful, planned."

"Then we shall make use of that," he said. "First, however, I think I need to take additional precautions. Since my photo is of a clean-shaven priest, I will no longer shave, and I bought a few well-used items from a fellow on the street," he added, showing her a Led Zeppelin T-shirt and a pair of grubby jeans.

"This should finish the makeover," he said with a smile, reaching into a bag and pulling out a soiled Greek fisherman's cap, putting it on his head.

Crispin almost laughed at the transformation the silly hat made to Roberto's appearance. The oversized cap was large enough to cover his hair and shade his face, but also had the unfortunate effect of causing his ears to sandwich outward, giving him a slightly goofy, down-on-your-luck look.

Chapter Twenty-Two

Crispin traveled separately to the public computer clusters at the Biblioteca Nacional, Madrid's central library. When she plugged in her laptop and logged on to check her email, she found that Carole had forwarded a wealth of biographical and contact information for the scientists involved in Shroud research projects with her dad. Many were long-forgotten people from another lifetime:

Steven Edinburgh, the guy with Coke-bottle glasses.

Joanna Carland, the tiny woman from Detroit.

Wayne Daughtry. Norma Morales. Conrad Watts.

Then Jefferson (Jack) Kinsey popped up. It had been years since she'd thought about the family friend from Turin. Her dad and Jack were opposites in temperament as well as style. Her dad was spit and polish to the point of finicky. The housekeeper who ironed his shirts used cooked starch so the collars turned crisp and rigid, the way he preferred. Jack's clothes, on the other hand, resembled an unmade bed.

The Kinseys often invited Crispin's family to Sunday dinner. Jack and his wife, Beth, doted on their black Labrador, Chance. During the cocktail hour, Crispin and Clinton drank ginger ale in stemware and Chance carried a small wicker basket in his mouth to beg for canapés. Trouble was, Jack would forget the command to signal Chance when to stop. Round and round the dog would go until one of them would stop laughing long enough to remind Jack of the command.

When Crispin typed Jack's name into the search engine, it turned up a long list of his published papers, a number of which focused on Shroud research. A recent *National Geographic* article said Kinsey was affiliated with the Satabo Foundation in Paris.

Roberto joined her before she could find out more about Satabo. "Uncover anything?" he asked, easing into the chair next to hers.

"Maybe," she answered.

The two spent the next hour reading the material sent by Carole as well as supplementary information Crispin had pulled from the Internet. There were only a few threads of commonality.

"Here's something interesting," Crispin said, tilting the computer screen toward Roberto.

The articles indicated that Dr. Leads was one such thread. He had strategic positions on several research teams when they made major discoveries.

"Until this moment I don't think I ever appreciated how pivotal his role was," she told Roberto.

"It's been years since he was directly involved in Shroud research."

"I know, but Lew told me they'd remained in contact," Crispin said. "I guess I can't blame Pirolla for being suspicious of me."

They mapped out several other threads, but the one that repeated consistently was the millions of dollars the Satabo Foundation funneled to support Shroud research projects. The Foundation's home page consisted primarily of a generic corporate mission statement and other dry information that did little to illuminate. One link supplied the names of the board of directors.

Crispin almost closed the site when she spotted another connection. Buried in an obscure news release that she almost overlooked was an announcement that the Satabo Foundation would play host to a gala at the San Giovanni Cathedral. When Crispin opened the link, it not only described the gala on the night of the Turin fire but also indicated that most of the Satabo Foundation Board of Directors would be on the guest list.

"Whatever happened that night, the Satabo Foundation was in the middle of it," Crispin said.

"In the middle of what exactly?"

Crispin broadened her search parameters and got thousands of hits for news and scholarly journal articles that mentioned the Foundation. Many referenced obscure biological and medical journals. Some also mentioned that the Foundation was responsible for research involving the Sudarium of Oviedo.

"Whew," Crispin said, as she scrolled through the search results. "It will take hours to make sense out of this mountain, and it may not mean anything."

Roberto suggested they take a break in the library's basement coffee shop. There they ordered espresso and settled in at a corner table.

"Before I left the hotel I talked to Angelo," Roberto told Crispin. "We may have a bit of luck for a change. The Sudarium has been moved temporarily to Toledo."

"There are so many connections between the Shroud and the Sudarium," Crispin said. "The key is in the bloodstains, which match up if, indeed, the Shroud covered a body and the Sudarium a face. It's important to those who believe in the relics since the Sudarium's history can be traced, unbroken and unquestioned, much further back in time."

"I do not know exactly what Sister Llewellyn was on to, but Angelo has arranged for me to meet the monks from Ovideo who travel with the relic."

"Did he say why they moved it?"

"Jubilee preparations, again."

"Don't worry about me. I'll get as much done as I can here, and when the library closes I'll go back to the hotel and lock the door."

"I'll leave immediately and return in the morning," Roberto said, leaning ever so slightly toward her as if he were about to give her a farewell hug, but he straightened up in an awkward correction of his posture. He collected his fisherman's hat and left her sitting at the table without a backward glance.

Crispin finished her espresso and went back upstairs, where she began to call up the articles in the Foundation web search, one by one. It was tough going since the jargon of each field was specialized. Most of what she saw was outside her area of expertise. It was mind-numbing work, but her years of graduate study had honed her tolerance for tedium. Crispin's attention was diverted by a soft "bing," indicating an incoming email from Carole.

"Your father checked in just now. He's traveling abroad. He didn't give a reason for his trip," Carole wrote.

"Great. Here I am in trouble with the law and he decides to take a vacation without telling anyone where he is. I'll just bet he's with That Woman," Crispin grumbled to herself. "Two can play at that game."

She dashed back a response to Carole, thanking her for the information and telling her that if her father touched base again to let him know that she would be out of reach for several days, but could be contacted via email.

Then, it was back to plowing through the articles about the Foundation. As Crispin flipped through her notes, she noticed one reference to a scientist in Spain who had identified the blood type on the Shroud as A-B positive. In the article, the scientist particularly thanked the Satabo Foundation for financial support in her research. The acknowledgement also mentioned the Foundation's interest in blood research. Going back through her notes Crispin saw that the Foundation had invested heavily in cutting-edge protocols dealing with stem cell research and cloning.

What an anomalous combination of interests: ancient religious icons and sci-fi biotechnology, Crispin thought.

It was time to bone up on cloning. The concept was much older than she realized. Although the term *clone* was first coined in 1903, the idea of creating a genetically identical offspring dated to ancient horticultural practices when snipping portions of plants was the preferred method of propagation. The idea of applying the technique to animals, or even humans, caught the imagination of filmmakers and novelists, who conjured up outlandish plots based on human cloning. Such stories were relegated to pop fiction since scientists generally thought, even as late as the 1960s, that it would be impossible to clone a mammal as complex as a human.

When they did begin working with lower animals, scientists reported mixed results on experiments with frogs and mice. With each failure they perfected the technique of extracting DNA material from one source, implanting it in an ovum, and creating offspring. One of the most publicized efforts came in the 1990s when Scottish scientists successfully cloned the sheep "Dolly."

All at once, debates about human cloning that had previously been confined to bioethics conferences made their way onto the public agenda across the globe. The United States moved to outlaw human cloning, but was unable to stop plans by fertility specialists in Italy, Japan, and elsewhere from continuing their work. The process is in some ways maddeningly simple. All you need to clone is a few drops of DNA, like the kind you can get from body fluids or tissue.

The barest whisper of an idea began to push its way up from Crispin's deep subconscious and form in her now alert mind: the blood on the Shroud. "Surely not," she said out loud.

* * *

Two Brothers of Oviedo greeted Roberto as he stepped off the train.

"Father Rossini," the taller monk said. "Will you come with us?"

Roberto was shown to a waiting car.

"Your need for discretion was explained," his escort said, offering Roberto the middle back seat. The monks wedged into window seats on each side of him.

"I am Brother Cameron," the tall one said, offering no introduction of the driver or his other companion.

They rode in silence during the brief drive to the historic center of Toledo, where they parked the car in an alley off Calle de San Roman. Their destination was a short distance down the alley to an unmarked doorway entrance. Roberto's escort unlocked the door and Roberto followed him inside and down a narrow hallway. They stopped at an open door.

"We assumed you would want to change before we begin," Brother Cameron suggested. Without waiting for an answer he left, closing the door behind him.

Inside was a washbasin, a shaving kit, and full vestments of Roberto's order. He didn't try the door after Cameron left. Something told him it would be locked. He turned on the faucet until the water steamed in the bowl. A hot towel softened the stubble on his face, and with the help of a bar of soap he was able to get a close shave. He stripped down to his underwear and changed into the clothes that had been left for him. He used a wet comb to calm his unruly hair. All that was left was to button his collar and shirt. He was nearly finished when the door opened and Brother Cameron returned.

"Do you require assistance?' Cameron said, in a tone of condescension.

"I can manage," Roberto said, completing the once routine task, made awkward because it had to be accomplished with one hand instead of two.

"Then, come with me," Cameron said, turning on his heel.

Roberto followed Cameron through a puzzling web of corridors until they came to one that emptied into a small chapel, where he was asked to wait. A shaft of light pierced through a high, stained glass window, illuminating the room and finally coming to rest on the altar.

There could be no mistake. The onion dome canopy over an alcove in the far corner. The lapis inlay. This was the chapel in the videotape. He walked over to the end of the railing, where the light was brightest. In front was a brass plate that read: "Restoration of this chapel was made possible by the generous gifts and continuing support of the Satabo Foundation and its benefactor, A. Sato."

Before he could fully appreciate the significance of the inscription, Roberto lost consciousness from a crushing blow to the back of his head.

* * *

The implications of the idea that was now screaming like a car alarm in Crispin's mind were preposterous. Yeah, right. Get a grip, she chastised herself.

Yet, she argued back, as crazy as the idea was, it did at least offer a line of reasoning and a motive for someone to first steal the Shroud and then return it. She turned back to the computer and typed in keywords to see if her ideas were already out there. To no surprise, the idea wasn't original. What she found were some paperback thrillers, Christian monographs, and a website that had all the earmarkings of an Internet hoax.

"Great, now I'm keeping company with goofballs who have Cheetos fingers and aluminum foil beanies. Dad would be so proud," she mumbled.

Just then her pen ran out of ink and she realized that students at another table were giggling and pointing at her. She'd become so wrapped up in her revelations that she'd been talking out loud to herself as she jotted down notes.

She fished around in the canvas bag for a replacement pen, then felt it slide into the crease at the bottom, where heavy cardboard supported the bag. Crispin ran her fingers along and under the canvas that surrounded the cardboard. She kept digging until she could feel her pen inside a slight rip in the canvas seam along the edge. As she tried to push it out from where it had wedged, she felt something flat and plastic. Crispin fished around with her finger but it only lodged deeper into the seam. Finally she turned the canvas bag inside out and used a pen to free it. It was a compact flashcard FC-8M used to store digital images. It was little wonder that they'd missed it when they searched the bag in the hotel; it wasn't much bigger than a postage stamp.

"Hot damn," she practically yelled, grabbing up her computer, notes, and the bag while trying to ignore the looks she received from those around her as she made her way to the front desk. The library clerks directed her to a peripheral device that she could use to read the flashcard. When she inserted it into the external drive of the computer, icons popped onto the desktop. Some were JPG files of photos. Others appeared to be copies of microfilm images.

Crispin opened each in turn. The first one was an image of a chronological list of events involving the Shroud. The second was a key code. It made no sense until Crispin remembered the odd symbols Sister Lew had made by the names on the guest list for the gala on the night of the fire. This must be hers. The final images on the disk were copies of documents that had been scanned into the computer. One was a work order from a company called Lievin Silversmiths to repair an ornate silver handle. Bishop Pirolla had approved the work order. But the casket handle was still broken when Crispin saw it at the convent.

"Why hadn't the work been done?"

Another file answered the question. It was an obituary for a Winold Latham. Winold was a silversmith and one of the last descendants of Lievin Latham, the artisan who'd crafted the original silver casket for the Shroud in 1509. Sarah Doyle's brother, Kevin, had commissioned a replacement mold for the handle from Winold. But the silversmith was almost ninety years old when he received the commission and died before completing the work.

There was a series of letters between Doyle and Father Mitchel regarding the delay in repairs to the Shroud casket while Doyle identified another suitable vendor. This explained the anomaly that had puzzled Roberto from the first. It had never made sense that after creating an exact copy of the Shroud that was detailed enough to fool the experts, the thieves would fail to notice the defective handle on the casket. If they'd known about the work order, they would have assumed the repair had been made.

"So Father Mitchel knew about the delay in repairing the handle. Kevin Doyle knew, and it's likely that he mentioned it, at some point, to his sister. But, whoever stole the Shroud and replaced it with a copy didn't know about the delay, so they made a casket that didn't match the authentic one," Crispin mumbled. "Wow, such an innocuous bit of information to result in three murders."

She couldn't afford to waste any more time in the library when the Satabo Foundation, and perhaps the answers she needed, were a train ride away. It took only a sigh to decide what to do next.

* * *

Roberto woke to a strong smell, like spoiled eggs, near his face. Someone was prodding him. "Father Rossini. Wake up."

When he opened his eyes he saw Estabin.

He was sitting on the floor of a basement, propped against the wall. In the distance, he heard a voice droning a mixture of Gregorian chant and monologue. He felt himself drifting away, but Estabin again prodded him. "Wake up. You must wake up."

When Roberto touched the back of his aching head he realized that he was bleeding. He tried to sit up, but he felt faint and slumped back down against the damp, stone wall.

"Where am I?" he asked. "What is that sound?"

A familiar voice emerged from the shadows.

"You are my guest," said Angelo, dressed in what resembled the pope's miter and cassock. Instead of white, however, his costume was purple. The fabric was embroidered by strange symbols. The most distinctive were an inverted gold cross and his family crest. He stood erect in an archway, holding a staff in his right hand and an orb in his left. In a loud, clear voice, he chanted in Latin, "I am God's Instrument on Earth."

He motioned to the monks who'd met Roberto at the train. Like Angelo they were now robed in purple. The hoods of their long robes obscured their faces. Their feet were bare, and long ropes of gold chain hung around their waists. Each had a vicious whip that appeared to be a demon version of a mortification scourge. The ones they carried were at least five feet in length, tailed at the end in seven cords knotted to hold metal rings and hooks.

Estabin stood aside while they grabbed Roberto under his arms and dragged him across the damp floor to a makeshift altar surrounded by what appeared to be medieval coats of arms. They chained him to the altar in a position of prayer. The wall in front of the altar was covered by crossed swords and shields, representing sigils of medieval knights, many of them polished to a high sheen. The monks manacled Roberto's hands in a fashion that caused them to hang away from his body, exposed over the railing. They took up positions on each side of him.

"You must confess," Angelo commanded.

"What am I confessing to?" Roberto replied in a dry rasp.

The words were no sooner out of Roberto's mouth than Brother Cameron's whip came down with full force on Roberto's disabled hand, slicing the skin through to the bone. Roberto screamed in pain.

"Auto-da-fé," Angelo commanded. "Confess your sins."

Before Roberto could say anything, Angelo signaled the second monk and he unfurled the full force of his leather whip on Roberto's good hand, opening deep wounds from his fingers to his wrists. In a measured rhythm the two monks repeated their strokes. First left, then right. Left. Then right. With each lash, Angelo commanded, "Auto-da-fé."

Roberto felt himself about to lose consciousness when the door opened and Estabin signaled Angelo that he was needed. Angelo held up his staff. "Hold. I will return," he told the monks.

Brother Cameron paused in midair and withdrew. Roberto prayed silently for forgiveness.

Forgive me, Father, for I have sinned the sin of envy. I thought I could outwit Angelo, but I am his prisoner.

Forgive me, Father, for I have sinned the sin of wrath. My anger at the bishop clouded my judgment.

Forgive me, Father, for I sinned the sins of sloth and gluttony. I stayed too long in Seville while my investigation languished.

Forgive me, Father, for I have sinned the sin of lust, for I have yearned to break my promise of celibacy.

Forgive me, Father, for I have sinned the sin of pride. I believed you called me on the night of the fire, but it has led me to endanger others.

Forgive me, Father, for all my many sins. Guide me. Show me what I must do.

As he prayed, he felt himself lose consciousness.

* * *

Crispin hailed a cab for the trip back to her hotel, and once safely locked inside the room again, she called Jack Kinsey.

"Crispy? Is that really you?"

"Jack, no one's called me that in years. How's Beth?"

"She's just fine. In the States at the moment. Now, surely you didn't call just to chat."

"No, I didn't. Jack, I need your help. I'm on my way to Paris to complete a grant proposal, but I need your advice about the best way to approach the Satabo Foundation."

While she talked, Crispin moved around the hotel room, packing a bag. She was catching a train early the next morning.

"What's the subject?'

"Guess."

"You've been bit by the Shroud bug too?" he said.

"You could say that."

"Good for you."

Crispin could hear Jack turning papers and smiled to herself at the thought of how messy his desk must be.

"Umm, I'm supposed to fly out of here. Hang on. Umm, the day after tomorrow. Yup, be gone a month."

Crispin thought quickly. "Can we meet tomorrow night?"

Jack laughed. "Of course we can. Where?"

"I'll try to get a room in the hotel where Dad always stays."

"The Regina?"

"Yes. And, by the way, please don't say anything. If Dad finds out about the grant and I don't succeed, he'd be very disappointed."

"Enough said. Mum's the word."

They arranged to meet in the Regina lobby the next evening at six.

Crispin shoved her laptop into the canvas bag and opened the closet. Lew's habit was folded neatly on the shelf. She spread it out on the bed and set up the hotel ironing board. After a steam press, it was ready to wear again.

She dashed out a note for Roberto, which she intended to leave at the front desk. There was no sense sharing her off-the-wall ideas with him until she had solid information. She felt deceitful, going on without him. But, what choice did she have?

That night she dreamed she was inside the Guernica. Although Picasso distorted the figures in his masterpiece to capture intense pain, in Crispin's dream one of the villagers resembled Roberto and another had the distinct features of her dad. Crispin was an airplane circling the unsuspecting crowds, who looked skyward before she dipped low and unleashed hell from her fuselage. The bombs rained down, leveling buildings and turning the air into a roar of explosions and smoke.

* * *

Angelo, now dressed in street clothes, was standing over Roberto. "Well, well, I thought we'd lost you, but I see you are back with us again."

Roberto didn't answer.

"Don't pretend you didn't know your girlfriend was going to run away again."

"Crispin?"

"Yes. That malicious American cunt," Angelo replied and spat on the floor. "She is up to her schoolgirl tricks. She didn't fool me the first time, and I'm ahead of her again. I have lost all patience."

Angelo turned to Estabin. "After you have his confession, finish things. Then join me in Paris."

"Yes, sir," Estabin said, leaving with his boss.

Roberto could see his distorted face, now covered in blood, reflected back at him in each of the seven shining shields on the wall above the altar. The skin on his hands and arms was shredded, and the two monks were poised to complete their task. They raised their whips, and in the reflection Roberto saw Estabin return with a gun and take aim.

"If this one is done, Father, find me another life," Roberto whispered, his voice cracking as the gun went off.

Chapter Twenty-Three

Icy water dripping on her feet from the air-conditioning unit above jerked Crispin back into reality. She'd been staring out the window at the misty green hills of Navarre, the northernmost state of Spain. The summer-ripened land seemed to say, "I am a country to be reckoned with." It was easy to see why Shakespeare described Navarre as "the wonder of the world . . . still and contemplative in living art." It was at once old and young, stable and in turmoil.

Crispin tried to hide her pea green Keds under the hem of Lew's habit and nodded at the grandmother in the seat across the aisle. She's too polite to question the outrageously inappropriate footwear, thought Crispin, pressing her nose against the window for fear that any further eye contact would be interpreted as an invitation to conversation.

A metallic clatter interrupted her concentration. Crispin turned around to see a conductor struggling to open the heavy door between her railway car and the one behind. Then he called out. *"Pasaporto."*

Her blood pulsated in her ears and echoed in tempo with the sound of the train's iron wheels as they rhythmically clattered along the track.

She wanted,
thumpity . . . thumpity . . . thumpity . . . thump
to get,

thumpity . . .thumpity . . . thumpity . . .thump
out of there.

Seven more rows.

Will he notice that I'm not the nun in the passport photo?

Six more rows.

Why didn't I change my shoes before getting on the train? Stupid oversight!

Five rows to go.

Crispin's paranoia was like a fulcrum, heavy and leaded, pulling her to a stillness, immobilizing her against action. She fought back, willing herself to overcome and to act.

Thumpity . . . thumpity . . . thump.

Two more rows.

"Pasaporto?" the conductor asked. *"Pasaporto?"* he asked again, with a bit of annoyance in his voice.

Crispin bowed her head as if in prayer. Steady girl. Remember the nun's habit is a disguise, not a vocation, she reminded herself and handed him Lew's passport.

Mistaking her nervousness for shyness, the conductor gave the passport photo a cursory glance. He then returned it respectfully to Crispin and tipped his hat. As he continued down the aisle he cheerfully said something to her in Latin, but it was drowned out by the laughter of the woman in the seat in front of her. Minutes later Crispin was again startled when she heard a rattle and a voice behind her. "Café?"

This time it was a porter pushing a snack cart toward her. Rubbing her stiff neck, she ordered a pastry and hot coffee with lots of cream and sugar. She inhaled the aroma of strong Spanish coffee, released when she removed the plastic lid from the Styrofoam cup. One whiff would be enough to keep her up as the train rolled into the night.

Out the window the horizon was hidden in blackness, and she saw only her face framed under her borrowed coif. With the cup still at her lips she gently blew the steam from her coffee toward her reflection. The image disappeared as the steam formed a circle of condensation on the glass. As it materialized, a faint rainbow illuminated the vapor ring surrounding it.

Am I still Crispin Leads? she wondered. Is it so easy to shed one's identity? Are the vestments of the Church so powerful that the mere act of wearing them changes who you are? Settling back in her seat, Crispin followed the line of thinking through the puzzle of the people who had touched her life since she landed in Rome. Everyone, she thought, is someone else. We all project one side of ourselves and shroud the others.

Even Ellen. She was Sister Lew to some but a childhood friend to me. But she was a keeper of secrets too. What secrets did she take to the grave?

Angelo, your Old World charm and masculine pride were, at times, irresistible, even sexy. Ellen loved you and you saved us in Turin. But something about your control of every situation is heavy, like a wool blanket that is inviting for a time but might smother you if you stay under it too long.

Crispin struggled to remember something, anything, that would bring balance to her impression of Bishop Pirolla. She had to admit that she disliked Bishop Pirolla from the minute she met him. Her impression of him from the beginning never wavered from that of a mean-spirited bully because he had a lethal combination of arrogance and chauvinism that she would have resented even if he hadn't been in a position to make her life miserable.

Crispin grinned at her reflection. Coming clean felt good, but more important it felt honest. My dear Ellen, is the residue of your goodness and honesty in this costume rubbing off on me? She could hear her dad, lecturing her that it is illogical to form an opinion about someone's character based on nothing more than the quality of a handshake or, in the case of the bishop, an ever-present smirk. Crispin realized that she could never tell her dad to his face, but she felt that logic was not all it's cracked up to be.

You can't explain everything by logic. Sometimes your head has to give in to your heart, she lectured herself silently, using an argument she knew she would never have the courage to make to his face. Then she continued to piece together her line of reasoning. After all, people aren't logical, so why should human reactions to them be any different? Maybe some people are hard to like because we only get to see one side of them. Crispin considered herself an independent, serious scholar. She knew, however, that many of her fellow graduate students dismissed her as a privileged princess or, worse, a lightweight because she enjoyed romantic comedies as much as the theater and was as likely to curl up with a cozy murder mystery as she was to reread one of the classics.

She didn't care so much about what they thought, but it did bother her that her dad accused her of wasting her time and talent when she watched television or read pop novels. He reminded her of one of her communication professors from NYU who had a sign in his office that read: "Theatre is art. Film is life. Television is furniture." When we pigeonhole people in our life to just one role it was another form of stereotyping, she thought. We become blind to their complexity. Crispin wondered if that's what she had done with Pirolla, forming broad conclusions about his character based only on a few volatile meetings.

Maybe if I got to know him, she thought, I'd find out that we both laugh at silly knock-knock jokes or that, like me, he has a secret love of hot dogs with lots of steamed onions and spicy chili.

"I'll never get the chance to find out now," she mumbled.

Her dad's voice mentally interrupted her well-ordered argument. "If that is the case, then is not the converse also likely?"

She wanted to pretend that she didn't understand the question, but she knew exactly what the question meant. If she'd disliked and distrusted Pirolla based on physical attributes, wasn't it possible that her trust of Roberto was also an emotional and, therefore, illogical response?

Roberto is all action and passion and, yet, something is out of reach. The collar doesn't always fit the fireman. The way he looks at me when he thinks I don't see him suggests an interest, but then a cloud passes over his gaze and I can't read him. One minute he is Roberto, helpful and available. The next he is Father Rossini, silent and remote. Who are you? Do you even know yourself, Father Rossini? If you don't know, how am I supposed to know?

My heart tells me to trust you, so I've ignored a lot of things my head has been trying to tell me, she admitted to herself. When Crispin thought back over the past several days, the number of unexplained coincidences connected to the young priest struck her. Was their chance meeting at the steps of the Vatican simply a set-up? Is that why Pirolla conveniently missed that first meeting? It did give Roberto a perfect chance to befriend her.

She had never fully understood his willingness to break the rules and help her with the Macken diaries. In retrospect, it seemed odd behavior for a man of the cloth who vows to be obedient to his superiors. Besides that, Roberto was the only one who knew where she would be when she was attacked the first time in Rome. He was with Ellen the last time she saw the nun alive, and he was the first to search her office.

Roberto had appeared from out of nowhere to rescue her when her ruse was uncovered at the Turin convent. He told her how he found her, but could she trust his explanation? And, it was strangely coincidental that he was right there at her door when the bedroom shadow attacked her in Seville. It was his idea to separate after they arrived in Madrid, which left her alone when she was attacked the second time.

Crispin rubbed her temples and mumbled out loud, "Stop it!"

Grandmother clearly heard her, but Crispin didn't acknowledge the stare. Crispin bent her head and folded her hands in prayer. I'm going around in circles, she silently lectured to herself. I've committed to a course of action. It is too late to turn back. If there is an answer, it is in Paris.

* * *

Roberto woke up to the pain of a nurse tending wounds on his hands.

"Try not to move," she told him as he struggled against the tangle of wires and tubes.

For a fleeting moment he thought he was back in the hospital after the Torino fire and everything in between had been a nightmare. He had trouble focusing, and when he reached toward his sore head he realized that his hands were heavily bandaged.

Hospital wires and tubes draped across him, giving him a sense of being trapped. He was connected to a heart monitor that was feeding a constant electrical pulsing beep to a machine above his head, and he could feel the oxygen support he was receiving through a nasal cannula. The IV leading to his right arm fed through a monitor, blending several bags of medicine at once. His vision was out of focus, and he had a taste of copper in his mouth. When he tried to speak again, his voice came out just above a whisper.

"How did I get here?"

"They admitted you last night," she explained. "And, a good thing too."

The nurse checked Roberto's IV, made a few notes, and left.

"I was summoned from Rome," a voice from the corner of the room added. It was Bishop Pirolla.

The door opened and Estabin came in carrying coffee. "I believe our young priest is going to make it," he told the bishop, offering him a cup.

"Bishop Pirolla. Estabin. What happened?" Before they could answer, Roberto drifted back to sleep.

* * *

J. D. Moss approached from behind and touched Crispin's shoulder. "Sister Crispin, I beg you for a moment of your time."

Crispin had just stepped onto the train station platform at Gare d'Austerlitz in Paris and was so skittish that she almost decked the British detective she'd first met in the Vatican. The two settled in at Café de Giselle, a nearby sidewalk café, and ordered. Strong black coffee for Moss; bottled fizzy water for Crispin.

After the waiter left, Moss presented Crispin with an entirely different business card from the one she had used in Rome. This one read: "J. D. Moss, Director, Special Operations, International Institute for Protection Against Scientific Espionage."

"I see you have an alternate persona as well. Why am I not surprised?" Crispin said. "Is this some kind of government agency brought in to help the police in Rome?"

"We don't think of ourselves as government per se. We draw from the private sector, but have access to every criminal investigative organization in the world."

After a few sips of coffee, Moss asked perfunctory permission to smoke. "May I?"

Without waiting for a response, she lit a small, dark European cigarette that smelled like a sweet cigar. "You left Rome with Father Rossini. Where is he now?"

Crispin ignored the question and sat in silence, sipping the water. Moss smoked and waited. The face-off lasted for what to Crispin felt like an eternity, then she finally asked, "What does 'J. D.' stand for?"

The detective was temporarily amused, but the smile melted quickly from her face. "Nice try, but we don't have time for casual conversation."

Crispin fingered her water bottle and took a long drink.

"Remember, you are the one who called me," Moss added, putting out her cigarette with force.

* * *

The man in the gray suit stayed a respectful distance while Crispin made her way along the Seine in the general direction of the Hotel Regina. It was not far from the Louvre. Tour buses lined the street. As she passed one, an American group was disembarking. A large man in his sixties was holding up the group. His tour director seemed ready to dispatch the man into the river. "No, they don't take American currency in the Louvre, Mr. Anderson."

"Why the hell not? They make their money on tourism."

Just then the American bigmouth noticed Crispin. "Excuse my language, Sister," he said, turning back for an answer from the tour guide.

The nun's habit that had been so useful as she traveled from Spain now only made her conspicuous. Crispin thought about ducking into a restroom and losing the habit so she could blend in with some of the college students she saw.

As she turned away, Crispin mentally lectured the tourist. "You're in Paris, Mr. Anderson, and you're treating it like a theme park full of places to check off a to-do list: Eiffel Tower. Check. Arc de Triomphe. Check. Sacre-Coeur. Check. Champs-Elysees. Check. Been there, done that. You and your friends will leave disappointed from too much sitting and not enough just getting around, getting lost, and figuring out. You may as well go to Las Vegas, Mr. Anderson. Don't you know that you can't find the real Paris on a bus?"

She felt that her dad would agree. After her mother died, Crispin liked to sneak into his lecture hall at Cornell University and sit in the back row, listening. When she was fourteen, she remembered him looking directly at her during a particularly important point in his lecture. It was as if he were speaking only to her. "You can't learn archeology from a book. To discover something worthwhile, you have to get your hands dirty."

Would he be proud, or dismayed, to see just how "dirty" I am willing to get? she asked herself.

Strolling the familiar streets of central Paris, Crispin was aware that her escort was never far behind. Finally, she was at the entrance to the Hotel Regina, so loved by her father for its central location, service, and classic elegance. When she was growing up, he always took her and Clinton with him to academic conferences. They'd stay over and explore the beautiful cities of Europe, South America, Australia, China, Egypt, and Japan. Both children had an early affinity for language that he encouraged. Some of her fondest memories were of the three of them on the streets of Paris, speaking French and laughing when anyone mispronounced a word or used a phrase incorrectly. The smile these thoughts brought to her face quickly faded, however, when the image of Laurie Pierce crowded into the tableau.

In the end, her head hurt, she had no new revelations, and she had appointments to keep, with Moss tomorrow and with Kinsey in a few hours. She checked herself into a modestly priced room at the Regina and called Madrid, but Roberto had yet to return to the Hotel el Prado.

"Where are you?"

After a quick shower and change, Crispin lost track of time as she read more of the material from her Madrid research. Before long it was time to meet Kinsey downstairs. She brushed her hair and put on soft pink lipstick and a lightweight sweater before dashing down the stairs. She was slightly breathless when she found Kinsey waiting in the lobby.

She was thankful for the Parisian style of dining that frequently went on through several courses and could easily stretch over hours. Kinsey was like a favorite blanket from childhood. It may be threadbare, but it was comfortable and familiar. Over wine and *pâté en croute*, they laughed and talked about Turin. By the time the *potage velouté aux champignons* arrived, however, she was pumping Kinsey for inside information about the Foundation.

"It's a political powerhouse," Kinsey said. "I swear there are times when I think that everyone even remotely connected to European money or politics is hooked up in some way with the Foundation."

"Where does the money come from to fund the research projects?"

"Certainly, the greatest single source is the patriarch of the Foundation, a Spanish capitalist."

"Spanish, but why locate the headquarters in Paris?"

"I say Spanish, but in reality the Sato family is Italian."

Crispin almost dropped her spoon into her soup. "Did you say Sato?"

"Yes, Angelo Vienti Sato. Have you heard of him?" Without waiting for Crispin to answer, Kinsey continued. "He's the most thoughtful gentleman. In fact, I talked to him right after you called. He had just returned from Italy. A death in the family. A real tragedy from what I hear."

Crispin began to eat again, calmly absorbing the latest bombshell. *Maybe nothing shocks me anymore. After all, is anyone who they pretend to be?* she thought. Then she asked Kinsey, "When you talked to Mr. Sato, where was he?"

If Kinsey was surprised by her sudden interest in Angelo, he didn't show it. He told Crispin that the Old Man had called him at his office on a routine matter. He thought he was calling from his private plane, but couldn't be certain.

"It's strange, but when I told him I was having supper with a former colleague's daughter, he asked a lot of questions. I'm sure he remembered your father from years back."

The memory of the near intimacy with Angelo on her last night in Seville caused Crispin to wince.

"You look worn out, Crispy. Perhaps, we should call it a night," Kinsey said.

Crispin regained her composure and assured Kinsey that it was no more than a touch of jet lag and she would soon shake it off. As the meal drew to a close over Sauternes, she asked him to write a letter of recommendation for her nonexistent grant application. He told her he would be delighted and they agreed to meet in his office early the next morning before he left for the airport.

"I hate to impose, but you've no idea how much help you've been," Crispin told him as she kissed his cheek and gave him a good night hug.

Back in her room, Crispin again tried, unsuccessfully, to locate Roberto.

"What has happened to you?"

Chapter Twenty-Four

Puffy-eyed and nervous Crispin strode toward the Satabo Foundation headquarters. Trees lined the streets, and Crispin guessed that the buildings averaged twenty stories. The facade of the Foundation was covered with black marble, etched to give an Art Deco appearance. It was at once modern and retro. An aluminum sculpture the size of a Volvo dominated the plaza leading to the front of the building. A Henry Moore, it only just hinted at the *Madonna and Child* in its clean, rounded edges and highly polished finish. Kinsey was waiting for her near the main entrance.

"Did you sleep at all, Crispy?" Kinsey asked.

Crispin assured him that she was fine, but the snatches of sleep she'd caught the night before left her with a mouth that tasted like chalk and a brain that wasn't firing on all cylinders.

Kinsey introduced Crispin to the security guard.

"This is Dawit. He's worked here for three years. He's from Ethiopia," Jack explained, signing Crispin in.

"Pleasure to meet you," Dawit said, extending his hand.

Upstairs, Kinsey's office was a study in the laws of gravity. Every flat surface was covered, and the path from the door to his desk was more precarious than a game of Jenga. Dog-eared academic journals, computer printouts, and reports formed stacks so unsteady that to remove even one sheet would surely start an avalanche.

"Can you find a place to sit while I type up the letter?" a bemused Kinsey asked.

Crispin teased him, saying she would wait in the outer office rather than disturb his filing system.

"It's a mess, but I know where everything is," he responded.

While Kinsey typed, Crispin conducted reconnaissance at his secretary's desk. It was home to a computer unlike any she'd ever seen: an IBM ASCI model with 12.5 teraflops and could work up to 512 nodes with four-gigahertz processors each. The forty-two- by thirty-six-inch plasma screen was less than an inch thick. It rested on Plexiglas legs that were so clear it gave the impression that the screen was floating in space. The usual tangle of wires and cords weren't needed because infrared connections linked the components.

The setup had the first triple keyboard she had ever seen. The boards were arranged like the keys on a church organ, each a little higher than the next. The brains of the beast were in two towers on the floor at either side of the desk. The casing in the tower was luminescent, blue and gray, reminding her of mother-of-pearl.

"You're a little beauty, aren't you?" she told the machine as she stared down at it.

Jack called to her from inside his office. "What did you say, Crispy?"

"Nothing, Jack. I'm just gaga over this computer."

"Really something, isn't it? They spare no expense. Everything is linked to a mainframe, but each machine has its own security."

Crispin studied the keyboards, experimenting and testing until she was confident of how each interfaced with the terminal. The keyboard on the first level was the one she needed to log on. She kept talking back and forth with Kinsey while she ran a few test strokes.

"Where's the mainframe?" she asked.

"You know, I'm not sure. My access codes are limited to those areas that relate directly to my work. I've never even seen the restricted areas."

"That would drive me crazy. You know how nosey I am," she said, folding her new designer jacket that she'd picked up at the hotel gift shop and pushing it out of sight under the secretary's kneehole. It had been an impetuous purchase that had taken a bite out of her budget.

"With what they pay me, I can afford to keep a check on my curiosity," Kinsey said as he joined her. "Voila! One glowing letter of recommendation."

Crispin spun in her chair to face him, and in doing so made sure that the chair's high back covered the screen so that he wouldn't see what she'd been doing. While his attention was diverted as he fished around on the desk for a pen with which to sign the letter, Crispin pushed the "back" key on the computer several times to make sure it escaped to a blank screen.

"Jack, you're a lifesaver," she said, hugging his neck as they left.

"Anything for Daniel Leads' daughter."

On the street, Crispin again thanked Kinsey and then waited until he pulled away in a cab before she returned to the building to talk to the security guard through an exterior intercom system.

"Hi, I hope you can help me. I was in here a few moments ago."

"Yes, I know, Ms. Leads."

"My friend just left and I forgot my jacket in his office."

Dawit offered to summon Kinsey on his cell phone so he could return and sign Crispin in once again.

"Please, Dawit, I'm so embarrassed. I've been enough trouble for him. Getting him here so early. He's on his way to the airport. If you call him he will be late for his flight."

The guard hesitated, so Crispin turned on the charm, doing her harmless-young-woman impersonation. "Dawit, please, could I just dash back up?"

The guard smiled and pushed the button to open the door. Inside the lobby, he gave Crispin an electronic passkey to hang around her neck. "That card is keyed to the seventh floor. If you try to go anywhere else, it will signal me here."

"No problem. I'll hurry."

Back at Kinsey's secretary's desk, it didn't take Crispin long to access the mainframe portal. "A password, a password, my kingdom for a password."

She tried all the obvious possibilities first: Kinsey's street address. Birthday. Wife's name. Birthday. Backwards. "Come on, Jack. You're not a complicated man. What's the password?"

Then it hit her. Lew always said, "Nothing is left to chance. The dog. Maybe it's the dog."

C-H-A-N-C-E.

She was in.

Crispin had spent most of the previous night thinking about this moment. She unfolded a sheet of paper from her pocket that contained rows of Boolean search combinations she'd worked out in advance. She needed one thing and one thing only. Where does the cloning research intersect with the Shroud research?

After a few rabbit trails and dead ends, she found the right combination of words and, suddenly, there it was. The cloning research was file-coded simply as DNA:X. The Shroud research was filed under a subtext series: CLOTH:Y. With a few more keystrokes she had it. Unfortunately, it was gobbledygook. Since she was almost out of time, she copied the file to a thumb drive, grabbed her jacket, and ran for the elevator.

Her luck held. As she exited the elevator the guards were changing shifts. In the distraction, no one asked for the passkey back. She blew a kiss to Dawit, waving her retrieved jacket in the air as she left.

On the street, a ribald group of Parisian cabbies nudged each other and made whispered comments that, from their demeanor, Crispin assumed were suggestive. Blushing, she stepped up to the black Citroen in the front of the taxi queue and gave the driver the address she needed.

"Hurry?" the cabby asked.

"No."

In true Parisian style he took Crispin's "no" for a "yes" and swerved onto a major street, all the while carrying on a nonstop monologue about his life, ending with a full interrogation of his passenger. "So why does the *mademoiselle* have business in that place?" he asked, pointing at the IIPASE offices as he pulled up to the curb.

"Sorry?"

"Does *mademoiselle* know what they do?"

"What?"

"Ah, how you say in Anglais? Like F-B-A."

He didn't get an opportunity to say more because, at that moment, the same man who had tailed Crispin the day before opened the door. She paid the worried cabbie and followed the man. Inside, her new mock strap loafers with shiny leather soles slid on the marble floor. Why didn't I wear my Keds? she thought. She followed him across an immense lobby decorated with Louis XIV period pieces, down a hallway lined with oils in ornate frames, and finally through a series of steel doors that each required a coded keypunch entry.

With the last step over the final threshold, Crispin left the warm, gilded world of French art and entered an ultramodern domain of cold science. The windowless laboratory was more than six times the size of the lab where her high school chemistry teacher had reigned. Like her high school science lab, this one was brightly lit and organized around rows of high counters crowded with experiments in progress. That was, however, where the resemblance ended. These counters were stainless steel rather than chipped Formica, and the walls were graced with television monitors instead of bulletin boards crammed with posters. These floors had polished, imported tile rather than linoleum.

"Not a Periodic Table or Bunsen burner in sight," she mumbled.

Men and women in crisp white lab coats worked in small groups scattered around the lab. The researchers nearest to Crispin were arguing about the significance of a newly announced scientific breakthrough. A group of quantum physicists claimed to have slowed the speed of light to a crawl.

A fellow who resembled a titmouse approached Crispin. "Dr. Raúl Olvares. I manage our research operation in Europe," he said, as his wide-framed eyeglasses slipped perilously to the tip of his slender nose. Olvares used his middle finger to slide his heavy glasses back up his bridge in a way that suggested the motion was required so often that he was no longer conscious of it. "J. D. has asked me to answer any questions you have about our operation. Please, have a seat."

Olvares pointed Crispin to a tall metal lab stool. He hopped onto one near her, his short legs dangling just shy of the supporting cross bar. His monologue sounded as spontaneous as those of a stewardess giving safety instructions before a flight.

"The International Institute for the Protection Against Scientific Espionage, I-I-P-A-S-E, or as we call it 'I-Phase' for short, has an investigative unit in London, but our main scientific lab, as you can see, is here in Paris," he said with noticeable pride. "While global communications are handled through our office in Washington, D.C., the organization has contacts and branch offices in most major cities and all universities with tier one scientific research functions."

Warming to his explanation, Olvares continued, "IIPASE was created as a bridge for science, government, business, and religion to present a unified voice on ethical questions involving biotechnology and similar scientific enterprises. The first governing board came up with three goals."

Olvares held up his fingers in turn as he ticked off each goal.

"First, is to form perimeters for the field of biotechnology based on multiple world views.

"Second, is to build a network of cooperation among the international scientific community.

"Third, is to set global ethical, moral, and legal standards for biotechnology."

"Who pays for all this?" Crispin asked, gesturing toward the high-tech equipment throughout the lab.

"Countries, like the United States, interested in biotech issues. Big foundations like Rockefeller. Sources like that."

"That's all very interesting, Dr. Olvares. But what does that have to do . . ."

"With you?" The voice came from behind.

Crispin turned to find Moss standing behind her.

"As I was going to say," Crispin responded, "with your interest in Father Rossini."

"Raúl is about to make a presentation that will help answer that question. Come with me," Moss said, turning her back to them and leaving through the same door she had just come through. Crispin and Olvares followed her a short distance into a large, darkened auditorium. On the screen at the front of the room, an image that resembled a giant zipper filled the screen.

Although it was hard to see in the dark, Olvares trotted down a short flight of stairs to stand in a lecture pit, where he could control the audiovisual equipment. As he tested his microphone, a young man in a lab coat handed Crispin a thick folder labeled "Human Genome" and motioned her to a vacant seat in the back. As her pupils adjusted to the dark, Crispin realized that about thirty men and women were waiting for the lecture to begin. Not wanting to cause a delay, she moved too quickly to the seat. Her haste caused her to trip over a briefcase and land in the lap of a man near the aisle.

"Dad?"

* * *

When Roberto regained consciousness, he had lost track of time. Pirolla was standing beside the bed and Estabin was at the foot.

"You fell asleep," Estabin said, grinning at the IV bags. "That stuff they are giving you is Class A."

"How long?"

"You've been in and out," Estabin said.

"I almost didn't recognize you," Roberto told him.

Instead of the obsequious manservant Roberto had come to expect, the Estabin grinning at him was a stylish man at least a decade younger, with perfect teeth and hair.

"Thank you. It is mostly stage makeup and a few actor's tricks," he said.

"None of this makes any sense," Roberto responded. "What happened?"

"I owe you an explanation," Estabin told Roberto. "However, I'm afraid that I don't have time to answer all of your questions."

"And, I owe you an apology," the bishop added.

Roberto used the hospital bed's electric remote control to raise his head so he was sitting up and eyed first one man and then the other.

"The short answer is that powerful forces within the Vatican have suspected Angelo for some time and wanted someone on the inside of his operation. You might say I was undercover," Estabin said with a self-satisfied grin.

"Did you know about my assignment?" Roberto asked Estabin.

"Yes."

When Pirolla addressed Roberto he was contrite. "I'm sorry, my son. I did not know."

"You have no reason to apologize, Bishop," Roberto answered. "I was asked to keep my investigation a secret. Very few knew. Who notified you?"

"I had a visit from a street vendor. You know him. Young, with a speech impediment?"

"Joey. He was in the Fire Service with me. I trusted him to be my courier since he was not connected with the Vatican," Roberto explained.

"He was afraid for your safety. Had a great deal to tell me," Pirolla said. "He was most persuasive. I still can't figure out how he got into my office."

"Several days ago I gave him a key and asked him to find some missing documents. He accidentally ran into Crispin. I know I owe you a better explanation but right now I need to know, Estabin, why didn't you tell me who you worked for?"

"Same as you. Strictly need to know."

"I must ask. Did you kill the Brothers of Oviedo?"

"You don't have to worry about that," Estabin said. "At the moment I need to go to Paris. Angelo is expecting me."

"Crispin is in Paris," Roberto replied, throwing back his covers and trying to stand. "I'm coming with you."

Estabin nodded to Pirolla. "Told you he would say that."

Pirolla grabbed Roberto's arm and helped him to a chair. It took all three of them to navigate the short distance because of the tangle of equipment that tethered Roberto to IVs, a heart monitor, and oxygen. Roberto plopped down heavily, realizing how weak he was.

"Do I have anything to wear?"

"We brought what you need," Pirolla said, opening the small hospital closet and laying out fresh clothes on the bed.

Roberto began to disconnect the tubes attached to his arms and chest, asking Estabin to make sure everything was turned off so he didn't trip any alarms.

Pirolla continued in his apologies. "I am so ashamed of my part in all of this. Angelo is one of the Vatican's great benefactors, and I could see no harm when he asked questions. His niece was doing the research and . . ."

"He was writing the checks," Estabin said.

"Did Sister Llewellyn know you were giving Angelo information?" Roberto asked.

"I didn't tell her because he asked me not to. I thought it was an innocent request. Because the Satabo Foundation had paid for the gala the night of the fire, I saw no harm in helping to ease his mind. Of course, when I told him about her theory regarding arson I was surprised when he came immediately to the Vatican. I had already decided to send the good sister back to Turin to get her away from Crispin's influence, so I saw nothing amiss when Angelo said he would escort her to her home convent."

"I couldn't protect her, although I tried," Estabin said. "He's quite mad, you know."

"Crispin's father is in Paris too," Pirolla said.

"Dr. Leads?"

"Yes, he came to Rome and, I fear, I treated him rather poorly," Pirolla said.

"Can we discuss this in the car?" Estabin said. "Right now we need to get moving."

With the help of Estabin and Pirolla, Roberto was able to finish dressing. They took a supply of antibiotics and pain pills before sneaking out a side door of the hospital just minutes ahead of a surprised nurse, who returned to Roberto's room to find the bed empty and the IV tubing dangling from the pole.

Chapter Twenty-Five

It was a peculiar trio that arrived at the private airfield in Toledo an hour after Roberto's unauthorized discharge from the hospital. Estabin had once again assumed his manservant role. Roberto had a raincoat draped over his shoulders and wore a hat low over his forehead to cover his bandaged head. He moved with an unsteady gait, leaning on Estabin's arm. The bishop led the way, barking orders and commanding attention with the full authority of his position. For once, Roberto was glad of Pirolla's bombast. No one dared to challenge them.

As they prepared to board the Falcon 900, Pirolla was again the penitent. "I wish you Godspeed in stopping whatever it is that Angelo is attempting," he told them. "I will never forgive myself for being so gullible."

"We were all taken in," Roberto assured him.

Pirolla promised to find a way to reach Dr. Leads and warn him.

"Make sure he understands that Crispin is in danger and that she must stay away from the Foundation and from Angelo," Roberto emphasized.

"I will do all that is in my power."

On the flight to Paris Estabin brought Roberto water and juice so he could take some of the pain medicine he'd brought with him. They had reduced the bulky bandages on his hands so he could grasp easier, but the wounds had bled through the gauze and his hands were painful and stiff. Estabin emptied the pills onto a napkin on the tray and offered to help Roberto with the glass, but he waved him off. He tried to hold the glass with his right hand, but he couldn't make his fingers function properly. He finally managed to grip the glass between both hands, but as he raised it to his mouth it slipped away and fell to the floor.

"Pour me another glass and let me try again," he asked Estabin.

This time Roberto swept the pills into his palm and put them in his mouth before using the heels of both hands to steady the glass. Success.

"This will take a little practice," he said.

"Yes, sir," Estabin said, bowing and leaving Roberto to rest.

Roberto studied his injured hands for a long time before praying silently: Oh Lord, help me find an honest end. If I struggle against my heart's pull, the light will go out and all that will be left will be bitter and mean and cold.

* * *

Crispin awkwardly climbed over her father and into the adjoining seat just as Olvares launched into his lecture. When she tried to question him, he signaled her to be quiet and turned straight ahead to give his full attention to the presentation, as if it were the most natural thing in the world to show up in Paris unannounced. Crispin flipped through the folder she'd been given when she came in the room. She tried to take notes, but kept glancing at her dad out of the corner of her eye. What she saw surprised her. On the Cornell campus her dad was known to be indefatigable. Well into his fifties, he was often mistaken for someone at least a decade younger, his hair only just beginning to show a hint of white at the temples. Between semesters he hiked the Appalachian Trail, and on archeological digs his reputation for tolerating long exhausting days in the sun and being the first to scale a cliff were legendary. Although he was dressed, as usual, in a perfect suit, crisp white shirt and silk tie, the man sitting next to his daughter seemed used up, as though he had been through an ordeal. Crispin had never seen her dad like that. Finally, she jotted a note and passed it to him.

"How did you find me?"

He read it and then folded it in half and put it in his jacket pocket.

"Later," he whispered under his breath.

Olvares had begun his talk by thanking the audience for taking time from their schedules to attend the presentation that would bring them up to date on commercial applications of cloning research to genetic engineering of food. He tried unsuccessfully to make a joke about street protests by French farmers because they were being sold genetically altered grain and corn from the United States.

"The French plowmen like their corn and their women the way Mother Nature made them: full and sweet. Yes?"

No one laughed.

After an overly long and dull review of ongoing global projects, applications, and predicted advances in genetic engineering, he opened the floor for questions. A woman in the audience asked Olvares to talk in greater detail about the genetic alteration of livestock.

"You have heard, maybe, of a new animal that would make a perfect mixed grill: half pig, half chicken?"

Again his lame attempt at humor fell flat. Flustered, he went back to the script.

He launched into a summary of the problems with the only documented case of mammal cloning, the famous Scottish sheep. Much of it was familiar to Crispin from her library research, but he added additional details and clarified some of the jargon for her. Then a man asked the question that was on the tip of her tongue.

"How far are we from human cloning?"

"Technically, that is not possible at this point."

Soon all the questions were answered and the audience began to gather to leave. Before Crispin had a chance to ask her dad what he was doing at IIPASE, they were joined by Moss.

"I trust you found that interesting. Now, come with me," she said, without waiting for a reply. She escorted them to her office and offered them a seat at a round conference table. "I assume you two want time alone so I will step out," Moss told them.

The second the door closed, Crispin turned, ready to bombard her dad with questions. Before she could ask the first one, he put his finger to his lips and mouthed the word "bugs," pointing to places in the ceiling where she surmised that there must be hidden microphones and cameras.

"I know you have a lot of questions, Crispin, but I think I can answer them more efficiently by telling you that I received a call from Vatican security searching for you. They said you'd disappeared. You can imagine my alarm, especially after the news reports regarding the death of Sister Mary Llewellyn. Of course, I flew immediately to the Vatican, where I had a, shall I say, 'highly charged' conversation with the bishop."

"Pirolla?"

"The very one. I'm sorry to report that he didn't express a favorable opinion of you or your efforts at the Holy See. I'm afraid he didn't have a much better opinion of my own work. He also said you were a person of interest in a police investigation involving the death of his administrative assistant. That's how I came to know Ms. Moss in her role working with the police in Rome. It was fortuitous since she later contacted me while I was at your hotel to tell me you were on your way to Paris. Naturally, I followed you here."

"I left messages for you. Did you get them?"

He did not answer her question. Instead, he removed his glasses. Reaching inside the breast pocket of his jacket, he took out his eyeglass case, opened it, and unfolded a black silk lens cleaner. He began to meticulously clean each lens. He didn't speak until he had finished the process, folded the square, returned the case to his coat pocket, and fitted his glasses back over his ears, careful not to disturb his hair.

"When I arrived in Paris, I came immediately to this office. Ms. Moss explained your situation. She told me that you called her before leaving Madrid. She said you had information that might help in the investigation of the death of Sister Mary Llewellyn."

The door opened and Moss joined them, pulling up a chair at the small table. "I suppose you have questions for me," she said.

"You can start by connecting your work with IIPASE to what happened at the Vatican," Crispin said.

"Fair enough. We've had the Foundation's operatives on our radar for some time. I had tracked several to Rome. When our friend, Thomas Cross, disappeared and I heard he might be in the Vatican, I asked if I could join the team that was called in to investigate the electrocution. I wasn't surprised when you identified him. But, when you hooked up with Angelo Sato, I had to wonder what you were up to."

"He's my friend's uncle and he offered to help when I got in trouble," Crispin said.

"Your little masquerade at the convent?"

"Yes, I know now that it was a mistake."

"Ms. Moss, you said you were in a position to help relieve my daughter of her current difficulties with the law," Leads said. "What do you propose?"

"It is the Satabo Foundation that we're concerned about. We have been monitoring their movements closely, but we need help from someone with access."

"You mean undercover information gathering?" Crispin asked.

"You have a gift for the dramatic, but in essence that is correct. You're bright, Crispin. You know about the Satabo Foundation. You were there just this morning with Dr. Kinsey."

"Jack Kinsey?" Leads said, dropping his composure for a microsecond.

Moss opened a folder and slid a group of surveillance photos across the table. They showed Crispin and Kinsey entering the Foundation building that morning; Kinsey leaving; Crispin waving good-bye to him; Crispin going back alone; and then Crispin coming out later, waving to the guards. Each one had a time stamp. They were professional and taken from several angles.

"I can explain," Crispin said, more to her dad than to Moss.

"That is not necessary," he responded, sliding the surveillance photos back to Moss.

"Please explain, in detail, what you expect from my daughter in exchange for your help with the police."

Moss addressed Crispin. "We need you to go back into the Foundation. Since you have inside contacts, it should be easy for you to get in without causing suspicion."

"Contacts? Jack left town this morning."

"There's your special relationship with Uncle Sato," Moss said.

"Why do you think that?"

Moss opened a second photo file. Inside were pictures of Crispin and Angelo at the nightclub and later on the street in Seville. Although nothing had happened, the lighting and angles were suggestive.

"We are convinced that illegal operations inside the Foundation are using harmful techniques and material that violate international ethical principles," Moss said.

"Okay, but why all the secret agent, double-o-seven flimflam?" Crispin responded. "Are you trying to steal the research?"

"Don't be foolish. We're trying to stop it. That's where you come in. You asked me to help you. It comes at a price."

Moss said that IIPASE investigators had reason to believe that significant data had just been transferred to the Paris office and there was more to come. She would show Crispin what to do. All she had to do was gain access to the Foundation computer.

"What makes you think I can do that?"

"You did it once. You can do it again."

"Okay, but I have conditions too," Crispin countered. "First, I don't want to be followed anymore. Second, I want you to be honest with me about Roberto—I mean Father Rossini. How is he involved and is he alive?"

Moss stood and went to her desk, where she opened her oversized handbag. She rooted around until she found a package of Benson & Hedges. With her back to Crispin and Dr. Leads, Moss slowly ran her thumb over the warning label on the package. "Smoking seriously harms you and those around you." She smiled before returning the package to her purse and removing her sterling silver lighter. After lighting the cigarette she took a long draw before returning to the table with a small glass ashtray.

"I would rather you didn't," Leads said, as he fanned the smoke.

Without answering, Moss took another, slow drag and exhaled before putting the cigarette out in the ashtray. She then turned to Crispin.

"What would you say if I told you that your priest friend arrived in Paris a few hours ago on a plane owned by the Satabo Foundation?"

Crispin felt her molars grind as she constrained a response.

"So be it," Moss said in answer to Crispin's silence. "He's very much involved. As to being alive, he was when he got to Paris, but we've lost him."

"And Angelo?"

"The Foundation does nothing without Mr. Sato's orders. His interests are vast and his pockets deep."

Dr. Leads interrupted. "I need assurance that Crispin will be safe."

"One of our men will stay close by," Moss said, casually overriding Crispin's request not to be tailed.

"You mean he'll watch me so you can be sure I do what you ask," Crispin said.

"The necessity of a bodyguard suggests there is danger," Leads added.

"I shouldn't worry," Moss said. "After all, Angelo Sato is clearly fond of you."

Ignoring the provocative comment about his daughter and Angelo, Dr. Leads focused on the business before them. "I'll have to insist on going with my daughter."

Crispin said nothing. She knew it was useless to argue with him. Apparently J. D. Moss still had a lot to learn about Daniel Leads, Ph.D.

"And you agree to get all problems with the authorities taken care of if I help you?"

"Yes, but I imagine you will still need to make yourself available to the police. They want to question you about the last time you saw the nun."

"What about the charges at the Vatican?"

"Unfortunately, that may be more difficult. The Vatican is an independent nation state with its own laws and judicial system. It is possible that you will be required to do no more than write a letter of apology, but they may require other forms of restitution."

Dr. Leads interrupted, "The only reason to consider this unorthodox arrangement is because we believe your organization to be legitimate. The Vatican, after all, holds a seat on your board."

"Still there is protocol to be followed. Crispin violated any number of Vatican statutes when she broke into the nun's office . . ."

"Please stop referring to her as 'the nun.' She had a name. Sister Mary Llewellyn," Crispin said.

"I meant no disrespect. As I was saying, you would have to disclose exactly what you and Father Rossini did after you broke into the nun's—excuse me—Sister Mary Llewellyn's office. Vatican officials will want assurances that the Shroud wasn't harmed by your little escapade in Turin. And, of course, there is the matter of a missing videotape."

Moss paused for dramatic effect, but neither Crispin nor Dr. Leads responded.

A caesura won't work this time, Crispin thought.

After a few moments of uncomfortable silence, Moss shrugged and paged Olvares, who had been waiting in the hall.

"Just one more clarification, if you please, Crispin," Moss said as she got up to open the door for Olvares. "What was the purpose for your initial visit to the Foundation, when you went with Kinsey?"

Crispin had read too many detective novels not to recognize that Moss was using one of the oldest tricks in the book by casually throwing a bombshell question in at the last minute, as if it were an afterthought. "Does our deal hinge on my answering that?"

"No, but it would show good faith on your part. Demonstrate that you can be trusted."

"Jack wrote a letter of recommendation for me."

"Such an innocent purpose? Very well, then let us begin," said Moss, as Olvares came in with an armful of folders marked "Confidential."

* * *

Crispin had always believed she had a better-than-average command of computers, but in the next few hours she learned just how much she still needed to know. IIPASE experts explained that the best way to track Foundation activities was through a cyber data link, or backdoor, that permitted them to access Foundation computers anytime, from anywhere.

"That doesn't sound legal or ethical," she told Olvares.

Typical of bureaucrats, his answer was evasive. Through an international agreement, IIPASE had the right to establish such links in cases of suspected scientific espionage. In many ways it was similar to wiretap authority granted to law enforcement in the United States.

"Except infinitely more sophisticated," Olvares said, with no small measure of hubris.

Olvares said the Satabo Foundation had an almost impenetrable firewall. IIPASE programmers had spent months of frustrating work and were beginning to doubt they would ever crack the code when they got some unexpected help from the Millennium. The Y2K scare had universities, corporations, and government agencies around the globe scrambling to refine their dated computer code to avoid a breakdown when the clocks rolled over at midnight, December 31, 1999.

Although the computer systems in the Foundation were generations ahead of most, they had links to several universities with ancient COBOL programming. To test the Y2K patches, the university programmers would periodically arrange for the Foundation to lower its firewall. It was during one of the tests that IIPASE was able to get sufficient access to design a link.

"That's what's on this disk," Olvares explained, holding up a compressed disk. He seemed reluctant to let go as Crispin reached for it. "Do take extra good care of it. We spent a lot of time and money to develop this program."

She asked him why they didn't just access what they wanted while they were in the computer. Olvares explained that the Foundation was moving so quickly and making advances so rapidly that data accessed months earlier was now agonizingly outdated.

"We need to monitor progress every day if we're going to stay on top of their work."

"Ms. Moss said you have reason to believe that significant innovations are soon expected at the Foundation," Leads said.

"That's right. We're sure that they are on the verge of a breakthrough. That's why we don't want a one-time download. We want . . ."

"A wiretap. I get it," Crispin said.

Olvares taught Crispin and Dr. Leads how to read the cipher and how to problem-solve downloading glitches that might arise. They would have to act quickly but, if it worked, IIPASE would have a real-time electronic mole feeding data to them on everything the Foundation was up to.

"What do you mean *if* it works?" Leads asked.

"Success is never certain," Olvares said, showing Dr. Leads a second disk. "That's why we have this."

The second disk contained a particularly nasty virus.

"I cannot condone the destruction of scientific achievement," Leads said.

"It is ultimately our obligation to act when action is required," Moss said. "It falls to us because we're here and because we can. We have sufficient information to know that what is going on at the Foundation is, at best, premature, and, at worse, extremely dangerous."

"Still, I don't like the idea of the virus program," Leads told Moss.

Olvares nodded agreement. "Normally, I would come down on your side of that argument. But, we also have an obligation to protect humanity and, in this case, that obligation takes precedent over the principle of scientific advancement. It is my fervent hope that you won't have to use this one," Olvares said as he gave Crispin the virus disk. "If the international scientific community is unable to safeguard against unethical practices by rogue outfits, we have no choice but to stop them. Dead in their tracks."

"It is of no use to worry about that now. We'll confront that possibility tomorrow," Moss replied.

"For the morrow shall take thought for the things of itself," Crispin said.

"Sufficient unto the day is the evil thereof," Leads said, finishing the Bible verse.

Chapter Twenty-Six

The taxi ride back to the hotel was miserable. Crispin wished her dad would yell, but, instead, he sat next to her in a silence so deafening that it drowned out any attempt at conversation. In the lobby, he finally spoke. "Come upstairs. I have some of your things."

Crispin's suitcases and laptop from Rome were stacked in the corner of his suite. She cringed thinking about him packing her bras and panties.

"We have a great deal to sort out. But, first we need to discuss this." He held out his hand. In it was her rolled-up sock with the razor blades from Rome. "I found it when I was packing your things."

Crispin sat down on the edge of the bed, her legs suddenly too weak to stand. "I can explain."

Leads laid the sock and razor blades on the bed next to her and then pulled up a chair and sat across from her. He didn't speak. While he waited he took out his glasses and began cleaning them. The gesture was so familiar to Crispin because it brought back all the times he had taken her to her therapy appointments, regardless of his schedule. Afterwards their special treat was ice cream in the summer and pizza in the winter. He never let her down or missed an appointment. She could see him there, just the way he was today, legs crossed, patiently cleaning his glasses, waiting for her.

Crispin picked up the package of blades, the cellophane seal crimped but still unbroken, and turned it over and over in her hands. It was time to plead her case to the High Court of Daniel Leads, Ph.D. She was ready.

"Do you trust me?"

"I want to."

"Then, I ask you to believe me when I tell you that this means nothing," she said, indicating the razor blades.

"Why did you buy them?"

"A moment of weakness, a lifetime ago."

Leads listened, without interruption, as Crispin condensed several days of adventure into what she hoped was a coherent narrative: Mitchel's death, Macken's diary, Pirolla's accusations, Lew's death, dressing up like a nun, her promise to Madam Sato, seeing Francine's hair on the Shroud, being caught by Pirolla, escapes first to Seville and then to Madrid and finally to Paris, her Kinsey escapade, and Roberto's disappearance. She intentionally left her encounter with Thomas Cross in Madrid out of her narrative. Ultimately, she got to the trickiest part of the story, her theory about the connection between the Shroud and cloning.

"Crispin, all this is mere supposition. It is, at best, the stuff of mystery novels and Hollywood film. I cannot imagine why you think . . ."

It was unheard of to interrupt Dr. Daniel Leads, but she did.

"Please hear me out. Lew's murder makes no sense if it isn't connected in some way to the Shroud and what she discovered about the fire at the Cathedral. Someone knew she was on to something."

"Maybe it's the missing priest. Both Moss and Pirolla believe he's hiding something."

"Pirolla doesn't trust anyone."

"Interesting that you bring up trust again," Leads said, in a tone as stern as she'd ever heard. "What about your trust in me? What I can't understand, Crispin, is why you didn't call me when this all started. Why didn't you tell me what was going on? Why did you run away from the Vatican?"

"I'm not sure I can answer."

"Can't answer or won't answer?"

Crispin the Advocate was ready to make her case. She just wasn't sure if Judge Leads was ready to hear it.

"Do you remember when I was in school and got stumped on a math problem and you would tell me that I had to work it out on my own? This is something like that, only much bigger. I feel like I have been given a challenge. A test. I have to figure it out on my own. If I don't solve it, I can't move forward. Does that make any sense?"

"This is not a game or a school problem," Leads replied, in an even angrier tone. "Someone could get hurt."

"Someone already has," she said, holding her ground.

"Enough!" Leads said, standing and going into the washroom, slamming the door behind him.

Crispin could hear him running water in the sink. She sat motionless. She watched the digital hotel clock as it registered 6:08. She didn't move but felt like time had been reduced to a crawl. No sounds were coming from the bathroom. She waited. The clock was now showing 6:29. Still no sound. Should she go to the door? Now it was 6:32. Just as she started to stand, she heard the door open and her dad came back in the room. She could tell by the damp hair around his face that he must have splashed it with cold water.

"We should eat supper," he said.

"Do you mind if I show you something first?"

Crispin booted up her laptop to process the data she'd gotten from Kinsey's office. She was surprised when her computer acted sluggish, unable, at first, to handle the dense file. After disabling a number of programs, she freed sufficient memory so her computer could read the file.

"I'll just freshen up a bit for dinner while it loads," Crispin said, digging a fresh shirt and toothbrush from her suitcase.

"Where'd you say you got this?" he shouted to her.

Crispin poked her head out of the bathroom. "I didn't say. Do you know what it is?"

"It's DNA, but there is something odd about it. You want to tell me about it?"

"At dinner," she replied, as she came back into the room.

"Agreed."

On the way through the hotel lobby, Crispin checked to see if there were any messages from Roberto. There weren't.

"You act like you've lost your best friend," Leads said, as he tucked his arm in hers on the street in front of the hotel.

"That's what I'm afraid of."

Crispin noticed that the Institute man who had tailed her the previous day was back on the job. Her dad saw him too. After spending most of the day cramped in front of a computer terminal at IIPASE, they welcomed a chance to stretch their legs. Occasionally they would stop outside a café and listen to the music, but neither felt like going in.

A familiar dull ache warned Crispin that a migraine was imminent. Her dad recognized the signs and suggested they grab one of the brightly lit dinner boats on the Seine that was just ready to embark. As the boat pulled away they saw the frustrated IIPASE operative standing on shore.

They found a quiet table where Crispin took a pill and ordered strong coffee. Dr. Leads started his meal with wine and escargot while Crispin let the medicine work its magic and watched the city glide by. While he ate, she told him about the data download from the Foundation that resulted in the unusual DNA strands she'd shown him back at the hotel.

"You'll need supercomputer capability to digest material that dense. A laptop will never do the job," he told her. "Stanford might be able analyze this for you."

"Will you help?"

"Now you need me?"

"I always have. Always will."

"You remind me so much of your mother. Leading with your heart."

"I am like her," Crispin said, smiling. "But I'm like you too. Isn't that the whole point of DNA, interwoven strands?"

"This conversation isn't over, but for now . . ."

"Sufficient unto the day?"

When the waiter brought Crispin an order of snails in wine and garlic sauce, Crispin held one up. "How would we clone this guy if all we had left of him was his tail? Could we use some of it or do we need his blood?"

"Blood, sweat, or tears would do."

"That's the thing about DNA. Each minuscule cell is a complete genetic roadmap, similar to the slice of a hologram. However thin, you still have the full picture."

The waiter refilled their glasses and delivered fresh baguettes and bowls of onion soup dripping with Gruyere.

"If IIPASE is a watchdog, who's watching the watchdog?" Crispin asked rhetorically.

"Now that is a genuinely interesting question. Some of my friends would say IIPASE is, by its very mission, an amoral agency since it is positioned to affect the global distribution of biotechnology," he answered.

"Global distribution. Do you mean turning the spoils of science into commercial products?"

"Exactly. That's who was at the meeting today at IIPASE. Potential international investors. They smell money in this line of research. I try to be pragmatic since much of what is happening in genetic and stem cell research eventually can be used to cure diseases, feed the hungry, protect the environment."

"And make someone very rich."

"That too."

"It sounds as though all of the pillars of society have a stake here: church, politics, science, and commerce," Crispin said.

"Their interests both intersect and collide. Always have."

Crispin swirled the Gruyere on her spoon, annoyed that something distant and illusive kept tickling the fringes of her memory. By the time the waiter delivered their warm salmon in a creamy saffron sauce, Crispin gave up trying to coax the thought free. It would come when it was ready. When she shared her frustration her dad suggested she break the questions about her theory down into parts. She started with the obvious. "Who would want to clone Jesus?"

"Not the faithful," Leads said.

"Why not? I'd think they'd be the first in line. A modern-day immaculate conception."

"Then you fail to understand the simplicity of faith. Think back to what you told me about Sister Mary Llewellyn. Would she clone Jesus?"

"No. She wouldn't feel the need."

"Even for the faithful, there would be metaphysical questions as well. Consider this one: Is God even in the DNA at all or was the body of Christ just a vessel?"

"So if the Church is off the hook, what about science?"

"Here I can speak with greater confidence. While some of my colleagues are not above choosing their research based on the likelihood that it would win them a place on the *Today* show or cover of *Time*, most in the community are much too serious to take on a highly theatrical stunt like that. If they're trying to clone, it is a general inquiry designed for broad application."

"That leaves commerce," she said

"Where is the potential for money in this kind of effort?"

"Televangelists generate plenty of Benjamins from the faithful."

"I find it hard to imagine that there would be enough potential payback from evangelical television to warrant the kind of up-front capitalization required. Again, if you're going to fund it, there is greater financial potential in an effort with broader application."

"It's irrelevant anyway since it can't be done."

"Perhaps, but let us not forget about the breakthroughs that Moss and her friends at IIPASE think Satabo is making."

"We're back to that."

When the boat landed they saw no sign of the man from the Institute.

"Guess he got tired of waiting for us," Crispin said with a smile.

They returned to the hotel, tired and ready to call it a night. Leads kissed his daughter on the forehead when the elevator reached her floor. "Good night. Tomorrow is a big day."

"Will you send the data I left to your friend at Stanford?" Crispin asked.

"I promised I would," he said. "But, don't get your hopes up. There may be nothing there to help your hypothesis."

"I know. Love you."

"Love you more."

Crispin stayed in her room just long enough to be sure that her dad was tucked in before sneaking out a side door of the hotel. She'd concocted a plan that would get her in and out of the Satabo Foundation long before either Leads or anyone at IIPASE knew what had happened. She'd made up her mind somewhere along the Rue de Saint Germain that she would do what she could to avoid dragging him in any deeper.

I made the mess and now I will have to clean it up, she told herself.

She found a twenty-four-hour copy shop down the street. It was the kind of office-away-from-home service center that had grown popular in big cities where business travelers frequently need access to computers, faxes, and sophisticated duplicating machines at odd hours.

Crispin prepaid for the use of a computer and was given an activation code. Her laptop had a variety of programs but, unfortunately, it didn't have the kind of desktop publishing software that she needed tonight. Besides, only a high-quality laser printer was right for the job she had in mind.

The mechanical rat-a-tat of computer keyboards and the faint hum of florescent lights filled the place. Crispin found a workstation along the wall that afforded her some privacy. She inserted a disk and opened a document from her Kinsey material with the Satabo Foundation letterhead. She then cut and pasted the letterhead, aligning the image until she had a perfect replication. That done, Crispin typed out a letter of introduction for herself on the Satabo Foundation template letterhead she had just created and then printed it on expensive paper she had purchased when she first came into the copy center. Using Jack's letter of recommendation as a guide, she practiced Kinsey's signature and copied it onto the letter. She then faxed it to herself at the hotel.

Back in her hotel room she admired her handiwork and allowed herself to lapse into a nanosecond of self-congratulation at her espionage skills before her lifelong companion, doubt, again knocked on the door. Will it be good enough?

As she pounded her bed pillow into submission, she thought about Roberto and what he was doing. Had he received the message she left for him in Madrid? What had he found out in Toledo? Why hadn't he called?

Before she drifted off she imagined a conversation she had promised herself she would have with her dad one day. She had started it tonight but there was so much more to be said. I am Crispin Two Threads. I am a rational fact-finder. I am a dream chaser. I am my mother. I am my father. I am Crispin the Weaver.

Chapter Twenty-Seven

Crispin didn't know how long the phone by her bed had been ringing, but she could tell by the light through the window that it was early morning. In her grogginess she couldn't find the receiver. She groped the nightstand next to the bed, knocking a full glass of water to the floor, where it shattered. She patted around until she located the light switch on the lamp's cord.

"Hello," she said, trying to sound alert.

"Is this Crispin Leads?"

Crispin tried to clear her throat, but it was dry. "Uh, uh."

"This is Sam Beckett. I'm calling from Stanford."

"Did you say Samuel Beckett?"

"Sam Beckett. Only my mother calls me Samuel. I'm a research assistant, not an Irish novelist," he said, chuckling as if he had never tired of the joke. "Sorry to wake you, but we did a rush analysis of the DNA data that Dr. Daniel Leads sent and I was told to give you a call. Should I call back?"

"No. No. No. I'm okay. Just give me a minute."

Wide awake now, Crispin propped the feather pillows behind her back and fished a small pad of paper and pen from the nightstand drawer. "Lay it on me."

"I don't know where you got the stuff, but the first report you wanted analyzed is totally bogus."

"Bogus?"

"Has to be. You see, usually only two, maybe three percent, of a DNA strand is clean information. The rest is what we call 'junk.'"

"Okay," Crispin said, absently writing "junk" on her pad.

"Your first data stream is just the opposite. There's almost no junk. Close to one hundred percent of it is pure information."

"Ninety-nine and forty-four one hundredths percent pure," she jotted. "So that means it's good stuff, right?"

"Wrong. It's not possible. You were probably the butt of some grad student prank."

"What do you mean a grad student? It didn't come from a university. It's from a lab right here in Paris."

"You may have gotten it from a lab in Paris, but this report was sequenced at the University of Texas."

He explained that all human DNA sequencing reports are required, by an international agreement, to carry codes that identify which labs they came from and whether the DNA sample was from a male or female.

"The code should also contain other basic info, like date and place of birth. Yours doesn't."

"What about the rest of the stuff we sent you?"

"The other samples are from all over the world. And, I mean all over."

"Sam, if you have those ID codes handy could you read me a few of the locator codes?"

"There are hundreds here. What you have here is an immense cross-sectional study." He called out about twenty and then stopped. Every report came from a different university or lab. "It goes on and on like that. I could see no pattern in the data."

"Is there anything else?"

"Well, there is one odd thing. The bogus report is male, but the rest of them are females."

"All women?"

"Yea, a real harem."

"Why do you think so many universities are involved?"

Sam said he couldn't be sure, but assumed that the originating lab had to farm the work out to vendors because sequencing takes days and hogs computer memory.

"I don't know what the lab in Paris is fishing for, but they have thrown a broad net. No pun intended."

"One more question, Sam. Do any of the female samples match the report on male DNA in any way? Any familial connection?"

"Why do you care? The report can't be real. I told you . . ."

"I understand, but can you check for me?"

"Sure. I can run it through the computer if you want. It will take some time since there's so much genetic information to process. But, if that's what you want . . ."

"I do. And, please get back to me as soon as possible. If I'm not available, you can send an email. And Sam, you have been a tremendous help. Thank you."

Getting up from bed, Crispin stepped where the broken water glass lay and cut her foot. The sharp, unexpected pain in her bare foot brought tears. As she dabbed with tissues, first her eyes and then her foot, she made the connection that had eluded her the previous night. Maybe it was seeing tears and blood so close in proximity. Maybe it was simply the kind of early-morning flash of genius that emerges from the subconscious on first awakening. But, there it was, the answer.

I'll be damned. So obvious. It wasn't good enough to just have the DNA from the blood on the Shroud. Satabo also needed the tears. Mary's tears.

It had been right in front of her the first day she arrived at the Vatican. In her mind she could still see the tapestry that nearly covered the wall in the hall outside Pirolla's office. She remembered it so distinctly since she toyed with the idea that the tapestry betrayed a closet feminist lurking somewhere in the Vatican because it was such a strong tribute to women. A plaque next to the tapestry offered a translation in several languages for the Latin inscription next to the tableau: "It was the women who came to claim Him. It was their tears that washed Him. It was their tears that stained the cloth that held Him."

Whoever was behind the bizarre scheme had to have Mary's tears. It was the only way to identify a genetic descendent that could be used in the cloning process. And it had to be a female relative. The revelation answered another of the questions that had tripped up Crispin when she first began thinking about the possibility of using the blood on the Shroud as a source for cloning. As her dad had pointed out, if all the conspiracy needed was Shroud blood, why didn't they simply steal the samples from labs that had cross-matched and typed the blood years earlier?

"That sort of sample is never destroyed. And labs such as those have far less sophisticated security than Turin," he reminded her.

She was stumped, and a little embarrassed, that she hadn't thought of it herself. Why go to all the trouble of duplicating a fake Shroud, stealing it, staging a fire, and returning it just for the blood if it was so easy to get from other sources? Now she knew.

Her euphoria was short-lived. Once you have the tears, how would you use them to find a female relative? She willed herself to be logical and to think through the possibilities. Work the problem.

She approached it the way someone who is trying to debunk a magician's prestidigitation might. Rather than try to figure out what was done, ask yourself if you were trying to achieve that effect, what would you do?

If I were trying to locate willing female subjects, how would I do it?

For a while she was again stumped. Not only would they need to find an egg from a living descendent of Mary, but they would also need an agreeable woman to carry the embryo to term. Crispin fidgeted and thought. The Foundation couldn't very well take an ad out in the newspaper: "Are You a Direct Descendent of the Holy Family? Call 1-800-"

Or could they?

All her life friends and family made light of her interest in movies, but once again her pastime came to her rescue. She remembered scenes in the movie *Creator* when Peter O'Toole, playing a Nobel Laureate, advertised on campus for a female willing to donate an egg for his cloning experiments. She'd seen advertisements just like that in her college newspapers back home. She'd heard one of her friends laugh when she saw it. "Guys have been selling sperm for years. Now it's our turn to earn a little extra shoe money."

The ads said that the women needed to be healthy and between the ages of nineteen and twenty-seven. If their eggs were viable they would get up to three thousand dollars. It didn't take a genius to figure out that the male strand must come from the blood sample. If it were actually from the Christ blood, that could explain the dense information load.

Using her computer and the hotel's phone modem, Crispin found the list of Satabo holdings and investments she'd copied from the Foundation website in Madrid. It was huge. The Foundation owned hundreds of enterprises around the world. She logged on and typed in a key word: I-N-F-E-R-T-I-L-I-Y. As the cursor spun like a beach ball and the computer searched through its vast pool of data, Crispin jotted down more possible search terms: obstetrics, gynecology.

Her computer screen lit up with thousands of hits. She began to systematically narrow the search until she had a list of infertility clinics. Several matched the names on the list of enterprises owned by Satabo.

She narrowed her attention to the ads. She typed in the keyword to pull up the national newspapers and magazines she thought might appeal to college students and then did a cross-reference for classified ads seeking egg donors. The computer told her that newspapers around the globe had been saturated with donate-your-eggs ads.

"Holy gravy!"

Assuming that only a tiny percentage of the women who answered the ad actually agreed to being tested, a campaign of this magnitude must have produced thousands of potential candidates. She reasoned that the female DNA samples that she'd downloaded from the Foundation database must be from blood tests of the women who'd answered the ads.

A knock on her hotel door startled Crispin. When she answered, a waiter rolled in a cart laden with the room service order she'd placed the night before in anticipation of an early start to her day. The waiter put her breakfast tray on the table by the window and, one by one, removed the silver covers from each dish, filling the small room with the aroma of grilled potatoes, bacon, and chocolate. Crispin opened the curtains on a drizzly Parisian morning while she poured herself a cup of hot chocolate and dug into the *pomme des terres* and an omelet cooked as only the French can. She slathered her croissant with blackberry jam. She even wet her finger so she could pick up all the golden crumbs that fell on her robe. As she popped them into her mouth she realized that she felt remarkably perky, even giddy, given the short amount of sleep she'd had the night before. Let's see, what's on the agenda today?

Go undercover.

Check.

Steal secret computer information.

Check.

Stop international conspiracy.

Check.

I may make it out of "Minor Works" yet.

Crispin called down to the front desk and asked if there had been any messages left for her. There hadn't been.

In the light of morning she was more convinced than ever that her simple, straightforward plan was brilliant. The letter she had printed at the copy center would provide her a plausible entrance to the Foundation. Add a sexy shirt and the plan is foolproof, she thought with a smile.

If her plan didn't work she still had the passkey they'd given her on her first trip to the Foundation. That would be more difficult to pull off, but it was a solid Plan B.

Feeling optimistic, Crispin selected a cotton blouse that was just sheer enough to be suggestive. It wasn't the kind she would normally choose to wear with her baggy khaki pants and sneakers, but today it served a useful purpose. She put both IIPASE disks into one pants pocket and the Foundation passkey and some cash in the other. Then she studied herself in the mirror. The pants were so loose that no one would suspect she had anything in her pockets.

* * *

Dr. Leads picked up the phone in his room six stories above her. The call was from Laurie Pierce in New York. She told him that she had an urgent message from Bishop Pirolla, who had been trying to track him down.

"He said he had left word for you at IIPASE that you must call him immediately. When you didn't call, he became frantic and called your office at Cornell. He finally convinced the girl who was covering for Carole to give him the number of someone who could contact you."

"Honey, slow down. What's the message?" urged Leads, as he absentmindedly glanced out the window at the street below in front of the hotel.

"Daniel, Pirolla believes that Crispin is in mortal danger. He said you should get her out of Paris right away."

At that moment Leads saw the doorman helping Crispin into a taxi. He tried to raise the window to call to her but it had been painted shut. Desperate, he banged on the glass.

"What's that racket?"

"I'll call back," he said, as he hung up and grabbed the elevator to the lobby, where he almost ran over the startled doorman. "Where did that young lady go?"

"Monsieur, Je ne sais pas."

"Mademoiselle, que?"

Attracted by Leads' loud voice, the elderly concierge came over to subdue the situation before it got out of hand. *"Monsieur* Leads, what is the problem," he almost whispered.

"Would you please inform this man that he must tell me where my daughter was going?"

The concierge explained that this was the young woman's father and he, therefore, had a right to make inquiries.

"Mai oui," said the doorman with a nod, winking as he told Leads that he had given the cab directions to take her to the offices of the Satabo Foundation.

"Get me a taxi," Leads commanded as he ran out of the hotel into the rain.

"Monsieur Leads," pleaded the concierge as he ran after him, pointing at Leads' striped pajamas and bare feet.

* * *

Roberto winced as Estabin pried the blood-soaked gauze bandages from his right hand. His left hand was submerged in warm water in an attempt to make the wound care less painful. Estabin kept up a continuous monologue while he worked, partly in an attempt to distract Roberto.

They had spent the night in an apartment across the street from the Foundation. The apartment was one that Estabin had used to stake out Angelo's business activities. It was equipped with Spartan sleeping quarters as well as basic surveillance equipment, including high-powered binoculars mounted on a tripod.

"I had perfect access to his day-to-day life, but I was excluded from a lot of what went on in the board rooms over there," he said, indicating the Foundation, which was in clear view through the large picture window. "Still, it was obvious to me that something big was about to come down."

"What do you think it is?" Roberto asked through clenched teeth.

"No way to know, but he got really agitated when his niece started asking questions about the Shroud and the fire. He said she was going to mess up his plan. Frankly, I couldn't see a connection."

"Why did she die the way she did?"

"I wasn't there, but he thought she knew something."

"What?"

"I don't know."

Estabin finished wrapping Roberto's hands in fresh gauze and offered the priest another dose of painkiller.

Roberto flexed his thumb several times and was pleased that he was able to grip the water glass without spilling.

"Thank you," he told Estabin. "This works better."

They moved to the large table in front of the window, where copies of the Foundation floor plan were spread out along with markers where Estabin had indicated a primary and alternate route for Roberto.

"I don't know what you'll find in Angelo's executive suite, but if Lew gave him anything, that's where he will have it. That's the safest place," Estabin said.

Out the large window, the city lights were just beginning to shut off as the morning dawned on the street below. As Roberto watched the last glow of light from the streetlights fade across the Moore sculpture, he was startled to see Crispin step out of the cab in front of the Foundation building.

Chapter Twenty-Eight

Crispin recognized the guard inside the Foundation offices as the Ethiopian who was on duty when she came to the offices earlier with Jack. Dawit seemed bored and tired as the night shift drew to a close. She waved and buzzed the intercom.

"What brings you here at such an hour?" he asked.

Crispin sighed and spoke into the intercom. "Dr. Kinsey asked a favor. He left behind some books and other materials that he wants me to bring him when I go back home."

Dawit buzzed Crispin into the lobby. She handed him the letter she had so carefully counterfeited and yawned while he studied it. "Excuse me, too much, ah, too much to drink last night."

He played along with the unspoken suggestion. "You're a good friend to come out so early for him."

"I'm the only one who can make sense of his filing system," she said.

Crispin guessed correctly that Kinsey's notorious disarray would be a legend in a dot-the-i's, cross-the-t's kind of place like the Foundation. She put her elbows on the guard station counter and cupped her chin in her hands. "Anyway, I owe him a favor and I make it a rule to repay favors."

"Now you will owe me too."

Crispin put a paper sack she had brought with her on the counter. From it she pulled a steaming cup of coffee, a fresh peach, and a cream pastry. She handed him the food. "Dawit, this is, perhaps, a down payment?"

"But, I'm doing a big favor. Am I not?"

"What do you have in mind?"

"A drink. Tonight?"

She nodded.

He handed her a pen and paper. "Your phone number. I'll call."

Crispin wrote down the hotel number, but reversed the last two digits. "I'll just run up and get the things Jack needs. Will you be here when I come down?"

Dawit was about to answer when his demeanor changed and he stood at rigid attention, addressing someone over Crispin's shoulder.

"Good morning, Mr. Sato."

"Good morning, Dawit."

Crispin froze. Ever since Kinsey mentioned that Angelo was in town, she'd been dreading this minute and worrying about how she might respond. She turned and gave Angelo what she hoped was a genuine smile and warm hug. "Angelo. What a surprise."

Angelo held on to her long after she released her end of the hug.

"I'm here as a favor to a friend," Crispin explained.

"I didn't realize you knew anyone here," he said, noticing her sheer blouse.

"That's two of us. I didn't know you were part of the Foundation until my friend, Jack Kinsey, mentioned it at supper."

"Kinsey? Don't think I know him."

"I suppose that you have so many employees it would be hard to remember them all. Kinsey and my dad are friends." Crispin was getting nervous and feared she might be babbling, but she persisted. "I have to tell you the funniest coincidence. You know my dad too. Dr. Daniel Leads. He remembers you. Just how funny is that? Imagine how I laughed when he told me. There I had been at your home. You, our savior, and you and I never made the connection. Not in Turin. Not in Seville. Now isn't that something?"

Angelo didn't say anything, but took hold of her arm and stood uncomfortably close.

"When I met you in Turin everything was so . . . ," Crispin said.

"Tragic?"

Angelo put his hand on the small of Crispin's back and began to lead her to the elevator. "Come, Crispin. We have a great deal to discuss."

"Aren't you forgetting something?" Dawit said, holding up the fake Kinsey letter.

Angelo let go of her so that Crispin could fetch the letter from Dawit. As she reached for it, she asked to see the note where she'd written the phone number. "Silly me."

Crispin scrawled out the correct hotel number and whispered to Dawit. "One more favor, Dawit. Call my father, Dr. Leads, for me. Tell him I won't be able to meet as planned because I've run into my old friend, Angelo."

"Come, Crispin," called Angelo, holding the elevator door open.

Fighting to maintain her composure, Crispin entered the elevator. The instant the doors closed and she was alone with Angelo, she realized she'd made a serious tactical error. In the close confines of the lift, Crispin's internal alarm system went haywire. It was as if she was alone with someone she'd never met. In appearance he was the same elegant man with the Vandyke beard and impeccable style, but there was no hint of the friendly and helpful Uncle Angelo of Turin or the handsome escort who flirted with her so openly in Seville. This Angelo emitted a menacing tension that was thick and oppressive. She opened her mouth, intending to ask a question, but her mind was blank. She could think of nothing to say or to ask as she watched the elevator floor indicator buttons light up one by one as they moved slowly from the lobby to the penthouse.

When the elevator stopped and the door opened, Angelo grasped her arm so firmly that it hurt as he herded her through the reception area and into his private quarters. Floor-to-ceiling windows graced one wall. A comfortable seating area, arranged around a coffee table, couch, and multiple chairs, was to the right. His desk dominated the other end of the room. He forced Crispin onto a narrow couch by the windows and returned to the office door to make sure that it was locked. Turning, he circled back in a predatory fashion. "So tell me, did Dr. Kinsey help you access files that you shouldn't?"

Crispin crossed her ankles and smoothed her pants, taking her time answering. "I thought you didn't know Jack Kinsey."

Angelo's voice ricocheted off the walls. "One more time. Did Kinsey help you access our research? Tell me!"

Crispin's instinct to protect Jack helped her find the nerve to stand up to Angelo. "No, he knew nothing. What you should really be asking me is who else knows what you're doing with the tears you stole from the Shroud."

Angelo took Crispin's chin in his hand and roughly pushed her head against the back of the couch, leaning close to her face. "What do you know about that?"

"Everything."

"How did you find out?"

She smirked and tapped her finger on her temple. "I used my brains."

"You're not that smart," he sneered, releasing his grip and standing up straight. "There's not a handful of scientists on the planet who could even imagine the kind of advances we've made. Our techniques for editing DNA and injecting it piece by piece into a donor cell puts us at least twenty years ahead of the idiots at IIPASE."

Crispin couldn't mask her surprise at the mention of the Institute.

"You think I don't know what they're up to? Trying to steal my work so they can sell it to the highest bidder."

"They are scientists," Crispin replied, realizing too late that she had only confirmed his suspicions.

"My work is for God alone, not for those greedy bastards," Angelo said, squeezing in next to her on the small couch and again putting his face close to hers. He'd been practically screaming at her up to that point but now he was quiet, stroking the back of her neck with his fingers. The silent room felt unnaturally cold and forbidding. "Crispin, Crispin. What have you done? Poor, curious Crispin. And no one to save you . . ."

"Save me?"

". . . now that Father Rossini is gone."

"Gone?"

"You didn't know? Our Father Rossini has died. It was a most horrible kind of death."

Crispin stared at him through red eyes. "I am not going to cry for you."

He slapped her, hard. "I'd be a little less cocky if I were you. Or, maybe you would like some of the same treatment Father Rossini received. Even your brave little fireman screamed like a woman in the end."

Angelo roughly stroked Crispin's cheek and seemed about to kiss her, but instead he stood up and went to a bar built into a wall cabinet, where he poured himself water and swallowed a handful of pills. When he turned back he had a self-satisfied expression, as if he had come to a revelation.

"No, for you, I think, it is more effective to hear about the pain of others." Angelo began to describe the painful torture of Roberto, relishing each graphic detail. "His hands. Now, that was genius. I could see it in his face when he realized what it meant. A man can make do with one damaged hand. How much more difficult life is when you lose the use of both."

"But, he didn't know about the blood." Crispin's voice cracked with horror. "He didn't know about the tears."

Angelo came back to where Crispin was sitting and grabbed hold of her knee. "My Sparrow knew."

"My God. What are you saying?"

"It took her a long time to tell me."

"You killed her?"

"She had to tell me what she knew."

"The police say she was tortured. How is it possible?"

"You know the answer. Remember what I told you. Auto-da-fé. Auto-da-fé," Angelo said in a chanting, hollow tone.

He squeezed his fingers into the tender part of Crispin's knee to the point of pain. "I didn't want to, but God demanded it. I am his instrument."

Crispin couldn't bear to hear another word. Angelo was right. No pain he could inflict on her was as damaging at that moment as the thought of the pain he had brought on Lew and Roberto. She had to push it away. She had to escape from his voice. The only way she knew to protect herself was to draw inside and shut out the words. She knew how it worked. Just stop listening to anything except your own breath. Stop thinking. Feel only the air slide into your nose and into your lungs. Fill them.

Let it out.

Pull air back in.

Do it again. Exhale. Inhale.

Don't listen.

Don't react.

Don't think.

Push all thoughts away. Push the bad down to that place where pain can be hidden and covered up. Lock the pain away so it doesn't exist anymore. I will not hear your words, she told herself, willing herself to close off the unimaginable. Someday, when it is safe, she knew she would have to endure. Not today. Not today.

The sound of the phone ringing cut through the silence. Angelo crossed to answer the call, furious for the disturbance. He listened for a minute before he responded. "Have him escorted to the board room and then send someone to entertain Ms. Leads for me. We must be hospitable. No, I won't need you."

Angelo retuned to Crispin and stood over her, his face close to her. She was aware of his breath. She didn't move a muscle,

kept her hands limp, and hoped that she appeared to have receded into a catatonic-like state.

"Where have you gone?" he said. Satisfied that she was harm-
less, Angelo left and locked the door behind him.

Crispin waited for a beat after she heard him leave. She took
a deep cleansing breath that sent a shiver through her body and
stood up. She assumed she only had a few minutes alone, so she
searched the office for something she could use to defend herself.
The bar offered no help, but the desk had a two-foot, crystal
statue of the Virgin. "Sorry, Mary, no disrespect, but clearly you
could do some serious damage to a person's cranium and I may
need you," Crispin told the crystal lady as she examined its heft
and gave it a practice swing. Armed with a possible weapon, she
took out her cell phone, intent on dialing Moss, but she could get
no signal. She walked around the office holding her cell above
her head, attempting to make a connection. Come on. Come on.
I need me some bars, she thought.

She heard someone trip the lock on the door and took up a
defensive position, hoisting the glass statue above her head, ready
to defend herself. She stopped herself midair. The statue slipped
from her grip and shattered on the floor when she realized that
it was Roberto who crossed the threshold. "I thought you were
dead?" she said, throwing her arms around him.

"Did he hurt you?" Roberto asked, as he cupped her face, still
tinged bright red where Angelo had slapped her.

"Don't worry about me. He told me what they did to you and
to Lew," she said, burying her face in his chest. "He's a monster."

Roberto pulled away. "We have to leave. Now."

He showed Crispin the way to the stairwell. Following him
down the concrete stairs she had flashbacks to their escape
through the underground tunnels in Turin. Was it only five days
ago? I feel as if we've been running from something since the day
we met, she thought. Crispin could see by his color and carriage
that Roberto was in pain. The bandages on his hands were discol-

ored and stained and he struggled to open the heavy, metal fire door when they reached the service exit that led to a side street.

The sky was heavy with India ink clouds that had rolled in over Paris. The winds picked up and Crispin held fast to Roberto's arm as the rain turned into a pelting assault, soaking them both. They moved as quickly as Roberto's injuries permitted to the safety of Estabin's apartment. Once inside, Roberto collapsed into a chair, gasping for air.

"Roberto, you should be in the hospital," Crispin said.

"There's medicine on the kitchen counter. Painkillers and antibiotics. If you don't mind."

Crispin found the bottles and brought them to him. Without being told, she opened the bottles and helped him with a dose of each. He swallowed them without water.

"I'll be fine when this is over," he said.

"Whose place is this?" she asked, sitting down on the arm of his chair.

Roberto explained Estabin's dual identity and his role in getting him safely out of Toledo.

"Do you know who he works for?" Crispin asked.

"We both answer to the same person."

"And, I take it, you're not going to tell me right now," she said, standing up. "I need to get out of these wet clothes and so do you."

Crispin scouted for dry clothes. Estabin's shirts were too big for her, but she found a guayabera in the closet. The traditional, white Spanish wedding shirt fit Roberto perfectly. She helped him dry his hair, and although at first he resisted her offer in buttoning the shirt, he realized that he had no choice. The shirt she chose for herself hung well below her hips almost to her knees, but at least it was dry.

"How about some tea?" she asked him.

"First, you must tell me everything that's happened since Madrid."

"I can talk while I boil water." Crispin filled Roberto in on what she had learned from the original DNA data and her hypothesis about the connection between cloning and the Shroud. When she got to the part about IIPASE, he stopped her in mid sentence.

"I cannot be part of anything that will benefit the Institute," he said. "I have a different assignment."

"Okay. I'm listening."

"You know what they have in there," he said, pointing out the window to the Foundation offices. "We cannot take a chance that it will reach the wrong hands. We must destroy it."

"I understand," she said, handing him a cup of tea and taking a seat next to him. "We'll need strong evidence before accusing someone as prominent as Angelo Sato of such a bizarre scheme. But, Moss will know how to handle it. Once she sees the files, she'll be able to make a case against Angelo."

"No. The information is too dangerous. No one can be trusted. This is not a matter for the law or for science. It is a matter for the Church."

Conscious of Crispin's sudden reluctance, he tried to explain his reasoning. "I cannot tell you everything, but my mission is to prevent the Foundation research from being completed. It is unholy. I hope you understand."

"I'm not sure I would use the word 'unholy,' but I agree that there are serious ethical issues that haven't been fully examined."

"Then can we at least agree to help each other stop the Foundation?"

Crispin returned to the kitchen, opening cabinets in search of something to go with the tea. She returned with a package of biscuits and a refill. The delay gave her time to think, but she still didn't have a good answer. If she didn't help IIPASE, they wouldn't help her. If she helped them, she knew she was potentially crossing an ethical line.

"Crispin, you know I cannot allow this idea or this research to . . ."

"I know. I know." Out the window, Crispin noticed that workers were beginning to arrive at the Foundation, some huddled under taut umbrellas along the sidewalk, others driving down ramps and through gates to underground parking.

"They must be paying a lot to have such a large workforce on duty."

Then she remembered what Moss had told her. "I bet they're getting close to their goal. That's why they're staffing up," she said.

"Then we cannot delay."

Crispin's cell phone rang. When she pulled it from her back pocket she recognized it as a Paris number. She showed it to Roberto before answering.

"That's Angelo's private line," he said.

Crispin answered, "Hello."

"I have Dr. Leads," Angelo said. "Let's make a trade."

Chapter Twenty-Nine

Roberto showed Crispin how to focus the high-powered binoculars. The sightline was aimed at Angelo's office. She could see everything clearly, even through the rain. Her dad was sitting where she had been. Angelo was yelling. Estabin was sweeping up the remains of the glass Madonna. As she scanned the room she got a jolt. Thomas Cross was standing next to Angelo's desk.

"Now it makes sense," she told Roberto. "Look who's with them." She stepped aside so he could take her place. "I'll bet he's been following me all along. He probably followed me to the Institute and told Angelo."

"Exactly what did Angelo say he wanted?" Roberto asked, showing signs that the painkillers were starting to do their job.

"It was garbled, but, apparently, he thinks I know more about the Institute than I do. He'll let my dad go if I rat them out."

"Do you believe him?"

"No. I think he intends to kill us both."

"I think you're right, but this time we have him outnumbered. Estabin will help us when the time comes and he's armed."

"Besides, we have the element of surprise since Angelo doesn't know you're alive," Crispin said, moving to the door. "I'll go in the front. Can you make it up the stairs again?"

Roberto nodded. As they exited the building, Roberto turned toward the street that would take him to the back entrance of the Foundation.

Crispin crossed the street and headed up to the main door. Dawit was no longer on duty, but his replacement buzzed her in when she waved at him as if he had been expecting her. The storm was in full force and the wind moaned and creaked, making it impossible for her to open the heavy door. The pressure difference caused by the rising storm sealed the door, and she couldn't budge it. Crispin hung to the brass door handle as the wind picked up to near-gale force. Just then a lightning bolt struck and a tree down the street snapped in half, crashing onto the sidewalk. Adrenaline percolated through Crispin, giving her the strength she needed. With one mighty pull the door swung open and the wind flung it parallel to the plate-glass window. Now that the door was open, it refused to close again. Sheets of rain and countless lightning flashes forced her into the relative safety of the inner lobby. She was soaked to the skin.

"Go straight up to the penthouse, Ms. Leads," the guard said, handing her a keycard and gesturing to the elevators.

Crispin walked as calmly as possible to the waiting elevator, her sneakers squishing with each step. Once inside she shook the oversize shirt loose from her body, but when she let go, it clung again, like a magnet, to her chest. Thomas Cross greeted her on the top floor.

"So we meet again," he said, gripping her arm and escorting her roughly through the empty reception area outside Angelo's penthouse suite.

As she approached the office it sounded like Angelo was engaged in a heated argument that her entrance interrupted.

"Ah, Daniel, here's your daughter," Angelo said. He was seated across from her dad in a large wingback chair.

From the expression on Dr. Leads' face, it was clear to Crispin that he did not know she was coming, but he said nothing.

"Crispin, we were just discussing the duplicitous Ms. Moss. I was explaining how she managed to play you both for the fool."

"Are you okay?" Crispin asked her dad.

"Why wouldn't I be?" he responded, patting the cushion next to him, suggesting she join him on the small couch, which she did.

Angelo pinched the bridge of his nose, squeezing it tight as if that would somehow neutralize the pain he was clearly feeling. "Estabin, do you have something for my head?"

Estabin bowed and excused himself. "Yes, sir."

"This is all quite civilized, Angelo, but you told me to come because you wanted to discuss a trade. What exactly do you want from me?" Crispin asked.

"I want you to tell me everything the little government grunts at the Institute know. They've been spying on me. They think they're smart, but I'm smarter. What have they told you?"

"We've been over all this, Angelo," Dr. Leads said.

Angelo had been focusing on Crispin, but turned his attention to Leads and pounded his cane on the floor.

"That's the problem with scientists like you, Daniel. You always think you're so clever. But, you're no more than an explorer, discovering a world already laid out by the hand of God," Angelo said. "Men and women of faith have waited for two thousand years for the return of Christ. There were times when I feared it would never happen. A second coming. An immaculate birth. How could it? Then God showed me the way. It was so clear. God has built within us the ability to be reborn again . . . and again . . . and again. To live on eternally, life after life." His voice faded in pain. "Thomas, go find Estabin. I need my medicine."

Cross left the room and Crispin and Dr. Leads were alone with Angelo, who continued his monologue.

"God knew that when we had reached sufficient scientific sophistication, we would find His plan, His blueprint for eternal life, hidden in our cells. And through it, we would know how to bring Christ back to us. He left it for us in the blood and in the tears. There is no other explanation. It is His Grand Plan."

Angelo's face was now contorted in madness. He got up from his seat, leaning on his cane, his back to them. As he stumbled across the room he continued talking, but it was clear that he was no longer talking to them. He was in a one-way conversation with someone only he could see.

"That was the Great Revelation He gave me. Eternal life is possible. Immaculate conception is possible. The blueprint he left for us is in our cells. He left it there for us to find. Every cell is a complete little manufacturing plant for another human just like us. All of the divine information is there. Did you know that? Every one of our trillions of cells. Can you imagine that? When I realized that, I knew I was truly God's instrument. All my money, all my power, was for one purpose only, to fulfill His plan."

A flash of lightning and loud clap of thunder filled the room followed by the unmistakable sound of a gunshot nearby. Leads jumped from the couch and grabbed his daughter's hand, and they ran for the door, as Angelo collapsed in pain over his desk.

* * *

The body of Cross lay across the threshold of the service kitchen next to the reception area just outside Angelo's private office. He'd been shot in the head. Crispin stepped past him into a scene of carnage. A ribbon of red from Cross' head wound moved in slow motion toward a pool that surrounded Roberto, where he sat on the floor pressing his bandaged hands against a gaping knife wound in Estabin's side.

"We've lost him," Roberto told her, gently easing the body to the floor. "Cross came in when Estabin was telling me where Angelo stored the samples from the Shroud. He stabbed Estabin, but before he could reach me, Estabin shot him."

"I assume you are Father Rossini," Leads asked from where he stood at the door.

"Yes, sir," Roberto responded, continuing to kneel next to Estabin's body.

"I'm calling the police," Leads said. "This ends now."

"Wait, Dad, we need time with the computers," Crispin pleaded.

"You don't intend to go through with that plan after all of this," he said, indicating the bodies.

"Now that we know for sure what Angelo is up to, we can't just ignore it," Crispin said.

With help from Crispin, Roberto stood and they joined Leads in the hall.

"You are both right," Roberto said. "Too many lives have been lost, but we can't trust the Institute any more than we can trust Angelo. The stakes are too high."

Leads spoke first to Roberto and then to his daughter. "There is a way, but then we call the police. Agreed?"

Roberto answered with a nod. Crispin removed the two IIPASE disks from her jeans—one was the virus and the other the wiretap program—and gave them to her dad. Crispin and her dad would find a computer to deal with the data issues, and Roberto would retrieve the samples.

"Estabin gave me several possible combinations to the safe. If they don't work, I may have to persuade Angelo to open the safe for me," he told them.

They agreed to rendezvous at Estabin's apartment and notify the police from there. Before they parted, Roberto gave Crispin a key to the apartment and an embrace.

"When this is over, I'll treat you to that *cavallo* you wanted," Roberto said.

* * *

Crispin and Leads found an empty office, and while he kept watch at the door, she sat at the computer. It was every bit as advanced as the one she had used in Kinsey's office. She typed in the first set of access codes that Olvares had given her.

Nothing.

She typed again.

Still nothing.

Muffled voices were approaching from far down the hall. Leads motioned to Crispin to hurry up.

She kept typing.

Finally.

Access.

"It's all yours."

Leads pulled out his eyeglass case. Inside, it was full of thumb drives.

"You planned this all along, didn't you?" Crispin said, as she watched over his shoulder. "I didn't think you could allow IIPASE to destroy this research."

Leads didn't respond, but inserted the first thumb drive. The system recognized the unauthorized stranger in its midst, and after a micro-beat initiated its programmed response. Alarms all over the building began to go off. At first Crispin thought it was a fire alarm. Then the computer screen before them flashed the words "Security Breach" in an orange and red box. The alarms grew louder and a voice on the public address system announced: "The security of our system has been breached and will self-destruct in fifteen minutes. Evacuate immediately."

Leads ignored the warning and continued to methodically copy files onto the compact thumb drives. The process was tedious, but he was systematic and the power of the Foundation's equipment moved the process with speed.

Crispin heard a commotion and stepped into the hall, where panicked workers were scrambling toward the stairwell. One of them pushed her aside, nearly causing her to fall. The momentum of the crowd propelled her down the hall against her will, and she had to fight her way back upstream to the office where Dr. Leads was working.

"Now for the final touch," he said, inserting the virus disk. "That should wipe out any backup systems." Leads pushed a button and the screen before him began to dissolve in a cascade of color that reminded Crispin of a time-lapse picture of a rotting flower on fast forward. For a second, the sight of the virus as it consumed the data held the pair captivated.

"I can't watch."

"I'm done," he told her, and they joined the fleeing stream of frightened scientists who poured down the stairs, through the lobby, and out into the torrential rain. They blended in and left the building, unnoticed.

Crispin showed her dad the way to the apartment, where they could watch the chaos unfolding across the street. She focused the binoculars until she could see Angelo. He was face down at his desk with his hand on a gun. As she scanned the room, Roberto walked in.

* * *

Fierce lightning filled Angelo's office with a pulsing strobe, and thunder synchronized with the wailing alarms. Angelo stirred, easing his head from the cradle of his arms to see an apparition. Roberto's white shirt and shoes were stained crimson, and his head and hands were bandaged and soaked through with blood.

"Has God sent you from the dead?" Angelo asked in a matter-of-fact tone.

Roberto, aware of Angelo's precarious mental state, avoided any swift movements. He eased into a chair across from him and spoke in soft, measured tones. "May I have the gun, please?"

Angelo aimed the gun at Roberto with a wobbly back-and-forth motion. "Maybe I'll give it to you this way."

Roberto knew it was best to avoid any response or movement.

Angelo's hand went limp and he began to rub his temples. "My head. My head."

Roberto eased the gun out of Angelo's hand. "I've come for the samples you took from the Shroud," he said. "I need the combination to your safe."

"I have what you came for, but first, Father, you must hear my confession. God talks to me, you know. His voice comes in my head. It is so powerful that sometimes I am weak from the pain of His voice. He insists on sacrifices," Angelo whispered, grimacing.

Roberto had to cup his hand over his ear and lean in close to hear Angelo over the alarms. He could feel Angelo's breath on his face. It was oddly cold as if the life were bleeding out of the man.

"He tested my faith to see if I'd be willing to sacrifice a life that was dear to me. I'm proud that I was strong in His service, even when my Little Sparrow begged for mercy. I tried to make her understand that it was God's great purpose, but she said a loving God would never ask me to do such things."

On the street below fire engines were blocked by the tree downed in the storm. Firemen with chainsaws were working to clear the massive twisted limbs entwined with the electric lines.

"Rossini, you of all people, know that God asks us to make great sacrifices."

Angelo rambled and became lost in his narrative, no longer acknowledging the alarms as they rose to a higher and higher pitch that Roberto too found painful. The warning sirens changed tone and the loudspeakers began to broadcast the mechanical voice of a computer signaling a final doomsday countdown: "This system will self-destruct in sixty seconds."

Roberto grabbed Angelo and tried to pull him from the chair. "Come, Angelo, we have to get out."

"God is calling me. I must finish my confession."

"Fifty seconds," said the computer.

"Angelo, time is running out."

Angelo would not budge. "He delivered me from my enemies, and from those who hated me."

"I will not leave you to burn," Roberto said, as he tried to force Angelo from his chair. For a man his age, Angelo was surprisingly robust.

"Twenty seconds."

Still weak, Roberto pulled Angelo's arm over his shoulder and tried to force him to stand. Roberto's knees buckled. He struggled again, unsuccessfully, to hoist Angelo to his feet.

"Ten seconds."

Across the street, Crispin watched Roberto's sudden, frantic activity. The rain stripped the scene of all color and turned it to shades of black, silver, and slate as Crispin's Guernica dream came to life. The Foundation building imploded in a wall of heat and fire, throwing jagged chunks of roof into the sky to mix with the wrath unleashed from the storm clouds. Office windows up and down the street, including those in the apartment, shattered as the blast sent a shock wave that, at first, caused a tremor and then rattle through the glass before dissolving it into a cascade of shards showering the streets below. The sounds of destruction drowned out Crispin's scream. Dr. Leads sheltered his daughter in his arms as they watched the heavens rain debris from an electric sky.

Chapter Thirty

The razor blade, dull from use, nicked the article Crispin was slicing from the newspaper. She added it to the box of clippings she had accumulated since Roberto's death. The collection had grown from a few articles to more than a hundred, cut from magazines and newspapers from around the world. They covered everything from Sister Lew's death to the explosion at the Foundation to her own exoneration. Not one of them told the real story. As she placed the lid back on the box, she added the razor blade to others in the chipped china saucer on her desk.

She had several hours before her overnight flight to Italy, so she decided to stretch her legs by walking around campus. There hadn't been a day in the last nine months that she hadn't thought about Roberto. She often replayed their conversations word for word. The clearest was their first memorable dinner in Rome, when they talked about the importance of saying good-bye.

I never got to tell you how much you meant to me, she thought. I hid my scars from you. You had scars too. I cut myself, but you were wounded. We thought we could hide by shrouding our inner self. That night in Rome we came close to the truth: "Life gets in the way of feelings. You think you have time and then you don't. Death can come dangerously quick. Unwelcome. Uninvited. Unexpected." She imagined she could see Roberto smiling at her the way he did that night. In her mind's eye she made him a promise: I will write about you someday. I owe that to you. To the masks we wear and to the scars we bear.

* * *

Pope John Paul II invited Crispin to view the Holy Shroud when it went on public exhibit for the Millennium celebration. Security at the San Giovanni Cathedral in Turin was tight. From her VIP vantage, she was able to see not only the Holy Cloth, but also the hundreds of worshipers patiently queuing. Many an arthritic hand clutched tight to a rosary as elderly women whispered prayers to the Virgin. Crispin imagined that Lew was sitting next to her, the way she had as a child, mesmerized by the transformative power of faith.

Later in a private audience, Crispin told the holy father that she felt responsible for Roberto's death.

"You take too much on your shoulders. You're not the author of this drama."

Sitting quietly for a moment, the pope selected his words with care. "I want to help you understand Father Rossini's work for me. You must agree that you will never reveal what I'm going to tell you."

Crispin nodded agreement.

"I came to believe that the fire in 1997 was intentional. Because I feared that some of my brothers could be involved, I turned to Father Rossini. Few, save the two of us, knew of his mission on my behalf. My special servant, Estabin, was in a position to help when the time came. As your investigation revealed, the fire was only a part of the story."

The pontiff filled in the blanks of the narrative, parts of which she had only guessed. "In the end, we are reminded that while fanaticism leads only to destruction, faith will bring redemption," he said.

Crispin asked permission to give him a package that she had with her. Inside were thumb drives of cloning data taken from the Foundation computers before the explosion. It also contained all of her notes and the DNA profiles she had copied from Kinsey's computer and Lew's key files, including the flashcard. "It's all there," she said. "We even recalled the material we sent to Stanford for analysis."

John Paul accepted the material and laid it on a side table. He closed his eyes and Crispin remained silent, unsure whether the old man was praying or drifting from the moment, the way seniors often do. Then he spoke again.

"Father Rossini and Sister Mary Llewellyn will receive the honors they have earned through their sacrifice."

Crispin thanked him for including her in the memorial service for Roberto. "It meant a great deal to me to be able to say good-bye."

The pope motioned to Crispin to come nearer and to bend over so he could whisper in her ear. He blessed her and gave her a notebook. "This is for you." It was a bound copy of the Macken diaries with a letter from John Paul and the papal seal, giving her unrestricted rights to its content.

The End

Turn the page for a sneak preview
of the next installment
In the *Crispin Leads Mystery Series*:

Digging up the Dead

Prologue

Valley of the Kings, Egypt, 1923

The boy heard his mother wailing but it came from somewhere far away. Diggers had pulled his broken body out of the limestone rubble and laid him on the hard sand not far from the dead and dying. He knew that soon he too would die. He wanted to tell them what he'd seen: the hand that had pulled down the frame that held the scaffolding in place, causing the cave-in. But his lungs were crushed and couldn't produce sound.

His fading thoughts were of his family and his fate. He strained to recall the teachings of his faith. What happens to murder victims when they face the final judgment, when every act and every desire must be accounted for?

Will the manner of my death erase the stain of my crime? Surely it was a small crime, to accept *baksheesh* to tell a lie. If I tell my secret now, will I be cleansed of my crime? But his throat was full of dust and his lungs were no longer able to hold air.

Then the water boy, who had become a local celebrity only a year before when he discovered the fateful stairs that led to the extraordinary discovery of the tomb of Tutankhamun, stopped breathing. He disappeared into little more than a footnote in history. His death and his secret would not be noticed again for more than seven decades.

Inna lillahi wa inna illahi rajeun.
From God we have come and to God we return.

Let Us Hear From You

Thank you for reading *Shrouded*. You can find out more about Meredith Lee and the future adventures of Crispin Leads at www.meredithlee.net.

If you liked *Shrouded*, please consider writing a review on Amazon. When readers take the time to review books they can and do make a difference in the success of the series.

If you have questions or want to be added to our mailing list to get updates and news about forthcoming books, drop us a note at 39starswrite@gmail.com.

Acknowledgements

We wish to thank all of those who helped make this story possible. Pat Hewitt and Jennifer Love Hewitt of Love Spell Entertainment were the first to enthusiastically back the project. The writers of the Joy of Revision, Pen & Fork, Sisters in Crime, Mystery Writers of America and Writers' League of Texas who offered valuable critique and support: Beth Sample, Gina Springer Shirley, Betty Bewley, Rodney Sprott, Gale Albright, Dr. Jack Swanzy, Gogi Hale, Lisa Mann, Diana Baker, Paige Bonnivier Hassall, Mary Hale Etheredge, and Blair Dancy.

We also owe a great deal to the editors and authors and readers who guided our work along the way, especially: Bill Johnson, Carol Dawson, Elizabeth Buhmann, Bethany Hegedus, Spike Gillespie, Donna Johnson, Michael and Stephanie Noll, Amy Gentry, Manning Wolfe, Debra Ginsberg, Katherine Moore, Sam Bond, David Aretha, Laurie Hunt, Suzanne Belser, Earl Wright, Becka Oliver, Father Walter Macken, and Kathryn Roberts, and members of the Tuesdays Are To Die For mystery readers group.

We also thank Dr. William Sofer who provided valuable comments and scientific guidance; academic colleagues, including Drs. Carol Babiracki, Gay Washburn and Jim Watts, whose insights on research and the life of a scholar were always helpful; Edward Pasterick and Mac McClellan who shared their special expertise; tech super hero Thomas Payne; and our financial wizard Terry Bleier Paul; and our cover artist Elizabeth Mackey.

But most of all we are grateful to our family and friends who have patiently supported us through this long but happy process: Chevis Cleveland, Todd and Michelle Hewitt, Taya and Sed Keller, Brenda Buck, Crispin Ruiz, Claudine Stone, Scott and Emily Cleveland, Charlotte Clayton, Shane and Bre Cleveland, Rebecca Palmisano, John and Connie Cleveland, Rosie and Hunter Swanson, Sandra and Jeff Ransom, Johnnie DeMoss, Lynda Bertram, Connie Sherley, Nancy Rogers, Don Herbert, and Richard K. Tanzmann. Look everyone, we have a book!

SHROUDED REVIEWS

"*Shrouded* is a masterfully written mystery novel, powered by well-developed characters and a sophisticated plot. Who stole the Shroud of Turin, and what do they want with it? And who kidnapped our favorite nun, Sister Mary Llewellyn? Crispin, our anxiety-ridden but determined young sleuth, is on the case."
—David Aretha, award-winning author

"When Crispin Leads goes to the Vatican to explore funeral rites she finds herself in a devilish world of intrigue. . . . Crispin must see through the shrouds many use to hide the heartfelt wounds that define us. *Shrouded* is a contemporary thriller that speaks to the mind and heart of its readers."
—Bill Johnson is author of *A Story is a Promise* and *The Spirit of Storytelling*

"Crispin Leads is a heroine I can get behind: bold, brilliant, empathetic and intelligent. Traversing Turin and the Vatican *Shrouded's* heroine will leave you breathless. It's the mystery, not a man, that Crispin is out to solve."
—Bethany Hegedus is an award-winning novelist and Creative Director of The Writing Barn

"I could not put *Shrouded* down. It had all the right things I want in a mystery novel, adventure, intrigue, and a driven, interesting female protagonist. Crispin is a role model for us all- persistent and smart as a whip. She made me keep turning the pages. Much like the Dan Brown books, "Shrouded", gives us new insight into religion and its inner workings and it left me wondering and thinking about many aspects of the Catholic church. This is the kind of book that makes you just want more. I can't wait for more of Crispin and her adventures."

—Katherine Moore, Editor and Ghostwriter

"Shrouded is well written, tightly plotted, and grabbed my interest. It would make a great film."

—Dr. William Sofer, Author. *Giants of Genetics*

"*Shrouded* is a really fabulous international jet-setting story with smart writing and a compelling plot. I enjoyed it thoroughly..."

—Sam Bond, award-winning author

CPSIA information can be obtained
at www.ICGtesting.com
Printed in the USA
FFOW02n2138200917
40187FF

9 780692 887608